THE
NEW
MEXICAN

WILLIAM
BURGDORF

A Division of Y&R Enterprises, LLC
PO Box 2283
Lindale, TX 75771

Interior Book design by Champagne Formats
Book production by Book Liftoff

Library of Congress Control Number Data
Burgdorf, William
The New Mexican / Burgdorf, William
Historical—Fiction.2. Historical western—Fiction.
Fiction. | BISAC: FICTION / Historical. | FICTION / Western.
PCN # 2017906677 2017

ISBN: 978-0-998932-00-2

www.waburgdorf.com

DEDICATION

This book is dedicated to Nancy who believed I could write
and kept at me until I did; and to my love of history,
especially U.S. history.

1

THE FOREVER MISTAKE

HEAT WAVES RIPPLE AND SHIMMER UPWARD FROM the desert floor in the midday sun. A cactus wren scolds loudly as it darts among the thorns. Alschesay hugs the base of the ocotillo, motionless.

The youth's obsidian eyes survey the landscape before him, they capture every movement in the desert. Short by Apache standards, Alchesays's sinewy body and unyielding discipline help him to survive in this harsh land of cactus and rocks. He keeps shoulder-length black hair from his face by a headband. A dark complexion, long breechcloth, and boot-like moccasins all blend into the landscape.

To his left, a Gila monster squirms from beneath a rocky outcropping in the scorching sun, contrary to its nature, and scuttles over to the next rock pile. Its beaded, striped black and orange hide sparkles in the sunlight.

Why does the lizard make a move in the heat of the day? What dislodges it from its slumber? Ground vibrations? Rattlesnake?

He watches as a figure moves out of the foothills, a silhouette rides steadily toward him. He remains immobile; the relentless sun pounds down, it cuts into his back like a dagger's angry blade. Remaining motionless means life.

Alchesay remembers enduring the "toughening" that prepares Apache youths to become warriors. Rising early, before the morning star, he ran, ran, ran for miles; learned to carry water in his mouth, and then spit the water into a bowl to show none is sipped. He learns to bear the unbearable and be oblivious to pain. In sling battles, struck many times, jagged rocks leave scars on cheek, arms, and chest; he gives as good as he gets. Carefully he listens and learns all the old warriors have to tell, it may save his life someday.

Watching the rider come nearer, he sees it's a pony soldier wearing a slouch hat pulled low over his brow, a dark blue uniform shirt, and striped trousers encrusted with many miles of dirt. A fold-over flap satchel hangs across his chest. He's a messenger. His face is covered in dirty thick whiskers, brown touched with gray.

Alchesay glances at a red-tailed hawk circle slowly above him. The raptor's slow gliding motion on air currents rising from the desert allows this predator to watch for prey. He feels a soulful kinship with the hawk. Any small creature that moves below becomes the bird's next meal.

Close now, the man dismounts. His tall dirty black boots raise a little dust as he loosens the saddle's cinch and waters his mount from a canteen using his hat. He takes care of his mount before himself. This land requires it and the land is merciless.

Alchesay wonders. *Where is he headed? Who does he think*

he will find in the desert? Who waits for a message he has to deliver? WHY does he dare to journey alone into Apacheria?

Alchesay sees his uncle, Dehkeya, slowly rise from his hiding place and walk toward the pony soldier. His stride is straight and strong. He moves silently in his boot-like moccasins. A blue cotton shirt is tucked into the belt holding his knife and he carries his rifle. His long breechcloth hangs to his knees, and he wears a headband to hold back his long hair. His face is granite-like, his dark eyes unemotional.

The two men face each other.

One belongs to this land, the other doesn't.

Alchesay quickly moves closer, like a shadow drifting near to the two men.

Neither the soldier, nor Dehkeya smile. If there is recognition, it speaks in their eyes.

"I'm headed for your village," the trooper states.

"What do you have to say?" Dehkeya asks.

"I carry a message from my General, the one you call Nantan Ba'cho, the Grey Wolf," says the trooper. "It is not good news."

"Why do you say that?"

"My army is ordered to arrest those involved with raids in the Santa Rita Mountains," the trooper says as he pushes his hat back on his head.

"You know the mountains are Apache land, the land of our ancestors and any you seek will not be turned over to white men," Dehkeya, says, clenching and unclenching his fist. "You are a very brave or very foolish man to come alone."

Taking a step back and moving a hand toward the pistol at his side, the pony soldier replies, "I'm not alone, many soldiers up in the mountains are coming fast behind me. Nantan Ba'cho leads them."

Dehkeya, struggles to contain his surprise, and glances toward the mountains for any telltale sign of an army.

The soldier says, "You can come with us peacefully, or we can drag you out. But, you are coming."

Alchesay hears the unbelievable. How can this white man insult his uncle, an Apache warrior, in such a manner? *The whites have much and want much more, they are never satisfied. They spread like flies over a dead animal.*

Jumping up, Alchesay charges the soldier; a bloodcurdling scream leaps from his lips. He yanks a knife from his belt and drives it deep into the soldier's throat.

The pony soldier grabs his neck; a gurgle escapes from him as he collapses to the ground. Blood pools onto the sand.

A tarantula ambles past and tests the blood with its two front legs.

Alchesay stands frozen, motionless, and watches a man die. He has never taken human life before.

He turns to his uncle for reassurance, "We will never leave this land."

Quietly, Dehkeya, corrects him, "No, we will not leave, but you must."

"I can not," Alchesay pleads. " Today I defended your honor and the honor of *The People*, the Apaches. Today I am a warrior."

Grabbing Alchesay by his shoulders, he turns him, and stares full in his face. Dehkeya says, "From this day until the sun sets on your life, you will have the blood of that soldier on your hands. You will also have the blood of your people on your hands."

"The soldier should not have come alone, he made a forever mistake," mutters Dehkeya. Looking at Alchesay he says, "Now, you must leave."

"But where will I go?"

"Take the pony soldier's horse. Ride south and join *The People* in the mountains the Mexicans call Sierra Madres." Dehkeya indicates the direction with his hands.

"Ride hard, when the horse fails, kill it and eat what is necessary to survive." He takes the soldier's rifle from the saddle, and pulls the pistol from the dead man's holster.

"What will you do?" asks Alchesay.

Dekeyah looks at the soldier then towards a distant cloud of rising dust. "I will cover him with stones," he says, "and pray the *Ga'an*, our guardian spirits, sweep his blood from the sand."

2

BORRACHO

"*B*ORRACHO, BORRACHO," THE GRINGOS SHOUT AS they throw me out of the *cantina* into the street. *Just because I'm short and lightweight, the grande gringo pitches me through the swinging doors. I am drunk. Yes, drunk, but I will remember.* He stares at the entrance with ebony eyes, and vows the big one will pay for shaming him.

Guillo, Guillo is my name no matter how drunk I am. The Anglos called me Billy.

Yes, I drink too much mescal, but no more than necessary. Maybe I drink to forget, maybe to escape, maybe…I remember too much.

Fortunately, they throw my sombrero out. I'll need it when the sun comes up and that's soon.

He mutters to himself, "They tell me, ride ahead and make sure there are no surprises. They say they'll join me later." *I have* no choice. *Well, that's not true. I can always ride away, but to where, and for what. They have the money.*

Dragging up from the dust, he brushes off his *pantalones* and thinks, *los idiotas* steal from the bank in Chihuahua, fight with soldados and *rurales, and now waste time drinking instead of riding for the border. Now, the soldados* will catch them. These gringos are *muerto, and not smart enough to know.*

Guillo recalls from early life-lessons the profitability that comes from hanging around *cantinas*. His sombrero, boots, and belongings are "contributions" from others in Chihuahua. *There are always some who need their purse, worldly goods, or clothing stolen and don't remember how it happens. Yes,* he thinks, *I wear the white pantalones and shirt of a peon, but I also wear boots, a multicolored vest, and sombrero of a vaquero. I may be born poor, but I have no intention to remain this way.*

Today, as the sun rises, he knows they are some distance from Chihuahua. He's back in the neighborhood of his birth – the foothills of the Sierra Madre Mountains. This *cantina* is in Casas Grandes.

He mounts his horse, begins to ride north, and watch for anything out of the ordinary. *Apaches claim this territory, my home, and my time on earth will be short if they capture me.*

Carefully he moves through the desert. By mid-afternoon he's covered fifteen miles and it's time to find shade and *siesta*. Circling around, he locates an arroyo with sheltering mesquite bushes. He dismounts, loosens the saddle cinch, and waters the horse from his canteen with his sombrero to hold the water. *It's a good pinto with endurance; I've "borrowed" it from an amigo in Chihuahua.*

He slides up along the arroyo bank, he places his sombrero on his head, now nice and cool after watering the horse, and pulls a collapsed telescope from his pocket, a 'gift' from a drunk Americano in Chihuahua. He extends the scope, and slowly scans the landscape in front of him.

Quietly to his horse, as well as himself, he says, "There should be little movement at this time of day, but I need to be sure. Apaches do not always do the expected."

His mind begins to remember.

The casa is warm. During the night, the small fire in the corner fireplace has burned down to coals. There is a frost as early fall arrives. I hear mi Madre move. This is home, small, compact, secure, and all I know. The village is named Ascension on the Rio San Pedro. Not much by anyone's standards. A dozen casas, fifteen jacales, thrown up to hold chickens, goats, and other animals, comprise the village. Oh, I recall, there's a plaza with a well and the ever-present cantina.

Light begins to sift through the shuttered window when the first piercing scream rends the air. It's followed by the front door being kicked open and in the doorway stands the Apache.

The indio's gaze sweeps everything at once and immediately he steps in and grabs mi Madre and throws her into the street. I did not hesitate, but slip under the frame that supports my corn shuck filled mattress, I lift two floorboards, and slide into the small tunnel. Dropping down a few feet, I crawl horizontally until I reach the Rio San Pedro bank. I shrink down into the thorn bushes that cover the exit of the tunnel knowing the thorns must cut less than Apache knives.

Screams, shouts, yelling, pain, anguish, and rifle shots are followed by a deathly silence. It happens so quickly. I hear Apache shouts and the sound of fire crackling. I huddle in the bushes until nightfall. It is terrifying to not know what happens, but mi Madre taught me well.

8

I don't go back into the village. If mi Madre is alive, she will find me as arranged. She doesn't.

During the night, I wander down the Rio San Pedro and am found at daylight by a Haciendado from a nearby ranchero. He sends me to Chihuahua.

"Now, I'm back," Guillo mumbles, his memory returns to reality. He looks behind him and in the distance spots a large dust cloud closing in on Casas Grandes.

"*Soldados*," he whispers.

If the *tres gringos* left already then they have a chance to make it to the border.

A faint whiff of dust in the distance assures him the *Americanos* are on their way ahead of the *soldados*.

Going this close to the Sierra Madres is foolishness. The Sierra Madres are Apache territory; they control the mountains, and have forever. No one ever goes in and comes out – alive.

The afternoon rapidly concludes and a soft evening breeze begins to stir across the desert. Once again, he scopes the landscape in front of him and anticipates being questioned about what he observes.

In the distance, he spots movement, slight at first, then more distinct. He spies a lone horse with a rider moves toward the mountains. Their movement, concealment, and stealth say only one thing…Apache.

3

THE CARBINE

LIGHTNING STRIKES ON THE HORIZON, AND ZEP FEELS the buzz in the air tingle the hair of his arm. Thunder rolls across the desert like cannon fire. His horse shudders, and he tightly holds the reins and strokes the animal's neck for reassurance. Since midmorning Zep's watched the sky. He knows nature is a tremendous and unforgiving teacher, and there's limited time to seek shelter from the approaching storm.

The scattered fluffy white clouds of morning became grey and low hanging. Dark clouds bunch closer and begin to tumble, boiling higher and higher they morph into black skulking thunderheads. By early afternoon, the clouds slowly devour the sun, and Zep feels the change in wind velocity and temperature.

He spots a boulder-strewn hill rising above a deep arroyo, and spurs his horse into a gallop. Carefully, he urges his mount higher, seeking shelter among the rocks. He maneuvers into a narrow cleft between granite boulders, and presses against the back wall under an overhanging ledge of stone. Zep slips from the saddle, shakes out a blanket from his bedroll and drapes it across his horse's eyes.

Strike after lightning strike rains down and slashes the earth like an angry sword, each more violent than the one before. The thunder reverberates off the boulders of Zep's shelter. Staying in the open, flat desert often means death at nature's unforgiving hand.

Then comes the rain. Wave after wave torrentially pours from the sky. *An honest to goodness toad strangler,* thinks Zep, as he stares at the unrelenting inundation of water.

A trickle of water begins to run through the arroyo below the hill. Rapidly it increases into a flow, and then turns into a churning, chaotic, consuming flood. Water quickly fills the deep gully brim-to-brim.

Zep spots a wagon bed as it gyrates toward the base of the hill. Ribs that once held protective canvas are now shattered broken pieces of wood stabbing toward the sky. Two wheels on one side are splintered, and their spokes slap the bank as if to strike back against the mauling water.

Zep watches the fractured wagon tongue slash back and forth through the flood as it jabs into the bank, forcing a shuddering halt of the wagon's forward motion. The back of the wagon swings into the bank, and the spokes of the broken wheels sink deeply into the muddy sides of the gully. It's a marooned beast, caught in the receding water.

As the sky clears and quiet returns, Zep steps from the cover of the rocks to watch the thunderstorm continue its eastward march. The wagon hulk clings, impaled to the bank of the arroyo.

Zep watches the departing storm fade into the distance. Leaving his horse ground tied in the stone cleft, he makes his way down to the wagon.

Pilgrim probably tried to cross the wash when the storm hit. Made the mistake of not watching the weather. Won't make that mistake twice.

Zep pauses in reflection about the wagon and thinks about his beginning.

Zepaniah. What a name to saddle a boy with. Yep, born in the hill country of Texas to a good German family. Pa did his best to teach the value of hard work to all five of us kids. Ma got us schooled in Fredricksburg. Guess they never figured on me becoming a mustanger.

Zep flexes his callused, weathered hands while he steadies himself against boulders as he walks downhill. He gives his shoulder-length brown hair a shake, re-settles his black felt slouch hat on his head, and takes a look around with steely blue eyes.

Then came the Comanches, he remembers. *Pa fed them from the farm and we never had any troubles. The best horsemen of the plains taught me about horses,* Zep smiles at the memories. *Some mustangers break a horse by beating and crushing its spirit. The Comanches taught me the best way is to gain the horse's respect, then they exceed expectations. Their will becomes one with yours.*

He shakes his head and steps into the front of the wagon. There are no bodies anywhere around. Whatever was in this wagon is scattered somewhere along the arroyo. He rummages through a remaining trunk, and then reaches deeply under the front seat. His hand grasps something metal and he pulls it into the sunlight.

"A Paterson carbine rifle, an honest by-God Paterson carbine, a .44 repeater. His loss, my gain." Zep shouts. "I've only heard about this rifle. Never expected to be holding one, especially here in the middle of the desert."

Zep feels the fatigue of three weeks hard riding into the Chihuahuan Desert on the hunt for men who burned down his ranch. He's followed their trail from his ranch outside of Mesilla. Returning from a small roundup of mustangs, he found the ranch burned to the ground, livestock missing or dead, corrals and water tank intact, but everything else gone. From the shod horse and boot tracks around the ranch, discarded cigar butts, and cast off clothing; Zep knows it's white men. *Indians aren't to blame. There are three of them that came to steal and destroy. Their trail points south to Mexico. A burned out ranch might seem small to some; but to a man who has little, any loss is important. They took from me; I'll take care of this scum.*

Zep follows their unhidden trail. They're selling his horses along the way. Tracking *gringos* throwing around money through *cantinas* and bordellos is a simple task. Conversation with locals in villages confirms what Zep knows, *tres Americanos--* Texans—passed through driving a small herd of horses.

As he rides into Chihuahua, Mexico, Zep thinks, *I'll be damned if any bunch of low-life Texans are going to get the better of this New Mexican. They may think they bested me, but comeuppance is comin'and it's bound to be a surprise to them. If they're here, I'll find them and finish this.*

He asks at *cantinas* about the trio, and verifies they are in Chihuahua. Before he can take his revenge, he hears that *tres*

Americanos rob a bank, initiate a gunfight with *soldados*, shoot up the local *rurales*, grab a Mexican boy, and appear to ride hell-bent for the border. Got to be the three he's hunting.

Quickly, he finds and follows their trail. It heads toward the Sierra Madres Mountains. From past conversations with prospectors and *soldados*, buying his horses, Zep knows nobody in their right mind, ever willingly travels by those mountains. It's an Apache stronghold. His survival and experience in this hard land teaches that Apaches are dangerous to one's health, to be avoided if possible.

These idiots are riding into the face of death. I wonder if I'm any smarter to follow them, Zep wonders.

He knows the trio races out of Chihuahua outrunning a detachment of Mexican cavalry. They push hard to Casas Grandes as Zep follows. They are headed for the border.

"No one rides as reckless and unguarded as they do unless they have 'eyes and ears' out in front of them," Zep convinces himself as he rides along. "As yet, I haven't located their scout. He has to be here, but where?"

Zep rides into a ravine and dismounts. He eases up to the top of the arroyo. Places the Paterson carbine repeater on the edge, and drapes a blanket across the barrel.

"No need advertising I'm here," mutters Zep as he adjusts the blanket. A sun dazzled glint or reflection from the barrel of the rifle could betray his presence.

He watches dust devils twist upwards in the desert in front of him.

Zep lies quietly beside his carbine. Slowly, pulling out a pair of binoculars, he shades the lens with his hands and begins to search. His sweep is left to right. Nothing. Desert stretches for miles, and purple mountains loom foreboding to the west.

Zep watches the sun migrate across the sky. The evening breeze begins to waft across the desert. He glances southward and sees a dust cloud moving away from Casas Grandes. He once again sights the binoculars.

At the top of an arroyo almost a hundred yards in front of him, something lies motionless. He adjusts the lens and can make out a…sombrero?

It has to be the scout for the trio. He is out in front and hiding. I've got him now.

Zep knows to get close requires stealth, using the horse is out of the question. He slides back down the slope, reaches into his bedroll, and pulls out a pair of Apache boots. He slips on the leather moccasins with tall leggings. Some time ago he traded horses for them with Mescalero Apaches. Now he can approach the sombrero wearer quietly. Zep retrieves his Paterson carbine and full-cocks the hammer.

He steps lightly, careful to not dislodge rocks or scrape his feet on any twigs or ground clutter. Patience, patience, walk, stop, listen, walk, stop, listen, and little by little the space between them closes.

The sombrero doesn't move. Zep is close, so close he can almost hear the scout's breathing. He moves forward with the quiet of cat's paws, and inches fifteen feet closer. At a bend in the arroyo, he creeps along the sand and knows his prey is around this corner. He drops into a crouch, one silent step after another, he moves nearer. In front of him stretches a young man silently sweeping the area with a telescope. He is completely unaware of Zep.

Zep raises the carbine and eases the barrel forward. It's an inch from the youth's neck.

"Hey, *amigo, como esta,*" says Zep.

4

NORTH COUNTRY

TOO FAR, MY GUN IS TOO FAR, FRANTICALLY THINKS Guillo. He senses a rifle barrel on his neck and knows his Sharps rifle hangs from his saddle. Can he make a leap for the gun? Muscles bunch, breathing increases, and eyesight sharpens. He glances over to judge the distance.

"Don't do it," hisses Zep. He stands poised with the carbine in his left hand; his right hand rubs the muzzle of Guillo's horse. "You'll never get off the ground."

Zep reaches over and quickly binds Guillo's hands behind him with a strip of rawhide yanked from his back pocket. Rolling the boy over onto his back, he pulls him and the sombrero down into the arroyo. Squatting on his heels, the rifle steady on the boy's torso, he quietly begins to ask questions.

"Who are you?"

"What are you doing here?"

"Who are you riding with?"

"Where are they?"

Still startled from his capture and being trussed up, Guillo stammers and stutters,

"Whhaat…whaat….what do you do, *señor*? *Que haces*, who are you?"

"Never you mind who I am, who are you, *amigo*?" asks Zep.

"I'm called *Borracho* by the *gringos* who drag me out of Chihuahua, but *mi llamo es Guillo*," says the boy.

"Okay, Guillo, what are you doing out here?" Zep continues.

"I ride ahead of *tres gringos* to make sure of no surprises," Guillo says. "I make mistake to say I know *del norte del pais*, the north country, when I get drunk in Chihuahua. They grabs me and make me hold their *caballos* while they rob a bank, then shoot at *soldados*, and ride to Casas Grandes."

"They're your *amigos* then?"

"They are not *mi amigos, señor*. But, I have to do what they say. They will kill me, and I know they can. They are *muy malo, señor*," the terrified youth glances at Zep.

He sees fright in the boy's eyes. "There's no mistake, the *gringos* are *muy malo*, very bad," says Zep. "So, Guillo, what have you seen?"

"*El indio*, Apaches," whispers Guillo. "They are a short distance ahead, and when you see *uno Apache*, there are *muchos Apaches, señor*."

Zep knows the youth is right. Seldom does an Apache let himself be seen without more with him. When you see one, you know there are others.

As Zep questions Guillo, another voice intrudes, "Pard, I'd like fer y'all to lower your shoot'n piece a mite. We'uns ain't wantin' to let light into your innards, but we ain't agin it neither."

Surprised, Zep lowers the Paterson carbine and it's quickly grabbed from his reluctant grip.

"Didn't rightly know if ya was gonna plug *Borracho* or not," says the voice admiring the new firearm.

"Orin, his name ain't *Borracho*. Member he hollered out he was G something. Ge-o, Geego, or Jehosaphat," another voice joins the gathering.

"Oh, Pard, forgive my rudeness," the voice says leveling the barrel of his Springfield musket at Zep.

"That joker is Clint, an over there is Thomas. Clint be my brother and Thomas is a cousin. Now, Pard, Clint is mean as a snake and Thomas is just evil. Me, I be Orin," the man says as he moves in front of Zep. His hand is rock steady holding the rifle.

"Sorry to drop in on you and such, but you was real busy with *Borracho* and it just seemed natural to take advantage of your situation," says Orin, with a smile.

Clint chimes in, "We had that young'un out here lookin' to make sure there weren't no surprises. Looks like you put the surprise on him."

All three men have the appearance of Texas trash. Some of those that drift up from El Paso and hang around. Zep's seen their kind in Mesilla -- loafers, no goods, thieves, and bandits. They are the low life that seems to ooze around the edges of civilized life. He glance at Orin, and sees greasy long hair under a gray, smashed, sweat stained hat, filthy trousers held up by suspenders over a white linen shirt long turned crusty brown from sweat and dirt. Clint, sits astride his horse, and doesn't look much better with his gray holey canvas pants, ragged denim jacket with the sleeves ripped off, and a preposterous black bowler hat. Ratty looking blond hair sticks out from under the hat. Zep has a sudden, uneasy, nauseous sense about Thomas, something's not right about him. His long brown hair is held back with a headband. A ripped blue-checkered shirt, that Zep recognizes used to belong to him, is tucked into dirty brown pants. All of the men wear scuffed up brown mule eared boots.

Yes, he thinks, *Guillo distracted me, but how did they manage to slip up on me unheard? I've managed for the past years to keep one step ahead of Mescalero Apaches, and that's no easy task. I didn't think my survival instincts could let me down. Yet, here they stand.*

Thomas, silent through the introductions, now softly says, "I ain't burnt nobody in a long time, Orin. It's hard to keep it under control and I feel a real hot fire comin' on."

"Now, Thomas, you ain't got a lick of sense, there ain't time. Look over your shoulder; y'all see the cloud of dust back there? It be them damned Mex cavalry fellers," says Orin. "You build a cooking fire and every Mex soldier and Apache for miles will know where we is. There ain't time to do a real good cookin', ya hear?"

"Maybe we can lose them soldiers and double back for a roastin'," says Thomas. "What if'n I was to tote them around the bend and cover them over with mesquite brush?"

"You do what you got to do, Thomas, but I ain't hangin' around here. You heard what 'G' said about Apaches, didn't you?" says Orin. "Well, we got to give these horses a restin' spell then we ride, and ride hard to put ground between us, the Mex, and any Apaches."

"Dump them round the bend and we'll come back. Reckon it'll be some fun to hear them squall and sizzle. It's been a while," Clint chuckles.

Rough hands grab Zep, snatch away his handgun, knife, and tie up his hands and feet. He's dragged around the bend of the arroyo with Guillo and both are covered over by mesquite limbs Thomas lops off of nearby bushes.

It is dark by this time, and Zep hears the men bring their horses in and settle down for some rest. He imagines they will be up at first light. He knows the Mexican cavalry can't be far behind, and Apaches might be in front of them or clear out of the area. *You never know with the Apaches. Don't try to second-guess them; you'll lose.*

The night gets quiet. The full moon lights up the countryside. Through the branches over them, Zep sees millions of stars ablaze in the firmament and hears a horse stamp and snort quietly.

"Roasting. Not about to happen to me." Zep mutters aloud.

Guillo lies quietly beside him thinking, *I once escaped this country. Now, it appears this is where I will be buried unless this gringo can do something. How do we get out of this?* He shivers as the chill of the night settles around him.

Zep drifts off to sleep in the early hours and jerks awake with a start. The soft, fluffy semi-light of predawn seeps into a cloudless sky. The horses are restless. Something moves around them, a coyote, wolf, puma, what? There is a bloodcurdling scream, then another, then more. From the sounds, the *tres gringos* are up and shooting. More screams, more shots, a horse on the run, then another, and then silence.

Shortly, Zep hears sounds of something tumbled and thrown about. A horse neighs and snorts, then quiet. There's more silence. The sun eases over the horizon. Birds settle in the brush around the arroyo and set up a welcome dawn songfest.

What's happened? What's going to happen? Zep pulls, tugs, and yanks at his bindings. The noise has Guillo wide-awake and doing the same.

"Stop yankin' around, boy. Lie back to back and let's try to untie each other. We're not gettin' out any other way," says Zep.

It seems like hours, maybe it is, but Zep's binding loosens. He works one hand out, then the other, and gets his feet untied. He reaches over he helps Guillo ғɪnish untying himself. Slowly he eases back the branches and slides out into the open.

5

JANOS

THE GROUND IS TORN UP, SAND SCATTERED, BUSHES ripped apart, dirt dug from the arroyo bank, and a body lies on its face. Looking closer, bloody spots on the bank and the sandy arroyo floor sparkle in the morning light. There's a body, it doesn't move. No rise or fall of breathing… it's dead.

Zep slips silently around the bend in the arroyo, and surveys the scene.

Stepping over, he kneels beside the corpse, grabs a handful of hair, and lifts the head. It's Thomas, the man-burner. He's Orin's cousin and evil no more…just plain dead. His throat cut from ear to ear.

Looking around, Zep sees and feels he and Guillo are alone. Still he whispers, "Guillo, come on out, everything's over."

Moving around the bend of the arroyo, Guillo takes in

the scene of savagery. "*Madre de Dios*," his face pales, "It's so bloody."

Zep nods in agreement. "Looks like the Apaches hit them before dawn, that's what all the ruckus was about."

"*Si, amigo*, they hit hard and fast, like Apaches do," muttered Guillo. "Some of them are wounded as well, see the bloody spots in the sand around the body?"

Zep agrees, "Yep. They haul off their wounded and dead. You never know how many there are."

"Bullets and arrows they fly thick, I think." Guillo stares and shivers.

Zep thinks the same. It was a blood bath. Yet, he knows there are two missing persons and he remembers hearing horses race away. *Did Orin and Clint get away, or did the Apaches haul them away? Thomas' horse is missing as well as all weapons. The body is picked clean. Guillo's horse is gone also.*

"Not much more we can do here." Zep realizes the man-burner was responsible for saving their lives instead of roasting them. By dragging them around the bend of the arroyo and covering them with mesquite branches, they avoid detection by the Indians. "So much for Thomas," Zep mutters. "He went out unknowingly doing a good deed."

"*Señor*, I do not want to bury *gringo Tomas*. We must move; the *indios* may be near."

"It's best we leave pronto," Zep says already in motion. "My horse and gear are over there a ways." He points the direction. "Move, now."

Scudding along the arroyo, they return to where Zep's horse is tethered.

"We need to switch off with riding and walking to get out of here," Zep directs. "Can't double up without doing in the horse and we are going to need him."

"*Amigo*, I know the way to a village, Janos; it's not too far," Guillo heads off at a swift walk. "If the *gringos* have a brain they will head there also."

Zep frees the horse from its hobbles and checks his saddlebags to find his spare Walker Colt and ammunition. The grub bag is slung over the back of the saddle as well. Changing his moccasins for boots, he leads the horse out of the arroyo, mounts, and quickly catches up to Guillo.

Zep paces his horse with Guillo's walk, "Let's keep on the move; can't burn daylight and wait for those Apaches to have a second look around."

Guillo, doesn't slow down, he rolls his eyes, and thinks in exasperation, *gringo.*

They intently scan the horizon, alert to the Indians' possible return.

Guillo and Zep alternate walking and riding; it takes all day. By evening, lights of Janos are visible in the distance. Both men and the horse are close to exhaustion.

They crouch in the brush outside town.

"I don't want to enter Janos tonight," says Zep.

"There will be beds and food. Better than out here, *amigo.*"

"No, there are only closed doors and shuttered windows in the village at night."

"Ah, you are right, *amigo*, but the *cantina,* she is open, yes?"

"Yep, and that worries me too."

"*Si*, we know what *hombres* are there at night." Guillo cringes as he recalls his nightly haunting of *cantinas.*

"We'll stop here and go in at daylight."

In a secluded low spot in the desert countryside, the travelers cold camp, no fire, hobbling the horse, Zep pulls out what's left in the grub sack, and passes Guillo some jerky. Shortly both roll up in blankets and are asleep.

Morning begins as a surly golden globe rises in the east. Janos comes awake as Zep watches the town. People are out and move between buildings, some go to the village well, others lead burros out of town, still others shake out bedding. He sees the village is twelve adobe *casas* arranged around a central square. Other houses with *jacales*, huts, are scattered at random outside the square. A well-worn rutted road divides the town. Everything appears normal.

Guillo and Zep approach Janos walking slowly out of the desert, leading the horse, and approach the cantina. Two other horses tied beside the cantina appear to have been there for a while from the piles of horse apples.

"*Amigo*, you see the *caballos*," asks Guillo.

"Yep, like expected, we know who their riders are. Let's go around back."

Quietly, Zep opens the backdoor to the *cantina* and they slip inside. The smells of fresh tortillas, fried chorizo, and tamales assault his nostrils. His mouth begins to water. He hadn't realized how famished he is. Escape, chase, and locating Orin and Clint drove appetite from him. Now, he wants food. Guillo, right behind him has the same look in his eyes. His belly is in control.

Both men step through the back room spotting Orin and Clint at a table in the middle of the *cantina* - asleep, their heads lying on the table.

The proprietor approaches Zep and Guillo. "*Señores*, you want something to drink?"

Guillo responds rapidly in Spanish and orders food, *muy pronto*. With a smile, the proprietor turns to comply and Zep stops him short.

"*Señor*, how long have those two *hombres* been here," he points to the middle table.

"*Muy horas, señor*. They ride in yesterday telling of escape from *indios*. They drink themselves *estupido*, and sleep as you see them now," the owner frowns. "*Perdóname, señores*, I will bring your food."

Moving to a table in the back corner of the *cantina*, Zep and Guillo devour the food set before them. Satisfied, Guillo decides to get up and check out the village. He groans with the load of food consumed, and moves to the front door. Standing momentarily in the doorway, he steps outside.

Zep moves to the middle table. Takes his pistol out of his belt, and raps it sharply on the table. Both men sitting there groan and begin to move. Orin squints open one bloodshot eye and focuses on Zep.

"Hey, *amigo*, you made it," he groans. "Good to see y'all in one piece and not sproutin' arrows."

Clint rolls from the table and tumbles to the floor, slowly stands, weaves, stops, and stares at Zep.

"Ol' pard, you still got a scalp with everthin' still workin.'"

Zep slams a fist into Clint's gut and sticks his pistol barrel into Orin's ear. Clint convulses to the floor. Orin is wide-awake.

Guillo careens through the *cantina* doorway almost colliding with Zep.

"*Amigo, aqui los soldados son*. The soldiers they here." screams Guillo.

"Where, how many?" Zep shouts back.

"They ride into town. I see maybe twenty *soldados*. They looking for *tres gringos* and me," shrieks Guillo.

The other *cantina* patronage slips quietly out the back door, or move deeply into the corners. They know soldiers do not necessarily bring good news.

Orin, pipes up, "Well, we got three gringos in this here *cantina* and him, pointing at Guillo, that means we fit the description. I ain't hangin' around to chaw the fat with no Mex soldier boy, or argue particular points of guilt or innocence, or attend a hangin', namely mine."

Jumping from his seat, he snatches bulging saddlebags from the floor, flings them on his shoulder, charges for the back door, and shouts, "*Adios*, y'all."

Clint's a step behind in full pursuit.

Guillo and Zep glance toward the *cantina's* front door, then race out the back.

The soldiers slow their trotting horses to a halt in front of the *cantina* as their *capitan* dismounts at the front door.

6

AMBUSH

GUILLO AND ZEP BURST THROUGH THE BACK DOOR OF the *cantina* to find their horse wandering down the alleyway. Running to catch it, both men fling themselves up on the animal. Staggering momentarily with the double load the horse regains it's footing and breaks into a ground-gulping gallop.

The double riders pass the outlying *casas* and *jacales* on the outskirts of Janos. Zep and Guillo follow the dust of Orin and Clint's horses. Slowly, the distance closes and Guillo shouts, "The mountains, head for the mountains."

All three mounts move into a single file covering ground at a blistering gallop. Zep knows the horses can't continue this speed for long.

"There's a valley that leads into a mountain canyon," shouts Guillo.

"So what?" Zep responds.

"The *soldados* may not follow. They fear the mountain and Apaches," shouts Guillo pointing the way.

All heads nod acknowledgement. Clutching Zep, Guillo glances over his shoulder. The *soldados* gain on them. Their dust cloud is only yards away. Zep knows this horse race will end in their hanging. He waits for a fatal gunshot.

Guillo shouts again and points to a nearby valley. All three *gringos* turn their horses that direction and see the yawning canyon mouth ahead.

The *soldados* don't falter and continue to close on the riders. Zep glances at the *capitan* waving his men forward.

"They mean to catch us before the mountain," he shouts to Guillo.

Into the valley thunder the *gringos*, Zep, Guillo, and the *soldados*. The trail suddenly turns sandy and their horses bog down. Their speed decreases rapidly as the horses struggle to continue charging forward. The riders kick, whip, and spur their mounts to move faster.

Ambush.

The first shriek is terrifying; the ground heaves up with a sudden, violent quake as sand flings skyward. Apache warriors leap from shallow graves on both sides of the trail. They drag Mexican soldiers from their horses. The trap is sprung.

Zep shudders as screams, shouts, curses, and cries flood the air. Horses shriek as they tumble to the ground. Gunfire, chaos, confusion, yelling, wounding, and dying are a cacophony of profane noises that shred the midmorning desert. The path turns red. Blood pools and splatters, sunlight sparkles on the brilliant red rocks and sand.

Riding hard to avoid being drawn back into the ambush,

Zep glances to see the destruction behind. What's in front of them? Whipping around, instinct tells him the canyon in front of them is not safe. He knows being spared is intentional.

Zep violently yanks his horse's reins to his right. The horse hunkers down hard into the sand on its hind legs; Guillo spills off onto the ground as the horse almost collapses. Leaping from the saddle, he grabs Guillo, and leads the horse by the reins into the mesquite, Rosewood trees, and creosote underbrush that line the trail.

Guillo yanks free of Zep, "*Idiota*, they have the bank *dinero, mucho dinero*." He points toward Orin and Clint.

"Much money or not, it's a trap. The trail was the first step to drive everyone into the canyon."

Zep continues to plunge into the brush. He stops and grabs a broken branch and quickly sweeps it across the sand to cover their footprints.

Thrusting the branch at Guillo, "Keep sweeping behind us, cover up as much as possible."

The mouth of the canyon abruptly erupts with shouts, screams, and shooting, the second part of the ambush. Guillo looks at the canyon, and begins to rapidly sweep the ground obliterating as much sign of their passing as possible. He glanc-es at Zep and thinks, *this loco gringo knows. His mind is like an Apache.*

The horse is panting, lathered, and staggers as it attempts to regain some strength. Zep knows his horseflesh and fi nd-ing somewhere to give their mount time to recover is critical to its survival. Breaking through the creosote and surrounding brush, he sees an open expanse of Mexican Redbud trees, oco-tillo, and Retama trees.

"Got to find somewhere to hide," mutters Zep as he sets out

at a jog with the horse in tow.

Guillo methodically brushes the ground to hide any presence of their trail. They jog, then walk, no talking, and hide their trail.

Mid-afternoon passes and the evening breeze stirs across the desert. Zep moves north, staying off the foothills of the Sierra Madres. As the sun initiates its slow glide into the western horizon, he locates a shallow depression where rock piles surround three sides. Tumbling into this refuge, the horse and two travelers collapse. If the Apaches find them here they deserve to be found. Night folds around them as they roll up in blankets and sleep.

A fiery sunrise eases up in the east and morning finds the travelers alive. Recovered and able to move again, Zep rummages around in his saddlebag and feeds some remaining oats to the horse. At least a little nutrition can help restore some of the energy spent yesterday.

They watch the sun continue upward, and decide their next step.

"If we continue to move north, we'll eventually come to the valley between the Peloncillo and Animas Mountains. Across the border is a *rancho* at Animas. A *Haciendado* settled and built a *rancho* there years ago, if I remember right. It could be either Mexican or Anglo now."

"There is no going back to Chihuahua," Guillo states.

"So, our direction is set; we go north. I'm going home and where are you going, Guillo?"

"*Amigo*, since I have no home, I think I will see Mesilla, otherwise I will just wander alone in this desert and wait for it to kill me. *Nuevo Mexico* might be a good place even if it is in *el Estados Unidos*."

"Water is what we need most. Are there rivers, water holes north of here?"

"*Si, amigo*, there are rivers--small, but water. Our travel will be from water hole to water hole until they run out. It is long way to go, but possible."

The farmer watches shapes wiggle and quiver as they rise on the heat waves from the desert beyond the field. Moving to his wagon, he reaches over the side and retrieves his rifle. Squinting into the heat he sees the squiggling shapes become human and animal forms. Soon, he identifies two men and a horse, alkali and dirt covered, stumbling along in a daze. Reaching into the wagon again he pulls out his canteen and slowly walks toward the men.

Zep is lost in a dream; he visions tall snow covered mountains around Santa Fe. They are sharp and clear in his mind.

One foot scuffs and stumbles in front of the other as he repeats a cadence. "Left, right, left, right, don't stop," whispers through his blistered and sunburnt lips.

Around him a length of rope ties to Guillo's waist. His horse's reins wrap around his right wrist. He rasps out the monotone cadence, "Right, left, right, left, don't stop."

The trio continues their stumble shuffle past the farmer.

Realizing the man in the lead is in a trance, the farmer begins to shout loudly, "Water, here's water." To grab an entranced man may mean instant death. Survival instinct is to shoot first, and jolting someone out of a trance is risky business. Survival reactions are automatic.

Zep realizes a voice shouts at him, the mountains of Santa

Fe vanish. Turning his sweat, dust, and alkali encrusted face toward the voice; he cracks his dirt-plastered eyelids, and squints at the farmer.

A canteen is extended and Zep snatches it greedily. Yanking off his hat, he knocks the dirt from it, pours water into it, and shoves it under the horse's muzzle. Loud slurping sounds from the animal are reassuring.

Zep tips the canteen and gulps down water. "Stop, stop, enough," shouts the farmer. "Drink slowly, I'll fetch more."

Zep turns to give the canteen to Guillo.

Realizing there is a change in their march, Guillo stops. He teeters at the end of his rope, his legs give way, and he collapses.

7

THE HUNT

S O CLOSE, I ALMOST HAVE THEM, HE SQUINTS AT THE figures standing beside the wagon. Notching his arrow he prepares to draw the bow.

It's been a long trail following their signs, losing them, backtracking, and finding them again. "These two are almost Apache in hiding their trail," Alchesay whispers in frustration.

"Little do my rabbits know the fox is ready to pounce." A satisfied feeling warms Alchesay.

They continued to elude me, recalling this long, frustrating chase began after the ambush.

Alschesay's arrival in the Sierra Madre Mountains a month ago is very visible. To not alarm or surprise any camp of *The*

People, he approaches in the open and stops when warriors appear. They are *Janeros*, cousins to his *Chokonen* band of the *Chiricahua* Apaches. Immediately, he's led to their camp where they feed and make him welcome. Around the fire there's much discussion.

"We killed white men in the foothills two mornings ago," a tall *Janeros* warrior shares. "When sun comes up, we see a large dust cloud of Mexican *soldados*."

An ambush is quickly planned to deal with the Mexicans and those who violate their mountains. Alschesay is invited to participate. Given weapons, he becomes part of those ready to spring a trap at a canyon's mouth. Other warriors will ambush along the trail and drive the *soldados* into the trap.

He travels with the warriors to the ambush site, as the trap is set.

Hidden between two boulders, Alschesay watches the horsemen flee the ambush and whip their reins from side to side to spur their mounts into the canyon.

"Get ready cousin," says a *Janeros* warrior pointing as the riders enter the mouth of the canyon. They ride furiously towards unknown but certain death. One horse, carrying two riders, suddenly stops, violently turns off the trail, and the riders and horse plunge into the brush.

The two remaining riders gallop headlong into the canyon. On signal, a wall of arrows flies through the air and cut down the white men and their horses. Desperately, they continue to fight on the ground firing their pistols at any moving thing. A second flight of arrows silences the gunfire. The riders die. The ambush is complete. Excitedly, warriors slip from the rocks in the canyon to examine their victims. A single rifle shot stills a thrashing horse. Some warriors collect weapons and ammunition, while others find saddlebags filled with useless paper and coins. The bags are unceremoniously discarded behind boulders. Those in the canyon wait for the warriors from the ambush.

"There were two who escaped," the *Janeros* leader comments.

"Yes, cousin, their horse stopped before the canyon and they fled into the brush," says Alchesay.

"They are gone by now," adds another *Janeros* warrior.

"I feel they must be found," Alchesay says.

"My cousin, that may be a good idea, but we have much success today," says the leader. "The Mexicans provide us with weapons, horses, and other plunder."

Others say it is time to return to camp and take care of their wounded.

Alschesay is adamant. "It is never wise to leave *wounded animals* to wander. If no one else goes, I go."

Not wanting to appear rude or uncivil, the leader of the ambush says, "If you wish to chase those who got away we will not stop you. Take the weapons and go swiftly."Alchesay leaves of the group of warriors, retrieves his horse, and goes to where the two men left the trail.

As he pushes through the brush, Alschesay surveys the inhospitable landscape before him. He thinks about its gravelly, sandy soil covered with creosote, mesquite, yucca, and barrel cactus. Observing the dark, purple mountains jutting skyward along the horizon, he knows his next stop is a *playa* water hole. Armed with his survival skills he prods his horse forward. He must move quickly to catch the white men.

The sun relentlessly blasts down its rays, but he is raised to endure the unendurable, and Alschesay will survive. Reading the signs, he confirms there are two riders and one horse, a poor arrangement. Finding their trail is difficult. The riders take great care to obliterate their signs. Finally, a broken branch and a dislodged stone point their direction. He follows.

Day after day, Alschesay follows their trail, loses it, finds it, and follows again. Dust, sweat, dirt, alkali cover him head to toe. Nighttime, he seeks rest and recovery. Regardless of his determination, skills, preparation, and strength, the desert is relentless and extracts its toll. All who pass through pay the toll. Dehydration drives Alschesay into hallucinations and seeing visions. His past, present, and future roll in never-ending dreams through his mind.

The last words of his uncle, Dehkeya, replay over and over. *From this day until the sun sets on your life, you will have the blood of this soldier on your hands. You will also have the blood of your people on your hands. I understand full well the soldier's blood. But what of my people, how am I responsible for my people? I must return home to know the condition of my people--find out where, what, and how they are. This hunt is my need to return home as well as kill the white men.*

Two days earlier his horse lies down and dies. No warning; just drops dead. Continuing on foot, he finally stares at those who elude him. Across the open field a clear shot is possible. He nocks an arrow, raises the bow, and draws the string. Concealed, he stands beside an ocotillo steadying his aim.

He pauses, *I have sought them for days; is it wise to kill now? Where are they going? What else can they provide me? I have followed this far, what lies ahead? I can wait.* Alchesay lowers the bow, sits, and watches.

I must discover the fate of my people.

He realizes a lucky shot from the white men's weapons could end his search, he whispers, "It is enough to be here. To wait for a short time is good. They are not going far."

8

HACIENDA

DROPPING TO HIS KNEES, ZEP CRAWLS SLOWLY TO Guillo. Underneath the grime, grit, and alkali there has to be life. We came too far across the desert to die now. Water ran out days before, the sun beat down unmercifully, and we walked, always forward. Zep reaches out and rolls Guillo's body over.

"Wake up, damn you, wake up," Zep pounds on Guillo's body. "You damn well can't die now, I won't let you die now." He screams at him while rocking the body back and forth.

"*Señor, amigo*, please let me die quietly," whispers Guillo. "I did not come all this way to have you beat on me."

The appearance of a smirk crinkles and cracks the dirt around Guillo's mouth. Zep lies back knowing he hasn't lost him. They survived and beat the demon desert. Reaching over, Zep extends the canteen, offered by the farmer. This time Guillo grabs it and greedily gulps down the life-giving water. Reaching again, Zep pulls the canteen back momentarily.

"Slowly, slowly, Guillo. You don't want to drown in the middle of the desert."

The farmer laughs at Zep's comment and moves to Guillo's side while Zep struggles upright and grabs his other side. They all stand together, and at the farmer's direction, climb on the back of the buckboard. It is a rough, jolting ride as the wagon turns around through the field and bounces out onto a trail. The horse tied to Zep's wrist, regains some stamina from the wa-ter, and follows behind.

"*Señores*, how long have you been in the desert? My name is Joe. They call me *Jose* around the rancho.

"Where did you come from?"

"Why are you here?"

"What happened?"

"Who are you?"

What did you do?" The farmer fires questions like bullets from a revolver.

Turning towards Joe, Zep sees dust-covered overalls, a dark shirt, mud covered brogan shoes, and a red handkerchief stuffed in a back pocket. The farmer looks to be about five and half feet tall with flaming red hair. His weather worn face is speckled with freckles, and his hands on the reins are calloused and dirty. He bounces on the spring-supported seat as they travel across the field.

"Easy, easy, Joe," Zep croaks. "We left Casas Grandes over three weeks ago. Got tangled up in an Apache ambush, and have been trying to get home ever since."

"Geeeehosephat. You've been in the desert that long?" Amazed, the farmer goes on, "It ain't no wonder you took to water the way you did. Y'all must be plumb dry to the bone and twice as hungry."

"Yep, you could say we are parched a mite, and I could eat," Zep agrees. Nudging Guillo who had fallen back into the wagon bed, "Hey, you could eat couldn't you? You ain't willing to pass up food are you?" Guillo groans and nods his head.

"We're aheading up to the *hacienda* right now," the farmer says. "*Don Louis* will want to hear everything you been through, especially about them Apaches. They continue to raid us killing livestock and *vaqueros*. He'll want to know what band they are. We get different bands of Chiricahua that hit us right regular like."

The bouncing, jostling ride feels like heaven compared to the stumbling, shuffling walk they just completed.

Joe pipes up, "I'll get cook to rustle up some grub, and we'll find space in a bunkhouse for ya. Just ride there and suck up some more water afore we get to the house."

As the wagon rumbles uphill, Zep turns to get a look at the *hacienda*. A thick adobe wall, ten-feet high, surrounds the compound. The main house sits on a slight rise in the center. They approach a thick wooden double gate that opens, as they get closer. Traveling through the portal, Zep sees parapets on the inside of the wall allow men to stand watch and defend the *hacienda*. The main house has a flat roof with two men patrolling across it as they watch the landscape beyond the wall. Inside the compound are a blacksmith, cookhouse, bunkhouses, stables, storage buildings, barns, corrals, and sheds for small animals all arranged along the wall. It's a fully functional city. Ten mounted *vaqueros* gallop past and out the double gates. Children play before *casas* grouped close to the main house. Laughter, talking, shouting, smithy noise, and singing are heard as the wagon comes to a stop.

Zep watches the main house doors open and a distinguished-looking man walk out onto the covered porch, and descend the steps to the wagon. He is past middle age, a head full of gray hair, dark eyes that have a hawk-like stare; he is almost six feet tall, with a walnut colored, weathered complexion. He wears tapered vaquero trousers, a white open collared shirt, a short-waisted multicolored vest-like jacket, and tall shiny black boots. His composure gives him an air of wisdom and dignity.

"*Buenos Dias, amigos.* I welcome you to my home, *Hacienda de la Colina,* the ranch on the hill. I am *Louis Estefan Antonio de la Vieta.*" Spreading his arms open he says, "Call me *Don Louis. Por favor*, get down, come in, and tell me of your travels." He turns and walks back up the steps onto the porch and into the house.

Zep slips off the back of the wagon. Guillo stands beside him holding his sombrero in front of him in obeisance to *Don Louis.*

Both men step up to the front door and brush off as much dust and grime as possible. Stomping both feet to shed dirt, they enter into the coolness of the foyer. Servants rush forward to brush them off, take their hats, and offer them glasses of cool water.

Zep surveys the interior of the house. The foyer is eight-feet square with a set of double doors going into the house proper. He notices gun ports in both doors. Glancing behind him, he sees gun ports in the outside doors as well. The roof soars ten feet above his head. Past the foyer, a main hallway extends straight for thirty feet and is twelve-feet wide. The walls and ceiling are all smooth plastered. There are eight arched doorways with double doors, four evenly spaced on each side of the hall. Each doorway is eight feet tall. Highly polished sconces with candles on each side of the doorways provide light. Large cabinets reaching almost to the ceiling sit opposite each other midway down the hall. A round table dominates the midpoint of the hallway with a short earthen jar overflowing with fresh cut flowers. All the floors are highly polished wooden plank. Even with lit candles, the temperature is still much cooler inside.

They're ushered into a room to their right that appears to be an office. It's twelve square feet. Taking seats in offered rawhide chairs they look at *Don Louis* across a large polished desk. A kiva-type fireplace fills the corner to the left of the desk. Light pours into the room from an open window that has folded back thick shutters with gun ports. Behind him is a large map of northern Mexico, Arizona, and New Mexico territories. Details on the map indicate roads, trails, mountains, plains, rivers, creeks, and habitation from El Paso to Tucson and Chihuahua to Santa Fe. A large area on the map is designated *Apacheria*.

"I am pleased you have survived the desert." The *Don* continues, "Yes, word travels quickly. No sooner did Jose climb off the wagon before chatter exploded."

"We are pleased to arrive here," says Zep, "For a few days we didn't think we were going to make it anywhere." Guillo nods his head vigorously in agreement.

"*Mi casa, su casa,*" offers *Don Louis*. "I would like to know who you men are, where you are from, and why you turned up on my doorstep."

"Well, Sir, my name is Zephaniah Bierman and this is my pard, Guillo," Zep turns to Guillo and under his breath whispers, "What is your dadburn last name, *amigo*."

"Zepato, *mi llamo es*, Guillo Zepato."

"Guillo Zepato, sir," Zep says to *Don Louis*.

"Welcome again, Zep and Guillo. Now, what are you doing in the Chihuahuan Desert?"

"Well, sir, I was in Chihuahua trying to catch three *hombres* who burned my ranch. I have a spread over near Mesilla. I came home and my place was torched. I followed the three who did it to Chihuahua. It appears they robbed a bank, fought some soldiers and a sheriff, ran to Casas Grandes, and were heading for the border."

"I see," says *Don Louis*. "So, you have been in pursuit for some time? What became of the *hombres*? Where are you from?" He points at Guillo.

"I am from Casas Grandes, *Patron*," says Guillo. "I was taken by the *tres gringos* to lead them through the desert. They are no longer alive. The Apaches kill them."

"So, Apaches. They are troublesome to us as well," says *Don Louis*. "We are constantly vigilant. We have lost cattle, horses, and some good *vaqueros* to them."

"We haven't seen any since the ambush north of Casas Grandes, sir," Zep adds.

"That does not mean they are not here," *Don Louis* interrupts. "You may very well have led them to this *hacienda*."

Guillo speaks up, "No, *Patron*. We have hidden our trail well."

"An Apache can follow you over solid rock, know when you stop, and for how long," *Don Louis* speaks forcefully. "The only way I survive here is think like they do. My family received this land as a grant from the Spanish, it is recognized in Mexico City, and now the *Americanos* attempt to rip it away from me."

"That's why men are on the walls and roof," guesses Zep.

"*Si*, my sharp-eyed, *amigo*. Men keep watch around the clock for *indios, banditos,* and *Americanos*. At this *hacienda*, we fight the world to keep our own."

"Meaning no disrespect, sir, Guillo and I only want to rest some and then be on our way to Mesilla. Will that be alright with you?"

"*Perdóname, señores*, I fear sometimes I become bitter and overbearing. You are welcome to the hospitality of the *hacienda*. Stay as long or short as you like. I will have a servant show you to a bunkhouse and you can catch up with *Jose* on our daily routines. *Buenvenido*. Welcome."

A servant escorts Zep and Guillo out of the house, across the compound past the *casas*, and points them toward a bunkhouse. Crossing a covered porch, they enter the building and see Joe sitting in a chair beside a table in the middle of the room.

"Well, *amigos*, you been talking with the 'He Bull' in these parts," Joe chuckles. "Looks like you faired well enough. Let me show you something over in the corner behind that there curtain." Joe moves over and pulls back a muslin sheet used for a curtain.

"Here sits an honest to goodness metal, high back bathtub. Full of water and a bar of lye soap sits on the table beside it," says Joe with a wave of his hand. "Looks like y'all can use this here device to cut some trail alkali. We'd appreciate your takin' a dunk before grub time. Grab a wash."

Zep quickly strips down and slides into the tub. It is heavenly. He scrubs vigorously to get the dirt out of every pore in his skin. Guillo impatiently waits his turn.

"*Señor*, Zep, please finish. I cannot stand the feel of this dirt no longer. Hurry, *amigo*. GET OUT."

Joe hollers, "When y'all get done, I rustled up some clean clothes for ya. They're stacked on your bunks. Let the dirty ones lay and I'll get them taken care of for ya. I'll see ya on the front porch when you're finished."

Shortly, both are bathed and sit on the porch admiring their new duds.

"I sure hate to give up my buckskins, but this vest, cotton shirt, and canvas pants do feel nice," Zep says as he knots a bright red bandana around his neck.

"*Si, amigo*, I was thinking the same," Guillo brushes at his tapered *vaquero* trouser, blue shirt, and short waisted jacket.

Sighing contentedly, they watch the slowly setting sun, and wait for the dinner bell.

Suddenly the doors on the main house open and a beautiful young woman steps out onto the covered porch. Taking a deep breath, she looks directly towards the bunkhouse porch, and smiles.

9

THE REASON

A CLANGING BELL SHATTERS THE SEARING BEAUTY OF both the sunset and the woman's attention. She turns and reenters the house. Joe hustles Zep and Guillo into a rapid walk towards the cookhouse.

Who was she, wonders Zep. *Was she smiling at us? I've got to ask Joe.*

Two vaqueros ride up beside them and slow their horses to a walk as their steely black eyes size up Zep and Guillo. Suddenly, they yank their horses to a stop and leap from the saddle landing in front of both men.

"Hey, *hola,* Manolito and Miguel, glad to see you made it in time for supper. These here *amigos* just wandered in from the desert," Joe says gesturing to Zep and Guillo.

Both *vaqueros* look at each other, and once again eye the strangers up and down. Then, they swing an arm around each of Zep and Guillo's shoulders. From beneath full drooping mustaches, they flash smiles of "pearly white" teeth. They sweep their *sombreros* off and knock the dust from their clothes and hats. Each wears tight-legged trousers, a dark colored shirt, a short waist jacket, and tall boots as *Don Louis*, but not as fancy. Their faces light up with humor and fun, and their black eyes show a twinkle of mischief.

"*Muy bueno, amigos,*" Miguel says. "Come, we eat, drink, and tell lies to each other about the desert. Then you must tell us about the Apaches. *Si*, we hear you escape an ambush."

They all walk into the cookhouse. Zep spies two long trestle tables with benches lining both sides. The table and benches sit side by side and stretch fifteen feet each. *Vaqueros* quickly fill the benches of one table and stable hands, field workers, and *hacienda* laborers fill the other table. Joe rushes with Zep and Guillo to sit with the *vaqueros*.

"If'n you don't have your own *casa* and *mamacita* to take care of feedin' you, then ya get your vittles here," Joe says. "It ain't bad, we have a good time, and are fed right well."

Soon pots with chunks of beef and *frijoles* are set along the tables. Next, platters of *tortillas* are passed followed by plates of sliced tomatoes, carrots, and corn on the cob. Jars of *jalapeño* peppers float from hand to hand. There is mayhem of reaching, passing, filling plates, talking, laughter, backslapping, shoving, and joking that speeds mealtime along. Soon the crowd around the tables begins to thin. Men drift off to bunkhouses, barns, and corrals. Some step outside to sit under the *ramada* cover around the cookhouse and light up cigarillos and pipes.

A servant threads his way past the men on the *ramada* and motions for Zep and Guillo to follow. They head directly for an arched doorway at the rear of the main house. The servant opens and holds the door; both men step into a lush, sequestered, quiet, garden surrounded patio. *Don* Louis sits at a table in the middle of the patio with a decanter and several glasses. He slowly sips a drink.

"*Buenos tardes, amigos.* I hope supper was satisfactory for you."

"Thank you, yes," says Zep.

Fascinated by his surroundings, Zep stares in amazement at the plants filling the patio area.

"*Don Louis,* how can a garden like this exist, so lush, healthy, and beautiful?"

"My friend, we sit on top of an ever-flowing spring. It is called an artesian well," says *Don Louis.* "It's been here for as long as I can remember. The water flows up from underground at a constant rate and same temperature year round. The spring is covered and enclosed. Water is piped under the wall and collects in a pond outside. From there it flows out a distance in a stream until it disappears into a large hole in the rocks of a nearby canyon. The well is what makes this *hacienda* possible, so desirable, and why others would like to take it for their own."

"Amazing," Zep marvels. "I once read about artesian wells, but this is the first time I've actually been to one."

"*Manana*, tomorrow, you will need to go to the spring house by the back wall to see the water flowing to the surface. We have water for all our needs: people, livestock, crops, and *even baths*," smirks *Don Louis.*

Zep flinches and recalls how great the bath felt. Getting the trail grime off makes him feel human again.

"Well, gentlemen, because I know she's already made her presence known, I will introduce you to my daughter." *Don Louis* stands up and extends his right hand. Along a foliage-hidden pathway, a beautiful young woman walks in and takes *Don Louis* by his extended hand.

"*Señores*, my daughter, Alassandra."

Zep and Guillo stand mesmerized. The woman from the porch stands before them with long auburn hair hanging to the middle of her back, an eye-appealing curvaceous body of feminine proportions, a pixie-like face, and deep mesmerizing brown eyes with golden flecks that sparkle in the torchlight illumination of the patio. She is as tall as her father with a cinnamon colored complexion. Her pastel blue, thin, billowy blouse flutters in the night breeze; a long multicolored skirt reaches the top of her sandals.

Zep somehow manages to recover his ability to speak, "Good evening, Ma'am. I'm pleased to meet you."

"*Si, mucho gusto, señorita*," stammers Guillo.

"Make yourselves comfortable, be seated, and call me Allie," she says.

"She is her mother's daughter," *Don Louis* says with dampened eyes. "Her smile, laughter, and actions are so like her mother's."

Zep holds her chair as all sit down at the table. *Don Louis* lifts the decanter, "Cognac, gentlemen?"

"Yes, thank you," they both answer.

"Anything for you, my dear?"

"*No*, Papa. But I would like you to no longer require a nursemaid to watch over me. Tell *Señora* Maria to leave me alone."

"It is for your own good and respectability sake," replies *Don Louis* casting an embarrassed smile at Zep and Guillo.

"Papa, I am no longer a child. I have no need for her being my constant companion. You raised me to be independent, think rationally, and take care of myself. What use do I have for a nursemaid? I can ride faster and shoot better than any *vaquero* on the *hacienda*. Please, let me be my own person. Mama would have wanted it so."

"Very well. No more nursemaids. Now, in courtesy, please ask these gentlemen's forgiveness for witnessing our personal discussion," says *Don Louis* indicating Zep and Guillo.

With a blush, Alassandra says, "Gentlemen, I apologize for my outburst and rude behavior in your presence. Please forgive me. *Mi Padre* and I have discussed this problem before. I understand you've had quite an adventure. Papa told me the details as well as hearing it from every wagging tongue in the *hacienda*." She smiles. "You are going to travel to Mesilla, yes?"

Zep replies, "That's home for me, and Guillo is going to help me rebuild it. I'm a mustanger and gather horses to sell for a living."

"Very interesting," she says. "I am familiar with those who chase the wild horses. It is a good living, no?"

"Well, ma'am, it seems to satisfy me."

Allie asks, "Have you ever considered traveling back east to see the cities and people there?"

"Well, ma'am, that has never really seemed important to me. You see it really doesn't interest me much." Zep mulls his response around in his mind. *What is this girl all about? She's fiercely independent, speaks her mind, and knows what she wants. Her spirit is enticing. What is she driving at about travel; there's more here than I hear.*

Standing and with a twirl, Alassandra curtsies and says, "Well, Papa, I will leave you men to talk. Gentlemen, again, I extend apologies for my behavior. Please forgive me. Perhaps you will ride with me in the morning, *señor* Zep. I would like that. Good evening." She turns and leaves without waiting for Zep's reply.

The men rise as she exits the patio and then settle back in their chairs at the table.

"Gentlemen, I need good men to assist me on this *hacienda*. Would you be willing to remain for a while? While you are here, I may share with you a problem you might assist me with."

"We've just arrived, *Don Louis*, but if we can help, we will."

"*Bueno*. As a mustanger, your horsemanship is valuable to this *hacienda*, *Señor* Zep. I will see you work with the *vaqueros*. Share your skills and abilities with them; make them better handlers of horses.

Señor Guillo, what would you like to do? There is much that needs attention."

"*Don Louis*, if possible, I would like to work in the barns and corrals. *Si?*"

"*Bueno*, it is settled. Now, gentlemen, I must apologize for my daughter's outburst."

"That's not required," says Zep reflecting, *this is some girl, speaks her own mind, and stands up for herself. She's like a wild mustang.*

"It must be apparent Alassandra challenges me so," says *Don Louis*. "Her mother, my wife Amelia, God rest her soul, was an *Americano*. We met and married in St. Louis; her family lives there. She came with me to this *hacienda*. Those were years of struggle and survival. She was my right arm, my strength, and support. A tigress in women's clothing, we built and prospered. Alassandra came along and life was good. Small pox took my Amelia from me when Allie was six years old. I knew I had to live for her, but swore that without my Amelia I could not go on. However, as you see we have gone on, yes?"

"*Don Louis*, you say Allie challenges you?" Zep attempts to get the discussion back on track.

"*Si, Señor* Zep, she's very much outspoken. It frightens many young men away. I don't think she'll ever find a husband. I don't know if she wants to. There are days I have no idea what she does want."

"Well is that all bad?" asks Zep. *It may be some challenge keeping up with Señorita de la Vieta.*

"*Amigos,* Alassandra has an overwhelming desire to go East to see the cities and visit her mother's family. I have promised to take her to El Paso, even Santa Fe, but watching over this *hacienda* keeps me from long departures. Allie is *Americano;* she embraces her mother's heritage. I must keep looking for a way to provide her with knowledge and understanding about America so in changing times she is prepared to continue what her mother and I began. You see this, yes? This is not just about her, but about all the other *familias* dependent on this *hacienda* for their very lives."

Zep rolls the information around in his mind as he replies, "I think I get the picture; but what does it have to do with us? Do you want us to take Alassandra to Santa Fe?"

"Oh, no, *mi amigos.* Maybe. At least, not yet. I must first get to know you, learn more about you, study you, if you will, before I entrust you with something I value above all else."

"Whoa, *Don Louis.* I don't know that we can agree to something of this kind," says Zep quickly looking at Guillo.

"Relax *señores*, we will take some time. You learn about me and I about you. But I need to make this clear. I'll need to act before things slip out of my control. I am afraid Alassandra will attempt something foolish, like trying to travel on her own."

"Yes, that would be a problem," agrees Zep.

"What I do like about both of you is that you are survivors. Your trek through Chihuahua demonstrates much about your character. You can tackle what lies before you and overcome it. Besides, I instinctively trust you."

Zep is taken back by *Don Louis'* frank confession and deliberates on his response before replying.

"*Don Louis,* we will do all in our power to respect and repay your trust."

"*Muchas gracias, señores.* I am in your debt."

"*Don Louis,* it is not my intent to appear abrupt, but it is late and my eyes aren't quite focusing. Right now, Guillo and I need rest. If it pleases you, we can discuss details *manana*? Tomorrow comes early. *Buenos noches.*" Punching Guillo to wake him, they rise to exit the patio.

"*Si, si,* we can talk later. *Buenos noches, amigos.* Rest well." *Don Louis* calls to his departing guests as he claps and rubs his hands together.

They walk to the bunkhouse, and spot Joe in a chair on the porch quietly humming to himself.

"Hey, boys. Saw you comin' across the way. Is everything all right?

"You gonna' hang around a while?"

"What did the *Don* have to talk about?"

"Gonna' to help the *vaqueros*?"

"Apaches could be by anytime, right?"

"Whatcha think?"

"I think you need to take a breath and give us time to consider all your questions," says Zep. "So, we are going to turn in. See you in the morning. Try to think up some more questions between now and then. I'd hate to see you run out." Zep smiles and enters the bunkhouse. Guillo smirks at Joe and waves.

Joe smiles and thinks, *they sure are all right, a good sort to have around.*

10

THE RIDE

THE HORSE SNORTS AND STOMPS, ITS SKIN TWITCHES AS the blanket and saddle settle on its back. The stable hand tightens the cinch and wiggles a bit into the horse's mouth. Suddenly, a dozen *vaqueros* trot past, their gear jingles and rattles as they pass. Most of them stare at Zep as he waits beside the corral. It is before dawn and the riders move rapidly through the opened front gate.

Zep smells the aroma from the cookhouse and still tastes the breakfast of *huevos, chorizo, tortillas,* and *frijoles* he shared with the just departed *vaqueros*. Shortly, he knows, another twelve riders will approach from outside and enter the *hacienda* grounds. They are the "night hawks" that watch over the ranch's cattle during the darkness. The returning riders will eat and then collapse in sleep.

The stable hand in his white *patalones*, shirt, and *zapatos* leads Zep's horse out of the corral and ties it to the hitching rail. The animal looks sleek, well fed, and rested. He's a good horse and stood up well under the ordeal in the desert.

"*Muchas gracias.*"

"*Da nada, señor* Zep."

An orange glow lightens the eastern horizon as Zep watches the steady flow of light sweep across the hacienda grounds. Noises rise from the *casas* as people move about going to barns, stables, and corrals. The "city" comes alive.

Zep unties his horse, walks to the front of the main house and reties him to the hitching rail. Stepping onto the porch, he finds a chair and sits to wait for Alassandra. She asked him to ride with her this morning and he doesn't want to make her wait.

Rocking slowly in the chair, Zep continues to observe all the activity that accompanies the start of a new day. He watches as Manolito and Miguel lead their horses to the hitching rail. They climb the steps and join him on the porch.

"*Buenos dias, caballeros.* To what do I owe the honor of your company this morning?"

"*Señor* Zep, you do not know that *Señorita* Alassandra may never leave the *hacienda* without us accompanying her? We are worse than *duenas. Don Louis* will skin us and nail our hides to a barn if we fail to do this.

Laughing out loud, Zep responds, "*Duenas,* chaperones, now that's a scary thought." He looks at the two *vaqueros* standing dressed as they were yesterday with the addition of bandoliers draped from their shoulders like an "X" across each chest. Two holstered pistols on each man, and rifles in scabbards on their saddles. Under their full drooping mustaches, big toothy grins light up both faces as Zep laughs.

"*Si,* Zep, should we curtsey?" They both laugh and grab the seams of their trousers to pantomime the motion.

The doors of the main house suddenly open and Alassandra walks onto the porch wearing a long dark riding skirt, short jacket, white blouse, a flowing red scarf about her throat, and a round brimmed *Caballero* hat on her head. Golden flecks sparkle in her eyes with the morning light, as she surveys the scene before her. The *vaqueros* snatch the sombreros from their heads and hold them in front of their chests. Zep removes his slouched, weathered, stained cowboy hat and runs his hand through his shoulder length hair as his nod acknowledges her arrival.

"*Buenos Dias, Señorita.*" Manolito and Miguel speak in unison, "We are ready."

"*Ay. Caramba.* What must I do to be rid of both of you?" She stomps toward the *vaqueros.*

"*Señorita,* you know *Don Louis* will not let that happen," cringes Manolito.

Spinning around, she looks at Zep, "I'm sorry for these 'babysitters' *Señor* Zep. My Papa constantly fears for my safety."

"I would enjoy their company this morning, *señorita.* I don't think they can spoil a day as lovely as this or a riding companion as lovely as you."

"Thank you, *señor.* What a nice compliment. Very well, for you two 'baby sitters', *vamonos,* we ride."

An unobserved stable hand brings Alassandra's horse around during the exchange with the two *vaqueros.*

As Zep steps down from the porch to mount his horse, he offers a hand to Alassandra. She waves him off and easily steps up and onto her sidesaddle quickly straightening her skirt.

Miguel steps quietly beside Zep and whispers, "*Gracias,*

amigo, Zep, sometimes she is *una diabla* to deal with." He springs fluidly into his saddle. Zep mounts his horse and they all ride through the open gate.

As the four horses move easily down the hillside, Zep takes in the activities going on outside the walls. Wagons make their way out to fields, farmers irrigate crops around the hilltop, and cattle roam with *vacqueros* constantly moving through the herd. Zep sees a *remuda* of horses driven from foothills toward corrals located close to the *hacienda*. They don't appear to be wild horses so he guesses they are *hacienda* working stock.

Moving around the hilltop, he notices a large grove of mature cottonwood trees, their limbs provide shade and relief from the constant sunshine. Riding a couple of horse lengths behind Alassandra and him are the two *vaqueros*. They appear to be ever vigilant as they watch and gesture between themselves at any unusual activity.

Alassandra turns, "*Señor* Zep, would you care to ride to the stream and rest under the cottonwoods? They have grown there by the water for as long as I can remember. The temperature is much cooler from the spring water flowing there."

"Anything you'd like, Alassandra, is fine by me."

"*Por favor*, please call me Allie. If you don't mind, I will call you Zep. *Bueno*?"

"Allie, I'd like to sit a spell under the cottonwoods. Would it be rude to talk about your family when we get there?"

"Not at all, Zep. I think you already know about my parents and what they have worked to accomplish, but I would like to tell you about my plans. Alright?"

"That's fine."

They rein the horses toward the grove. Alassandra waves to Manolito to ride ahead and check out the grove. Both *vaqueros* spur their horses, pass the two riders, and quickly disappear among the trees. They wait on Allie and Zep's arrival and assure them all is safe.

Dismounting, Allie draws a blanket from her saddlebag along with a sack of apples. Letting the horses graze, Zep and Allie sit down on the blanket. He takes an apple from Allie, pulls a knife from his pocket and begins cutting slices.

He offers a slice to Allie, and says, "This is a mighty special treat. I don't often get apples."

"It is special for me as well," Allie replies. "My Papa brought apple tree cuttings from St. Louis when he returned with my Mother. He planted them beyond this grove of Cottonwoods. Watering and nurturing them, they grew. Now we have a large orchard of apple trees. You may have seen the two apple trees in the patio garden. They are special also; one each for my Mother and Papa."

"So, from a few cuttings your father started an orchard?"

"*Si*, he worked with them for many years. In springtime it is wonderful to see the orchard explode in white apple blossoms and we watch the harvest closely to make sure we beat the animals to the fruit."

"Your father is a man of many talents, Allie. You do know his concerns about your desire to travel east and visit your mother's family?"

"*Si*, Zep. That is my wish. I want to travel to St. Louis, meet my family, and spend time to learn all I can of American customs and ways. Is that so wrong?"

"No, Allie, it's not wrong at all. There is a lot to learn, and meeting the rest of your family is worthwhile. Just one word of warning, not all Americans are good just as all Mexicans aren't. Don't be blinded by a compulsion to learn so much about one way of life that you sacrifice the great way you have now. Wow, that's more opinion than I've given in months."

Giggling, Allie replies, "It is good to hear you say more than just a few words. I do respect what I have, but know times are changing. With changes I need to know what to expect and how to prepare in order to be a better custodian of what my mother and father have created. I won't be tricked or cheated out of what we have, but I need to have more knowledge in order to be prepared. This is reasonable, yes?"

Standing up and moving to the horses, Allie reaches into the bag and brings out two apples. She begins feeding her horse an apple and passes one to Zep for his horse. She motions to Miguel and he moves quickly to Allie's side.

"*Si, Señorita*. What can I do?"

"Miguel, I want to apologize for being short and snippy with Manolito and you earlier. You both are a treasure to me and I rely on your protection. Forgive me."

"Oh no, *Señorita*. It is Manolito and I who need to apologize for when we cause you discomfort. We have all grown up together from *ninos*, children, to now. You are more than *Don* Louis' daughter. You belong to Manolito and me. *Perdóname* for being so forward."

"*Gracias*, Miguel. Here, takes these apples and share them with Manolito. We will leave shortly."

"*Muchas gracias, Señorita*. We will be ready to leave whenever you are."

Turning back to Zep, Allie looks past him at the beauty of the Cottonwood grove. She seems to be absorbing the coolness, colors, and atmosphere. Zep watches entranced by her appearance and countenance.

This is a lady, thinks Zep. *I feel like Miguel; I will do anything for her. All she has to do is ask. Yet, can I handle all her direct-ness? I want to gain her respect.*

Allie refocuses on Zep and in a steady voice asks, "Zep, will you take me to Santa Fe? I will travel from there to St. Louis."

"Allie, I will be happy to take you, but first your father must agree. We discussed working at the *hacienda* for a period of time so we can learn about each other. Guillo and I agreed to stay here. I will not be party to a dispute between you and your father because it will place me between a rock and a hard place."

Her brown eyes flash as Allie tosses her head and laughs, "You are a wise man, Zep. Papa will come to trust you and we will make certain he is in agreement. Now let's ride back to the *hacienda*."

She picks up the blanket and stuffs it back into her saddle-bag. Quickly mounting, all four riders start uphill toward the *hacienda*. Manolito rides in front and Miguel rides behind.

11

DECISIONS

Alassandra and Zep ride slowly toward the *hacienda* when suddenly four *vaqueros* charge up and surround them. They are rushed through the front gate and to the main house. The riders turn and gallop outside, as the gates slam shut.

Don Louis steps out onto the porch and spreading his arms offers an explanation. "Two riders have spotted an *indio* crossing a field north of the *hacienda*. He was headed west, but I take no chances."

"Papa, if it was just one *indio*, I have Manolito, Miguel, and Zep to escort me. It is not necessary to call out an army." Alassandra says with exasperation.

"What's done, is done," says *Don Louis*. He motions to Allie and Zep. "When you both are settled from your ride, please join me in my office. I have details to discuss with you, *gracias*." He turns and goes inside.

A stable hand helps Alassandra from her horse then leads the animal back to the barn. Zep follows to the barn and dismounts, leaving his horse in care of the stables. Going to the bunkhouse, he finds Guillo and Joe pondering over a game of checkers.

"A nice ride this morning, Zep?" Joe inquires as he deftly jumps two of Guillo's checkers. "It appears you had the best company in the whole dadburn place riding with you."

"Just so you know, and can spread the word," Zep smiles. "I had a great time, wonderful companion, and it is none of your business."

Guillo rolls his eyes, "See, Joe, I told you he would say something like that. You have to know my *companero* is very silent about what he does."

"Shucks, I wasn't prying, just asking, that's all," Joe smirks.

"I'm heading to the main house for a meeting with *Don Louis*. Do you want to come along Guillo?"

"No, *amigo*. I have Joe ready to be beaten and it will be the first game in five. So, I think I will stay and finish him off."

"Alright, I'll be back later," Zep says, walks out and heads toward the main house.

Stepping up on the porch he approaches the front door, knocks, and is ushered inside. A servant leads him into the office where *Don Louis* waits, standing at the window.

Without turning around he says, "Zep, if I know my Alassandra, she has approached you about going to see her Mother's family. As I have shared with you she challenges me regarding this regularly. As we discussed, I will never allow her to travel with someone I do not trust. Last night, you agreed to work at this *hacienda* so we can better learn about each other.

Do you still agree?"

"*Don Louis,* our agreement last night stands. Yes, she asked me to take her, and her reason sounds right. It will be a dan-gerous task. During our time of getting acquainted, we can meet to discuss supplies, the route, and protection."

"It is good to plan. Let me share with you what I've considered. Crossing to Las Cruces is not the right direction. I think the better route is out of the desert and up into the foothills and forests of the Mogollon. By this route, it assures water and better travel conditions. It is the way I would select."

"We both know the state of affairs with the Indians, so going north to the mountains and turn east to the Rio Grande River can work."

"That's the beginning. Now let's go onto the patio, have Alassandra join us, and eat our midday meal." *Don Louis* turns from the window and leads Zep out.

Alassandra joins the men; her long hair is pulled back into a ponytail swinging with every step she takes. A long pale green dress enhances every curve of her body and makes her auburn hair seem to blaze. Aware of her appearance she stops and twirls for her Papa.

"*Muy bien, muchas gracias, mi hija,* very good, thank you, my daughter," says *Don Louis.* "You continue to make me smile. After our meal we need to retire to the office and discuss details. I understand you have asked Zep to take you East, and he has agreed."

"*Si,* Papa. I know you cannot because of your responsibilities. So, I have asked Zep."

"*Bueno.* I then have a couple of additions to our plan that must be taken into consideration. Manolito and Miguel will go as well. Ah, ah, ah, no debate."

"But, Papa, surely Zep and Guillo are enough to accompany me. You agreed no other nursemaids."

"*Mi hija,* these men are *vacqueros,* not nursemaids."

"Ohhh, Papa. Will you never let me be independent?"

"*Don Louis,* I think having those two *vacqueros* along is a good idea, " Zep agrees.

Flashing Zep a quick glare, Alassandra smiles, "Alright, I acquiesce. It will take four men to make sure one woman arrives safely." She smirks.

Warm *tortillas,* fresh fruit, cheese, thinly sliced ham, and *pan y mantequilla,* along with a decanter of red wine make a filling meal.

All three move from the patio into the office and *Don Louis* stands before the large map behind his desk.

"We are in agreement, Zep and Guillo will work at the hacienda for the next few months. This allows us time to plan for the trip as well as know each other better. *Bueno?*"

"That's what we agreed," says Zep. Alassandra nods in approval.

"Just to show I haven't disregarded your desire to go, and to make it clear you need not abruptly decide to do something on your own, here is what I've been working on."

"Thank you, Papa," says Allie.

"The route should go like this. North skirting Animas Peak by the *hacienda* to Mexican Springs, next to Birchville and the Mogollon country, then east until you reach the Rio Grande," says *Don Louis.*

Zep studies the map, walks up to it, points at the details, and says, "It might be better to go from Birchville into the Mogollon country and travel north along the headwaters of the Gila River, to South Baldy Mountain, and miss the Black Range and the

Jornada del Muerto altogether. I know for a fact the Mescalero Apaches raise hell along the *Jornada*. Then we'd go east to Socorro, the Rio Grande River, and north to Santa Fe."

Considering the map, *Don Louis* pauses and then responds, "*Si*, Zep, that may be a better route. Avoiding the *Jornada del Muerto* from Las Cruces to Socorro can be much better. The only problem is the Mogollon is all Chiricahua country."

"It's all Apache country from here to there." Zep points at Santa Fe on the map.

"Alassandra, I know you are not familiar with the territory we are talking about, but there is wisdom of experience in Zep's suggestions." *Don Louis* looks at his daughter.

"*Si*, Papa. I rely on those who know the land by their experiences."

"*Bueno*. Now we have work to do around the *hacienda*. We will continue to meet as we prepare for the journey. Now, I have work to do. Go, go." *Don Louis* moves to this desk.

"Planning is fine, *Don Louis*, but don't forget it's mountains and we must travel light and fast. No pack train, only what we absolutely need goes with us. One mule, that's it. Okay?"

"*Ay*, you know you'll have a woman traveling with you, no?"

"Yep, she will have to tough it out like us *caballeros*."

"*Si*, what you say is probably best. Only one mule," agrees *Don Louis*. Alassandra looks at both men and shrugs.

Zep excuses himself and leaves the main house, heading to the bunkhouse. He spots Guillo on the porch.

"Well, *amigo*, how would you like to see some country?"

"Zep, *mi amigo*, have I not seen enough country already? Do you forget about the desert? My body is only beginning to become alive again and you talk about more travel. *Ay, Chihuahua*, what is the matter with you?"

"Oh, I just like to see scenery. No desert this time. We're heading for the mountains. You'll love the bears, cougars, wolves, and bobcats, not to mention Apaches."

"*Amigo*, are you not content to kill me in the desert? Now, you want wild animals to tear me apart? Apaches. When do we run out of Apaches? *Ay*, okay, *muy bien*, we go to the mountains."

"We've got a few months to get ready, so make yourself handy around the *hacienda*. I'm going out with the *vaqueros* to wrangle horses. How about you help in the corrals, barns, or cookhouse. Sound alright with you?"

"*Si*, Zep, I will find ways to repay the hospitality that has been given to me," says Guillo.

12

RETRIBUTION

ALCHESAY WATCHES THE TWO MEN, CLIMB ABOARD THE famer's wagon. He is covered in alkali, his black hair is multishades of grey from dirt, his long breechcloth is dirty and bedraggled. The sun has baked and caused his skin to peel from his shoulders, lips cracked, and eyes bloodshot. He has come far across the desert trailing them as a fox does rabbits. Yes, they are his 'rabbits.' Not wanting to lose them, he quickly begins to parallel the wagon as it rolls along the trail. He moves from bush, to shrub, to trees using all the cover available so his presence goes undetected. As the wagon begins to climb a hill, he sees the *hacienda*. It is a formidable place. The high walls, men on guard, observers on the roof of the central building, all indicate this is not a place easily surprised. The wagon with his 'rabbits' approaches and enters the compound. He rapidly moves through a field of tall corn almost stumbling into two *vaqueros*.

Silently, slowly, he eases back into the corn stalks. Sinking to the ground he slowly exhales and whispers to himself, "You fool, how could you not pay attention? You are watching those white men and the *hacienda*, and almost lose your life."

The *vaqueros* sit dismounted and resting at the edge of the cornfield. Their horses stand quietly. Shortly, they remount and continue their slow perimeter ride around the *hacienda*. Alchesay knows they scout for intruders. He is one.

Suddenly, twelve *vaqueros* dash through the open main gates. Alchesay goes immediately on defense. Notching an arrow, he throws his bow into a position to release the killing shaft, and then notices the riders veer away rushing down the hill following the trail. A quiet exhaling of breath stabilizes the adrenalin rush Alchesay feels. Sitting down, he allows the corn stalks and leaves to cover him.

What do I do now, he wonders. *The hacienda is more than I need to deal with. Revenge on my two 'rabbits' still burns in me. They escape the ambush and my tracking them. They will not elude me; they are as good as dead right now.*

As Alchesay deliberates what to do, he quickly remembers the other goal of his quest, *my people. What is happening to my people?*

The white eyes will be here for a while, he concludes. *They are in no shape to continue without rest. They are not Apache. I will leave them here and search out the condition of my people. If they leave before I return, I will find them.*

With his decision made, Alchesay moves back into the cornfield and, rises to look around, and spots a grove of Cottonwood trees. He knows they only grow where there is water. Quickly, he stealthfully makes his way to the stream in the trees.

From the protection of the grove, Alchesay views wagons moving through the fields that surround the *hacienda*, shepherds with herds of sheep, fowl, and other animals, *vaqueros* wrangle cattle and horses, and riders guard everyone outside the walls. He knows the stream draws every living thing to it. Once refreshed and revived with water, he looks for a place to hide. Searching the rocks at the end of a box canyon, he spots a ledge well above a hole where water flows into the ground. The ledge appears to be deep into the rock and affords a concealed hiding place away from all but intense investigation. Climbing up onto the ledge he at last relaxes and sleeps.

Awaking in the dark of the night, Alchesay moves down to the stream and waits. Shortly, two rabbits move cautiously to the water. He kills both and climbs back to the ledge, goes to the deep end of it, starts a small consealed fire, roasts, and devours his quarry.

As daylight approaches, Alchesay is startled by noise below. He slides to the edge of the ledge and peers into the grove. Two *vaqueros* rush their horses into the trees and furtively search the brush and bushes along the edge of the stream. They thoroughly check the wooded area, and then rest their mounts as two other riders join them.

Alchesay squints, focuses, and whispers, "It is my white man, one of my 'rabbits.' He is with a woman. Ah, he will be here for a while." Smiling, he slides back from the ledge edge, and waits for them to depart.

After the visitors leave, Alchesay begins to run swiftly around the *hacienda*, and heads west toward the mountains. As he always has, he runs miles before midday. Stopping for water in a *playa*, he resumes his travel. By nightfall he approaches the mountains and finds a place of concealment. Catching small game in the morning, he once again is nourished and runs on. By night he's well into the mountains and begins searching for signs of *The People*. Someone can tell him what has happened to his *Chokonen* band.

On his third day in the mountains, Alchesay approaches a watering hole the white men call Apache Pass. It is here he finds signs of another band. After filling up with water, he begins to follow their trail. They are moving southeast and at twilight he spots a warrior, a sentry watching over the back trail of the band. He moves into the open and approaches the warrior who is well aware of his presence.

"My cousin, I am Alchesay of the *Chokonen* band, a *Chiricahua*. May I approach your camp?" he asks.

"Traveler, I heard your approach from a distance. You are very sloppy or want to make sure I know you are there," the warrior responds.

"I have no intent to sneak up on you, my cousin. I only want to share a fire and seek answers to questions about my people," Alchesay replies.

"Approach the camp. We too are *Chokonen*. You may find relatives in this camp." The warrior waves Alchesay ahead into a small valley where he sees a few campfires burning.

He is welcomed with hospitality, civility, and warmth from the band. They acknowledge they indeed know his people. A distant relative, that Alchesay respectfully calls an "uncle," approaches him to talk.

"My warrior, I know of your band, they were mine at one time as well. My knowledge of them grieves me and my heart breaks to tell it to you," he says.

Alchesay is beyond distraught, "My uncle, I know we do not speak the names of those who are dead out loud. I would never ask that, but can you share what happened?"

"My nephew, the pony soldiers came, led by the soldier general, Nantan Ba'cho. The warriors of your band met him at the pass leading to their camp. Nantan Ba'cho had with him "wagons that roar," what white men call cannons. Your warriors die when the rocks exploded. Old and young warriors are blown apart. Some women and children of your band flee and join our relative Cochise deep in the mountains. A few flee further to the Sierra Madres in Mexico. They scatter to the winds."

The message crushes Alchesay. He asks, "Why would the soldiers use 'wagons that roar'?"

His uncle says, "A pony soldier who carried a message of surrender was killed. Nantan Ba'cho found what was left of him as he approached your band. Some say this is why the soldiers killed first."

At that moment, Alchesay remembers the words of his uncle, Dehkeya; *you will have the blood of our people on your hands.* Dropping to his knees, in grief he pulls his knife and slashes both arms. His warm blood flows freely and drops from his fingertips.

He feels strong hands lift him up, move him closer to the fire, and lay him on a blanket. Other hands bind his wounds. He sleeps. Dreams disturb him all night as he thrashes and mumbles in his sleep. When the sun creeps over the horizon he rises to see the band load their belongings getting ready to move. He searches out the band's headman and expresses his appreciation for their hospitality and care of him. He stands beside a burned out fire and watches them move toward the southeast.

His arms throb, his mind tumbles over and over. *My people scattered to the winds. What should I do? How can I do anything?*

In Alchesay's mind the two white men, his 'rabbits,' become

all that is wrong and evil. He accepts he has his people's blood on his hands, but the whites are the reason it happened. They are responsible for what happened to his people. His quest is now more than killing white men; it becomes "blood" retribution.

"No matter where they are or where they go, I will find my 'rabbits.' Their end will not be pleasant or fast. They will suffer as I now suffer. I will wait here a few days to heal and grieve, then I will find them again." Alchesay vows aloud.

13

MEXICAN SPRINGS

ZEP STEPS UP ON THE PORCH OF THE *HACIENDA'S* MAIN house, knocks on the door, and enters the foyer. Standing directly in front of him is a stranger with a soft slouch hat pulled low, head down, a draped *serape* covers front and back, worn boots, and gripping a Colt revolver. The handgun slowly rises and Zep takes a step back, reaches for his pistol, and remembers it's in the bunkhouse.

Who is this? Why's he here? Where is anybody? Why'd I forget my pistol? Got to find something to use to defend myself.

His eyes rapidly search for *Don Louis* or servants. No one but the stranger and Zep are in the hallway. Slowly, the stranger's head tilts upward. A broad, beautiful smile greets Zep. Alassandra stands before him, quickly lowering the weapon.

"So, Zep, do you think I will pass for a *caballero*," asks Alassandra.

"I'm sure you'll pass, you almost scared a year's growth out of me," Zep replies. "If I had my sidearm, I might have even drawn down on you. That's scary. Where did you get those duds?" *This woman continues to surprise me.*

"They're mine. Do you think I always stay in a house? I've ridden this land more times and more places than you, *amigo.*"

"Okay, okay, you're quite the *vaquero*; and if this is what you're wearing as we travel, then you're good to go." Zep says.

"I added the *serape* in order to shed rain, intense sunlight, and in case it's chilly in the mountains," Alassandra comments. "It's a great covering. I seldom ride without it."

"Looks like it's what this trip needs," says Zep. "You'll appreciate it in the mountains. Is your father in his office?"

"*Si*, Papa waits for us."

The past months of riding with the *vaqueros* and managing the *hacienda's* horse herd have been time well spent. Zep feels success in gaining the acceptance of the wrangler's *jefe* and *Don Louis'* trust. He's shared his horse breaking knowledge with the *vaqueros,* gained their friendship, spent time roping replacement horses for rider mount changes, kept the herds from straying too far, and drove livestock into the *hacienda* corrals each night.

It's been exhausting work but enjoyable, thinks Zep. *The evening meetings with Don Louis and Alassandra have prepared us for travel to Santa Fe, and this morning we finalize everything. We'll depart tommorow.*

Zep and Alassandra enter the office. *Don Louis* sits behind his desk closely checking the ledgers spread out before him.

"Ah, Zep, you have been busy, no? I am pleased to be such a good judge of character. Both Guillo and you have proven to me beyond any doubt you are men worthy of trust."

"Thank you, *Don Louis*," says Zep. Allie stands to the side smiling.

"Now, we are ready to ride north. I have supervised, packed, and repacked one mule. *Ay.* You have no idea how difficult that assignment was. You have what is needed for the journey and not one item more."

"One mule and riders are all that stand any chance of making it through the Mogollon Country, *Don Louis*," Zep says.

"*Bueno, bueno*, you are right. You need to travel light and fast. So, you will leave *manana por la manana,* tomorrow morning?"

"Yes, *Don Louis,* first light we ride north."

"Once you are past Animas Peak you will come to Mexican Springs. *Americanos* try to make a village out of the Butterfield Stage station located there. The stage line contracts with me to provide horses and I rent them land to build their station. The *gringos* now think they own the land. I will deal with them soon," *Don Louis* says.

"Once Americans get their hooks in something, they are difficult to convince to give it up," says Zep.

"Ah, well, I will deal with it in time." Moving to the wall map *Don Louis* traces a route. "You will ride north from Mexican Springs to Birchville. It is in the Mogollon area, a mining settlement. It is rough and uncivilized. Take care while there. Some time ago, three *amigos*, heading for the gold strike in California, stopped and found gold in Mule Creek. Another miner, Birch, he finds more gold and this brings more miners. The Chiricahua Apaches drive them away, but only temporarily. Now, other miners are back to gouge gold out the ground. The Apaches continue to threaten all those in the mountains."

"We will watch Birchville carefully, *Don Louis,*" Zep promises.

"*Bueno*. From there you have to survive the Mogollon Country. Locate the Gila River and travel the East Tributary. Follow it north to Mount Baldy and east to Socorro. Then, it should be an easy ride north to Santa Fe. Manolito and Miguel are ready to ride in the morning and will bring the pack mule. *Via con Dios*."

"I always hope God rides with me, *Señor*. Thank you. Because it will be a while before Alassandra and you will see each other, please take this evening to enjoy each other's company with no interruptions. I will see you in the morning, Allie. Be ready to ride. *Don Louis*, I have one request before I leave you. Are you able to provide me with firearms? I have only my pistol. My other weapons were taken in Mexico."

"Come my friend, let's go into the hallway." *Don Louis* moves to the tall cabinets in the middle of the hallway. He opens the doors and displays an armory of weapons. "This *casa* is a fortress, *amigo*. Please take what you need and enough ammunition as well."

Zep surveys the selection of firearms. He pulls a new Paterson carbine .44 from the cabinet; this replaces the rifle he lost. He also grabs two short barrel muzzleloader Greener shotguns, good for short distance and spreading shot and two Walker Colt .44 revolvers. Next, he grabs a supply of shot and caps. Finally, he finds two well-worn holsters for the revolvers. Now, Guillo and he are equipped. Thanking *Don Louis*, he leaves the father and daughter to say their goodbyes, and heads for the bunkhouse.

Guillo waits for him as he enters the bunkhouse. "So, Zep, we leave in the morning, no?"

"Yes, Guillo, we ride in the morning. Here is something to weigh you down a little as we ride." Zep tosses a holstered Colt and Greener to him.

"*Ay, amigo*, these are *muy bueno*, very good. I know we are ready to ride now," Guillo says.

"Your gear ready to go? First light comes quick," Zep asks.

"*Si*, my saddlebags are stuffed, bedroll, cooking utensils, and ropes are ready."

"Good, my horse is loaded also. Manolito has a pack mule ready to go in the morning."

"Zep, I also have a couple of *serapes* for us. One of the ladies in the *casas* makes them for us. They may come in handy in the mountains," says Guillo.

Zep rolls onto his bunk and is quickly asleep. Guillo lies down and shortly begins snoring softly.

14

ON TO THE MOGOLLON

ZEP LEADS HIS HORSE TO THE HITCHING RAIL IN FRONT of the main house where three other horses and a mule await. Manolito and Miguel sit on the steps. He sees Alassandra standing at the end of the porch. The soft light casts an aura around her momentarily taking Zep's breath away. *How will something this lovely survive where we are going? Will any of us survive?*

Zep knows during the past days, her appearance, conversation, laughter, and presence all affect him. He understands what drives her, a devotion to the people and land of this *hacienda*. Her character, inner strength, and independence, as well as beauty stir him. She is willing to make this hazardous trip, risk her life to learn more about her family and Americans, only to return and apply the knowledge to this lonely spot in New Mexico.

Hearing Zep approach, she turns and smiles at him. "*Buenos dias*. It is a good day to ride, yes?" She is dressed in the trousers, slouch hat, shirt, and serape that greeted him yesterday in the *hacienda* hallway.

Zep, entranced by the smile, stumbles in his reply, "*Si*, yes, yep…it's a good day." *There is something special about this girl,* thinks Zep. *What is it?*

Guillo breaks the trance by walking up and says, "Let's ride while it's cool. It will get hot soon enough."

"Mount up," Zep replies.

Everyone mounts and moves single file out of the *hacienda* as the gates are opened for them.

On the trail, Zep immediately gives directions on how to proceed, "Manolito ride to the left side out far enough so you can still see us. Miguel, you take the right side. Guillo, ride the point, up front, far enough forward but keep an eye on Alassandra. I will ride in the middle with her and lead the mule. We will switch positions every couple of hours. Sound about right to you?"

"*Si*, Zep," is a unanimous response and the three riders quickly move in separate directions.

"Zep, why do you send them away when we could all ride together?" asks Alassandra.

"From here to Santa Fe we must take all the precautions we can. Riding together almost guarantees an ambush. With riders on the flanks and point we stand a better chance of stirring up something before we get in the middle of it. We kick up less dust and leave multiple trails making it harder to follow," says Zep.

"I am beginning to see why Papa agreed on you taking me to Santa Fe," Alassandra smiles.

"Yes, Ma'am, I promised your Father to escort you and see you get there safely. I'll do that or die trying," Zep says earnestly.

"I know we will arrive safely. I do not want to lose you, Zep," says Alassandra.

He wonders about her response.

The desert stretches before them; a thin purple line is visible on the horizon. It is the Mogollon Mountains.

After two hours the outriders shift positions and Guillo's horse settles in beside Alassandra.

"Guillo, what do you know of *Señor* Zep?" asks Alassandra.

"*Señorita*, I know he rescued me from *malo gringos*, an Apache ambush, and led me across the desert. There is nothing more I need to know. He is a man who says what he will do, and does what he says. He is my *companero*. Why do you ask?"

She turns her head and smiles. "He escorts me, I need to know."

Guillo smirks and responds, "*Si, Señorita*, it is always good to know."

Another couple of hours and Zep calls a halt. Waving all the riders together they collect and check their equipment. Guillo looks over the pack on the mule to make certain it does not rub sores on the animal's back. All drink from their canteens, water the horses, and share some *tortillas*.

"We are about half way to Mexican Springs," Zep says. "We should be there by evening. Let's keep making good time. *Vamonos.*" The riders rotate positions and ride out. Manolito rides with Alassandra.

The next four hours pass as the riders rotate positions and walk along through the heat of the day. Early evening, the group is on a rise looking down at four adobe *casas* and two large corrals.

"Mexican Springs, Butterfield stage stop," Zep points. "I was here a while back chasing mustangs. Not much to it then, not much now. Let's move back down this rise and make camp. Don't see much reason to announce us, nothing to be gained by that. Miguel, take care of stock. Guillo set up camp. Manolito and I will ride out a ways to see what can be scrounged for supper."

Everyone sets about the tasks. Guillo has Alassandra's tent set up, campfire going, and cooking utensils spread out when Manolito and Zep return.

Zep slips off his saddle and turns his horse over to Miguel. Manolito drops a fifty-pound javalina off his saddle and takes his horse to the picket line.

"I have never seen anything like it in my life," Zep says. "We ride out a ways and Manolito spots something moving in the bush. He tells me to wait, rides into the bush and flushes out this here javalina. He steers it to the open, then rides it down, drops off his saddle, and with his big "pig stickin" knife slits its throat slick as can be. I never saw that before. No gunfire, no noise, just dead javalina."

"I will skin it and cut up what we can eat and leave the rest for the desert. Then, I put meat in my skillet with onions, peppers, and spices, *ay, es bueno*. Then I shred the meat and we can have it with *tortillas y frijoles. Fabuloso*," says Guillo.

After a day of riding, supper is good and filling. Clean up goes quickly and everyone shakes out their bedrolls to turn in for the night. Alassandra stops Zep.

"Zep, do we have a longer day tomorrow?"

"With luck, we'll have a ten hour ride tomorrow to get close to Birchville," says Zep. "I want to get close to the town but not in it. We'll camp outside town and ride through in daylight. It's a rough place and we need to see everything that might come our way. Sleep well."

"Zep, thank you for today," Alassandra leans close and kisses Zep on the check. "Sleep well also."

Zep moves over by Guillo and lays down on his bedroll. Guillo turns toward him. "Sleep well, Zep." He puckers up and waves a kiss with his hand. Guillo grins.

Zep glances at Guillo, "One more pucker, Amigo, and your next one will be with a busted lip." He smiles, rubs the spot of Allie's kiss, and rolls over.

Before daylight Zep rouses everyone. Last night's fire coals are stirred to a new blaze for coffee and warming *tortillas* for breakfast. Camp is packed and the riders head toward Birchville at sunrise.

Alassandra realizes how the landscape changes. More trees are seen, mesquite, oak, and some piñon pines. The land rises and they climb from the desert into the foothills. What was a purple line on the horizon the other day now takes shape as tall rugged mountains and cliffs.

Zep rides beside Alassandra this morning and she asks, "What makes this Mogollon country so special?"

"Well, it's special land for the Chiricahua, it's their *Apacheria*, and they protect it fiercely, have for years. Their lands used to stretch from the Arkansas River into Chihuahua, Mexico, and from Central Texas to middle of the Arizona Territory.

These mountains run at least fifty to sixty miles across this corner of the territory. Why, they must jump up near a thousand feet from the desert to the highest points. The sandstone and limestone been blasted by wind and water through the ages and erosion creates canyons, valleys, rocky out-cropping, buttes, and overhangs all along the mountains. It's beautiful and dangerous; amazes you and can kill you. I guess it's the majesty and mystery of it that makes the Apaches fight so hard to hang onto it. Wow, now I've probably told you way more than you wanted to know, but they sure do get my attention."

"No, no, please tell me more about this land, Zep. I want to know about all of it."

"They are named for a long ago Spanish governor of New Mexico, *Don Juan Mogollon*. The Apaches and whites have fought around here since *1849*, and Apaches and Mexicans mixed things up for generations. During the war between Mexico and the U.S., the Chiricahua Apaches allowed American soldiers to pass through the Mogollon area. They were fighting the Mexicans, and the Apaches been fighting Mexicans forever. There was a truce, kind of like 'your enemy is my enemy.' After the war, Americans began to move into the Mogollon and all bets were off. It's been warfare ever since. Okay, I'm done. Way more words than I ever speak."

"Zep, I thank you for telling me about this area. I want to learn all I can," says Alassandra. "Will Birchville be dangerous?"

"No, I don't expect anything; still have to be careful. However, once we start into the Gila River area things might get interesting," said Zep.

The trail continues to rise and soon the jagged face of the Ponderosa pine covered mountains fills their view; the Mogollon Mountains stretch from east to west. Pines proliferate the landscape and rocky scree piles up at the base of cliffs and buttes. The trail winds through a valley floor climbing upward. The riders are forced into riding single file through the overgrowth of juniper trees, manzanita, and creosote brush. Stopping every two hours, the day passes swiftly, and by nightfall the smell of pines overwhelms the group. Setting up camp in a small valley beside a brook, supper is quickly prepared and eaten as night's darkness consumes them. A million stars light up the heavens above and a lullaby of night wind rustles through the pines.

Alassandra comes over to the campfire and sits beside Zep, linking her arm with his and laying her head on his shoulder. "It is a lovely place, Zep, no?"

"Yes, Allie, I think this land is as close to heaven as one can get."

In the dark, a cougar screams and snarls. Alassandra flinches and grabs Zep's arm tightly.

"He smells us and the horseflesh," Zep says. "He wants us to know he's watching. It's his backyard we are passing through."

"How can you not be afraid?" she asks.

"Oh, he don't want to bother us and we don't want to bother him. He's being respectful. Besides, he'll be here when we're gone in the morning."

"You know this land well, don't you?" Allie says. "Did you ever want to see other places?"

"Well, I did see other places when I was a kid. Austin, Houston, San Antonio, and Indianola in Texas. Albuquerque's okay while Santa Fe is special, El Paso is not so much. I'm really at home here." Zep shares.

"I have to see St Louis and other American cities," says Allie. "I need to see what progress looks like and be able to bring what I learn back to my *hacienda*."

Alassandra thinks about this man her arm is entwined with. *Since his arrival at the hacienda, I know he is something special. His silent strength, sense of protection, and goodness are what I appreciate. I know this is the kind of man I could be with. But, my life includes going and seeing things beyond where he wants to go.*

"I know you have to go and see places," says Zep.

Startled, Allie looks up at Zep. *Does he read my thoughts? How can he know what I am thinking?*

"You have a mission, a cause, and it makes sense. That is one of the reasons I agreed to escort you. Guillo, Manolito, Miguel, and I will help you accomplish it," says Zep.

He wonders, *what future is there with one so driven and compelled. What can New Mexico territory offer compared to St. Louis?*

Zep breaks their thought filled reverie, "Tomorrow will come early; its time to turn in. We don't know what waits for us in Birchville. Better get some shut eye."

Allie leaves Zep and goes into her tent. Zep looks around the camp, spots Manolito sitting beside a tree taking the first watch. Zep will relieve him in a few hours. He moves to his bedroll and sees Guillo watch him. Guillo winks and throws a kiss. Zep picks up his saddlebag and tosses it at him.

15

ALCHESAY'S WAY

I T HAS BEEN A LONG THREE MONTHS FOR ALCHESAY. HIS run from the Chiricahua Mountains back to the *hacienda* ends in waiting. He needs a horse. During the wait he plaits a halter from fibers he has stripped off yucca leaves. For the past three days he lies on an arroyo bank seducing horses to move closer to him. The *vaqueros* continue to ride around and manage the horse herd, but daily Alchesay entices the horses to move closer. Today he will get his horse. He is ready as a chestnut colored gelding moves closer to him curious about the way the halter flips back and forth on the ground. He slides down the bank into the deep ditch; the horse follows. As the horse steps onto the sandy floor of the arroyo, Alchesay leaps onto its back and wraps his hand in the horse's mane. Steering the horse further into the arroyo and keeping it in the sandy soil, he gallops away. A *vaquero* suddenly rides up and looks in the arroyo. Shouting at the other riders, he gallops along the edge and pulls out his rifle as he rides.

Kicking the horse in the sides, Alchesay lays flat against the animal's withers and neck, he wills himself to become one with the horse. Throwing up sand, the horse explodes into a ground-gulping gallop as it eats up distance. Not wanting to risk other Apaches being in the arroyo, the *vaquero* slows up and throwing the rifle to his shoulder snaps a shot at the fleeing Indian. Alchesay manages to round a bend in the arroyo as the rifle fires and the shot misses. He continues to ride hard until the animal's sides start heaving and coat begins to lather. Alchesay stops, slides off, and slips the halter onto the horse's head. They begin to walk to the nearest water seep.

His arrival at the *hacienda* is opportune and coincides as five riders leave and head north. Waiting to capture a horse frustrates him but risking *vaqueros* in the open is not an option. He knows the riders' direction, now has a horse, and begins to track. It will not be long before he has them.

The slashes on his arms over the loss of his band heal well. There is little discomfort from the self-inflicted injuries. His heart is still burdened with the loss of his band, and retribution burns intensely within him. *The white men in front of me must pay the price for what I've lost,* he thinks.

Alchesay feels a certain sense of respect in tracking the riders. The leader is not without knowledge. It takes him some time to realize the riders have divided up and ride to avoid an ambush. He almost loses their trail until it becomes clear what happened. *This is something an Apache would do.*

"I don't follow a foolish white man," he whispers. "This will make catching him even more satisfying."

Alchesay discerns the riders are headed toward Mexican

Springs. It is the only close white man village. It isn't much of a village, but whites occupy the *casas*. He is halfway there and decides to gamble on Mexican Springs being their destination. Spurring his horse ahead he will get there as direct as possible.

He arrives at a hill above Mexican Springs and hides to view the activity below. After an hour of watching, he knows the riders are not in the village. He begins backtracking to find their trail. Covering the desert back and forth, it takes another hour to find the cold camp of the white men. The signs say they stopped before arriving in Mexican Springs and continued their journey going around the village. He will not try to outguess them again. From now on he is going to follow their trail until he catches up with his prey. Once again, he is impressed with the leader of the riders. He becomes convinced the white man knows Apache ways.

Alchesay follows the trail as it leads toward the Mogollon Mountains. He smiles a knowing smile. "The *Apacheria*," he says to himself. "The land of my ancestors and home of the Chiricahua people. I know the spirits will support me in my quest."

The changing landscape is noticeable as he rides into the foothills. He enters the Ponderosa pines as dusk creeps over the land. Suddenly from among the trees he hears an owl hoot. Two, three, eight times the owl calls. Involuntarily, Alchesay shivers. An omen, and not a good one, owls have forever heralded bad happenings befalling a hearer. Big Owl is a dangerous and malicious being among Apache spirits. He is in human or animal form. All Apaches know owl is the adversary of the War Twins, Born for Water and Killer of Enemies, heroes of *The People*. The number of calls signifies the intensity of impending trouble.

"This is not good. What does Big Owl plan for me," whispers Alchesay. "Do I continue to follow, stop, wait on other signs?" His horse continues to move quickly through the woods parallel to the well-used trail. The pines continue to thicken as the trail begins to rise. The rocky face of mountain cliffs stare down at him as Alchesay dismounts and looks for a concealed place to overnight. No fire tonight. Hobbling his horse, he finds an overhanging cliff to provide cover.

Alchesay tries to find release from overpowering worry.

The morning sun creeps into the mountain valley and under the overhang where Alchesay feels its warmth he sits thinking about how to proceed. The riders are still in front of him, he thinks they head to the white man settlement of Birchville. Warriors drove the white eyes away from this part of *Apacheria* a few years ago, but the vermin continues to return. They tear up the land, cut the timber, ruin the creeks, destroy the wildlife, their villages stink, and they do as well. Alchesay decides before falling asleep he'll continue the hunt for the riders. They must pay for his loss. The spirits can do with him, as they will.

Unhobbling and mounting his horse, Alchesay resumes tracking. The trail leads upward and into thicker pine forests following the valley until it opens onto a flat mesa-like area. In the distance he sees the white man settlement of Birchville. He will not make the same mistake as at Mexican Springs. This time he follows the riders' trail to the outskirts of town and knows they have entered. Outside of the town, he finds a place of concealment that gives him excellent visibility. He studies the village to ascertain that his prey is in this place.

There is a rush of activity in the white man's village. Alchesay sees his riders. Four mount their horses in front of a large building and ride to the opposite end of town. The fifth one rides toward Alchesay where he stops, rushes in and out of a building, and confronts another white man in the street. One of the four riders now moves down the street, points a weapon at the white men in the street, one man mounts a horse and joins the other rider as both race to the end of town to join the other three. All five ride out of town. The white man left in the street is irate. He stomps, shouts, and screams at the departing riders.

Alchesay moves quickly back to where his horse is hidden, unhobbles it, mounts, and begins to ride a wide circle to bypass the village. He will be on the riders' trail soon and follow to where they stop. He can almost smell their blood.

16

BIRCHVILLE

THE *CANTINA* DOOR HANGS FROM THE TOP HINGES. THE bottom swings freely away from the frame. Standing inside and looking out, Brody watches Main Street while thinking, *riders approach from the south. Strangers can be carrying something I want.*

He shoves the batwing doors open, steps out, and slides his Colt up and down in its holster making sure it moves easy.

I came here after hearin' about gold while I was in Las Cruces, and I'm gonna be in on a big strike in these Mogollon Mountains if only them Apaches would quit bothering us miners. Some fools say the Injuns think miners are invading the Apacheria and there'll be no peace.

Watching the road, he mumbles, "I ain't even got two coins to rub together. Before comin' here, I'd saved some money, but since buyin' my claim outside of town, I'm pert near broke. At least I'm lucky, I've got an *arrastra* where my horse pulls big stones around crushing the ore I dig up. Then I gotta splash some mercury into the muddy mess to snatch out any specks of gold. Damn, this mining is way too much work. It's way easier to save all that effort, and take gold from them who already got it. Besides, bushwhacking dumb miners is just plain fun."

Standing on the boardwalk in front of the cantina, he absentmindedly scratches at the filthy ragged canvas pants he wears. Suspenders hold up his trousers and a faded threadbare flannel shirt and greasy leather vest barely cover his protruding belly. The mule ears of his worn-out boots flap as he steps into the street.

Waiting for the riders, he leans his six-foot frame against the cantina wall, and spits a stream of tobacco juice through gapped front teeth leaving a stained, dripping trail on his scrag-gly beard. His body odor is enough to choke a goat.

Zep looks closely at the settlement they approach. A rutted dusty road runs the short length of the village. It's bordered on both sides by raised wooden sidewalks allowing persons to get out of the muddy quagmire the street becomes with a little rain. People move about, cross the street, enter and exit buildings. They pass single story adobes and a few log cabins.

"Looks kind of slapped together don't it?" Zep asks Allie.

"*Si*, there are two substantial buildings," Allie responds pointing at a wood structure with a roof covered extended porch that is likely the mercantile. Up ahead is another building with four archways, an overhung roof, and Saloon painted along the top.

Zep looks toward the far end of town. "There's some reminders of Apache attacks. See those charred ribs reaching for the sky?" He points past a couple of intact adobes to four other burnt out remains.

Zep leads into town. Manolito and Miguel ride on either side of Alassandra, and Guillo in the rear leads the mule. A bearded, grubby, stooped-shouldered miner in tattered denim pants, a filthy red long johns shirt, and worn out boots crosses the street in front of the riders.

Zep asks, "Friend, can you tell me where the General Mercantile is at?"

"First, I ain't your friend; second, look at the sign damn you, it's right down yonder." With that the miner stomps away.

"Friendly cuss," mutters Zep.

He waves his riders on toward the store, dismounts, and ties his horse to the hitching rail. The others stay on their mounts. Yanking a canvas bag from his saddlebags, Zep goes into the store and spots the clerk behind the counter.

"Howdy, stranger," says a store clerk.

"Howdy, yourself," says Zep walking up to the counter. "Need a few supplies."

"I'll try to help you."

"Looks like you've had some Indian troubles."

"Yep, a while back some Chiricahua came into town. Plumb surprised us. Killed a couple of folks that lived in the adobes and burned the houses."

"Saw the remains riding in. Still got troubles going on?"

"Been kind of quiet since then. 'Course, never can tell with injuns."

"I reckon not. Say, need to find a place to eat. Anything in town?"

"Only got the saloon down the way, but it's passable."

"I need these supplies: a package of coffee beans, four cans of Gail Borden's milk, three pounds of flour, and a slab of bacon, if you got it. Can I leave my tote sack for you to fill up? I'll be back directly to pick everything up."

"Sure, I'll take care of your needs. See you shortly."

Zep walks out of the mercantile, and scans the street looking for the saloon. Spotting the building, he motions toward it. Guillo understands and moves the riders that direction. Zep follows along leading his horse.

When everyone is dismounted and tied up at the hitching rail, they enter the Saloon. Zep heads toward a corner table inside the front door. The table is large enough so no one sits with their back toward the entrance. Alassandra is positioned in the middle of the group. A bartender walks over.

"We don't allow no Mex in here," he gestures at Manolito and Miguel and squints at Guillo.

"Sorry you feel that way, barkeep. See, we just rode in; we're hungry and thirsty," Zep says as he lays his Walker Colt on the table in plain sight. "My friends would like tequila, and I want whiskey. Then we would like some food, so bring us what you have cooking in the kitchen. It smells good. Is that okay with you?"

"Well, since you asked polite like, and are making a point with your shooter, I believe I can accommodate y'all this once." The bartender backs away from the table and disappears into the kitchen.

"Zep, do you think I'll get rat poison in my food?" Guillo asks. "This is not a place I would like to die."

"Why would someone act like that, Zep," Alassandra asks. "He doesn't know us, yet he says some people can and others can't be in here."

"Welcome to Americans, Alassandra. This time it's minor, the next time it might be even more ugly," Zep assures her.

"Give some of your food to Miguel first, Guillo, to see if its poisoned," Zep motions to Miguel.

"You kid me, yes, *señor* Zep?" Miguel asks in wide-eyed shock.

"*Si*, Miguel. I'm kidding, but I'd watch Guillo just the same."

"*Ay, caramba*, Zep, you are a *muy malo hombre*, very bad man," says Guillo laughing.

The bartender returns with drinks and a large bowl of food. He distributes smaller bowls and spoons and says he will return shortly for refills.

As Guillo serves everyone at the table, the front door opens, and Brody stomps into the saloon. The bartender shouts at him.

"You're not allowed in here. The last time you broke tables and chairs. Clear out before I get the owner."

"Shut up you old coot. Go get the lily-liver in here," says Brody. "Tell him I'm sitting over here with these strangers." Brody moves over and pulls up a chair at Zep's table.

A stench washes over the table as Brody arrives. Allie gags.

"Howdy, y'all. Saw you ride into town. Don't know if you know but this here town is a right bad place," Brody smiles. He notices the Colt on the table. "I see you have a calling card on the table."

Zep knows trouble when he sees it, and this *hombre* is trouble.

"Yep, glad you noticed." Zep stares steely eyed at Brody. "Don't know that I invited you to sit down, so pull in your horns and move along, mudsill."

Anger and evil flash in Brody's eyes as he glares at Zep and says, "Well, can't say you did. Just trying to be friendly."

"I ain't your friend. So mosey along and leave us be." Zep lays his hand on the Colt.

Rising from the table, Brody slowly looks at everyone sitting there. "Well, I believe I'll have me a little drink at the bar. Plan to see *you* later." Brody points at Zep, moves away, and shoves the men standing at the bar aside to make room for him.

"Zep, I don't know if I want to continue to learn about Americans," Alassandra looks determined.

"Don't let him buffalo you. Let's eat, pick up the supplies, and put Birchville behind us."

Zep knows staying longer can only cause complications. They finish, leave money on the table for the meal, and head outside to their horses. Zep mounts and rides quickly back to the mercantile to pick up the supplies. He motions for Guillo to start out of town with the others.

Jumping off his horse, Zep walks quickly into the store, retrieves his full canvas sack, pays for the goods, and rushes out the door. Brody waits beside his horse.

"You know, you didn't even offer to buy me a drink in the saloon. You didn't even let me offer to buy one for you," says Brody as he moves away from the horse so he can face Zep. His right hand slides toward his revolver.

Zep knows there's no avoiding this confrontation. Sitting the supplies bag on the ground, he slowly moves to face Brody.

"Been a while since I've put someone in the ground," says Zep. "You think your powder loads and percussion caps are good? I've checked mine earlier and know they'll fire."

"Don't you worry about my Colt," says Brody. To his right he hears a horse slowly approach. Glancing, he sees a Mex on horseback with a double-barreled Greener shotgun pointed at him.

"That's my saddle pard, you mudsill," Zep says.

"If you reach for your pistol, *señor*, I will make little pieces of you out of your great big piece," says Guillo smiling. "*Mi amigo*, it is time to go, no? Pick up our supplies and we *adios*."

Zep walks up and pulls Brody's pistol from its holster. Turning to his horse he ties on the supplies bag, steps into the stirrups, and says, "I will leave your shooter down the street a ways. Let's ride."

Zep and Guillo rapidly ride to join the other three at the outskirts of Birchville. Zep tosses Brody's Colt into a nearby horse trough.

Miners across the street, watch and anticipate gunplay, after Zep leaves, they begin to laugh like braying jackasses.

Livid, clenching and unclenching his hands, Brody cusses a blue streak, and screams at the departing riders. He stomps up Main Street and fishes his pistol from the horse trough. Shoving through the batwing doors of the Mexican *cantina*, he kicks chairs around the room and sits down at a table. He shouts for the bartender to bring him black powder and shot. Pulling the cylinder from his Colt, he knocks out the wet power, wipes down the pistol, and reloads.

"I'll find him and put him down," Brody threatens under his breath. "No Mex, or Mex lover, gets the best of me." He scatters black powder on the table as his hands shake from the anger that consumes him.

17

GILA RIVER

TALL SPIRES OF PONDEROSA PINE SENTINELS CLOSE around the five riders leaving Birchville. The canyons grow deeper and the cliffs climb higher as Zep leads his group towards the Gila River. Their back trail, visible in the pine needle covered ground, is followed by a lone rider quickly making up lost time, the flaps of his mule ear boots slap time with the trotting of his horse.

Zep pushes his group rapidly along the pine-encircled trail. Reaching the Gila is important. His goal is to put distance between his people and Birchville. Not leaving the town under the best of circumstances, he knows there is a high probability trouble follows them.

The trail weaves, rises, and falls as they ride. Ragged, rocky outcroppings and buttes rise before them as they travel along the valley chiseled by erosion of the sandstone. Deer scatter and turkeys scramble across the trail as riders approach. Guillo motions at the fleeing birds and licks his lips as Zep motions him forward. By midday they are almost halfway to the Gila when Zep calls a stop. The horses and people are ready to rest.

"Miguel, ride back down the trail and look for anyone following. Here, take these binoculars with you," Zep says reaching into his saddlebag. "See but don't be seen."

"*Si, señor* Zep, I will look good," says Miguel. He turns and trots back the trail just traveled.

"Guillo, ride forward to see if the way is safe. Watch close for Apaches," Zep instructs.

"Zep, you remember the last time I did this, *si*?" Guillo looks at Zep. "A *loco Americano* sneaks up and puts a rifle to my head."

"Yep, I remember. So, don't be caught napping this time, *amigo*. Ride, and keep your eyes open."

Zep turns and motions for Manolito to lead Alassandra off the trail into the woods.

"Dismount and give your horses a breather. Climbing these hills takes a toll on horseflesh."

"*Si, señor* Zep, I will move *señorita* and me into cover and give the horses a rest," Manolito replies. Soon both are concealed in the woods.

Zep ponders on his next move. *If the Apaches are out and about, I don't want to stumble into any ambush. If we can make it across the river, then I'll wait and watch for any following trouble. Got to keep the group moving. Sitting still we're too easy a target.*

Alassandra walks over to Zep. "You are worried, yes? Are we in danger here?"

"No, Allie, no danger I can see. I'm worried about the

dangers I can't see."

Quickly, she throws her arms around Zep's waist. "You are a good man, Zep. I trust you." Releasing her grip, she moves back to her horse.

Zep is momentarily at a loss. *No woman's ever done that before. Do I like it? How should I respond? She trusts me. I can't let her down.*

"Thank you for your trust in me Allie," he replies.

Miguel rides rapidly up to him.

"*Amigo*, I watch and saw a single horseman follow us. Through the glasses I saw him good; he looks at the ground reading our tracks."

"Did you see who the *hombre* is?" asks Zep.

"*Si,* it is the *loco gringo* from the saloon. The *muy malo grande hombre.*"

"Big and bad, it's the mudsill sure as shootin'," says Zep. "How far back?"

"He is maybe one hour behind us," reports Miguel.

"Mount up everyone, we have to ride for the river," Zep orders.

Everyone mounts, moves back onto the trail, and heads the direction Guillo departed. Ten minutes later they ride down into a depression and find Guillo sitting beside a huge pine tree.

"I hear you coming; sounds travel very easy in these mountains, especially in this valley. Any Apaches will know we are here and how many we are," Guillo says as he moves his horse around and mounts.

"Yep, I know we're makin' all kinds of racket stompin' through the woods," says Zep. "Here's what we are going to do. Manolito, hang back and keep your eye on the back trail.

Miguel, ride with the señorita and wait for five minutes. Guillo, you and I are going to try to make sure we don't stumble into trouble up front. Let's ride a few more hours and we'll reach the river. *Vamonos.*"

Guillo and Zep take the lead and weave around trees, boulders, and rocks in the trail. They strain their eyes looking for every possible trouble spot and listen for any unnatural sound.

"Listen, Guillo," whispers Zep as they pause along the trail.

"*Si*, I hears some bushes break."

"Quietly, get your horse off the trail. We've got company ahead of us."

Both men slide off their mounts and move into the undergrowth.

No sooner have they placed a hand over the muzzles of their horses than seven mounted Apache braves plunge out of the brush and cross the trail ten feet ahead. Moving rapidly, the Indian's don't seem concerned about noise. They seem focused on a mission and in a hurry to get there. As quickly as they appear they are gone.

Slowly exhaling, Zep and Guillo stand patiently waiting for a few minutes then move back onto the trail.

Got to put the river between them and us, thinks Zep.

Miguel and Allie catch up and he tells them to wait for a few minutes as he and Guillo move forward.

The trail becomes steeper switchbacks as it winds down the mountainside. Guillo acknowledges hearing rushing water crashing over rocks.

"The river, Zep, it's just ahead," he motions and points.

"Sounds like it. Keep working your way down and get out of these trees. When you get there, find a place to ford. I'm going back to bring the others up here. Keep your eyes peeled. If anybody's going to hit us, the river is the best place."

Zep stops Miguel and Allie. "The river is ahead. You're coming up on a tough stretch, hold on tight, and give your horse its head going down the hillside. I'm going back to fetch Manolito."

Moving back along the trail, he spots Manolito. As the riders pull up beside each other, Zep asks, "See anything of our follower?"

"No, *señor* Zep, *nada*, nothing."

"A band of Apaches crossed the trail over there," he points into the woods. "They can be anywhere. Keep a sharp lookout. Let's ride for the river it's just ahead. I'll follow you."

Manolito spurs his horse into a trot and they ride to the hill and carefully traverse it to the river.

Zep knows the Gila River is fed from tributaries and watershed of the Mogollon Mountains. He pauses, waits on Manolito to ford, and watches the river churn and tumble its way through the narrow canyon. Water sprays and showers as it collides with boulders in the waterway. Rocks of every size, tumbled downstream from the force of spring floods, litter the waterway. Today, the flow moves rapidly, but it's crossable. Guillo's located a good ford and Zep spots his group moving single file up the far hillside.

Out of habit, Zep shouts above the roar of the water, "Kick out of your stirrups, hold onto your saddle horn, and give your horse its head." Realizing he is shouting directions at a *vaquero*, Zep sheepishly smiles and Manolito grins back.

Gingerly, carefully, the horse picks its way through the chilling, rock strewn, rushing water.

Zep is the last to cross. He begins, stops, stands in his stirrups, and quickly looks around. Satisfied everything seems okay, he settles in his saddle, and guides his horse into the water. Urging his horse onward, it suddenly stumbles throwing him forward in the saddle. An arrow streaks across where his body was only moments before.

18

CLIFF DWELLING

U NEXPECTEDLY, ZEP FEELS THE ARROW PASS AND hears it. He continues to fall forward, slides off the right side of his horse, and into the river. His left hand clings to the stirrup. Both he and the horse plunge through the water and onto the opposite gravel bank. Thoroughly soaked, he keeps the horse between himself and the direction the arrow came from.

Leaping up, he grabs the reins and runs leading the horse into the woods. Throwing a glance over his shoulder, Zep sees only a mountainside of brush and pine trees on the opposite canyon wall. Up ahead, Manolito guides his horse along the steep trail.

Running to catch up and shouting to get Manolito's attention, Zep closes the gap on his friend. "Apaches," Zep gasps pointing across the canyon, pressing his other hand against the horse's withers as he steadies himself.

Manolito quickly slides off his mount, pulling out his rifle at the same time.

"Arrow, over there," Zep rasps out.

"I see no one, *señor* Zep. We should move quickly."

Rather than mount and make larger targets of themselves, both men run up the trail leading their horses. They catch up with the others at the top of the canyon. Zep motions Miguel and Guillo over.

"Apaches down there." He points into the canyon. "One took a shot at me. Now we're discovered, we've got to run."

"Zep, if we try to run through the forest we can be easily shot," says Guillo. "We can hold up and hide behind trees, but so can the *indios*."

"You're right, *companero*. We have to find a place to make a stand and have them come to us on our own terms. I know just the place to give us an advantage."

Zep moves to take the lead and the other riders fall into single file behind him. Quickly, they weave and wind their way through the forest. Leaving the trail they're following, Zep moves toward the northwest breaking a new path as he goes.

"Zep, where do you take us?" Guillo shouts.

"There's a place this direction. It is an old cliff dwelling; it can give us cover while taking away any surprise the Apaches might plan for us. Stick with me and ride hard. It's not far."

The five riders redouble their efforts and follow Zep as he works his way through the forest.

Eventually, the riders come upon a sheer cliff towering above them. Zep begins to move along the face of the cliff and stops.

"There; see it?" He points into the distance and up on the cliff face.

"About halfway up the rock wall you can see the cliff dwelling." All pause and scan the cliff; there is excitement among the riders upon seeing the structure.

Zep knows the horses are problematic for them. He motions for Guillo to ride forward beside him.

"I have a dangerous job for you *companero*. We can't take the horses into the cliff house with us. Someone needs to take them and ride like the dickens to try and draw the Apaches away. They may go after the *remuda* or they may not. At any rate, the horses need to be led in a big circle and come back here to pick us up. It won't be easy; it's a tough, risky job that has to be done. These horses are our only way out of this place. It means life and death for us, and I am counting on you so we all can live. Will you do it?"

"Zep, why does it seem every time you have a *magnifico* idea, I get the hard job? Sometime, just sometime, you could say, 'Guillo, take the easy job, no?'"

"I guess it's just the way the cards are dealt, *mi companero*," says Zep. "Will you take the horses and keep them safe?"

"*Si,* I will ride a big circle. It may take two or three days before I am back. That should be enough time to deal with whatever follows us. Pray I do not find more Apaches along my way."

"*Muchas gracias, companero.* We absolutely must have the horses back. Oh, and you too." Zep grins at Guillo.

Zep spots a rocky outcropping, and has an idea. A flat stone almost the same height as the saddle's stirrup is a short ways from the cliff dwelling. He directs Guillo to ride past the stone and stop. Zep stops his horse beside the boulder and steps from his horse onto the rock. He hands his horse's reins to Guillo and explains his plan.

"I'll step off here. You take my reins and lead my horse once

I've removed everything."

"*Si*, I wait for you to unload," says Guillo taking Zep's horse's reins.

Leaving no footprints on the stone, Zep reaches over and retrieves his weapons and supplies. He sets them on the stone outcropping. Next, he pulls his lariat from the saddle, ties one end around the saddle horn, and strings out the rope as Guillo moves both horses forward. Zep motions the next rider to approach the rock where he stands.

Miguel moves his horse in position and steps off onto the boulder, lifts all his supplies onto the rock. Zep hands him his lariat. Miguel ties the end to his saddle horn, and taking his rope ties one end around the horn as well. He drapes the reins around the horse's neck, and his horse follows Zep's as the rope is strung out.

Each rider repeats the process until all the horses and mule have been unloaded onto the windswept rock outcropping. Guillo leads all the animals away. The riders gather up their equipment and supplies and move toward the imposing multi-level stacked-stone structure.

The large complex rises three stories tall. The entire structure is constructed out of stones and built into a shallow curvature of the cliff. A towering overhang shelters the structure from above and its ample ledge supports from below. The building looks centuries old, part of it's eroded away, there are rooms with collapsed walls and roofs, and a tower in the middle overlooks the valley below.

They arrive at the base of the cliff and climb up over the accumulated rocks, rubble, and scree. Looking from the bottom of the cliff, the house is twenty feet above them. The structure rises at least forty feet higher and stretches 50 - 60 feet along the ledge.

"Zep, this is a big stone house, yes?" says Allie. "How do we get in?"

"Over there," Zep points to the left. "See the handholds carved into the rock? We will climb those like a ladder. In the cliff dwelling, we can make the Apaches come to us."

Almost as one, they turn and watch as Guillo leads their horses away, each lost momentarily in their own thoughts. "*Via con Dios, companero*," Zep whispers.

"Now we climb," he says breaking the spell. "Gather the equipment and supplies and carry everything into the cliff dwelling. It may take more than one trip."

Everyone grabs something and they begin to pull themselves up the rock wall using the handholds.

As soon as they enter the dwelling, they see all the rooms are connected. Equipment and supplies are piled together and Zep assigns tasks.

"Miguel, take the binoculars from Manolito and climb up in the tower. You can keep a watch on everything below us. Manolito, move back and cover the entrance to make sure we don't have unwelcome visitors. Alassandra, start a very small fire in the back corner for some coffee and grub. I'll check out the rest of this place to see where we can best defend ourselves. Everybody has a weapon, right?"

All nod in answer and move off to their appointed tasks. Zep climbs, crawls, and walks over collapsed roofs, walls, and piles of debris scattered throughout the cliff dwelling as he travels its length. Assured by what he sees, he feels it is nearly impossible for anyone to enter except the way they did.

Coming back to where Alassandra busily arranges cooking utensils and prepares food, he sits down and is suddenly overwhelmed with physical and emotional fatigue. His shoulders slump and he sags his head against his chest.

I hope I've made the right decision, he thinks. *Everybody depends on it. Guillo is beyond brave. He is alone and risks everything to make sure we have a way out. Be safe, companero.*

Alassandra walks over and hands Zep a freshly brewed cup of coffee.

"Smells good, been lookin' for this all day," he says with a smile. He takes a sip and savors the taste, then sits the cup beside him.

"You are worried, no, about Guillo? I know him leaving with the horses troubles you." She sits down beside Zep and takes his hand in hers. "We are here. We are safe. You are a good leader. Guillo will be safe." Taking his face with both hands, she stares into his eyes. Her deep brown eyes seem to engulf him. He sees the golden flakes glitter.

Miguel stumbles over debris in the adjacent room, and then steps through the doorway as Zep and Alassandra separate.

"An *indio* on horseback, *señor* Zep, tracks our trail below the cliff," he reports.

19

TOGETHERNESS

ALCHESAY DISMOUNTS HIS HORSE AND VIEWS THE cliff house. I know we have no spiritual issue with places where people have died. It's not where one needs to spend any time, but there are things left behind that are useful, he thinks. He watches the activities of the riders entering the structure. While concentrating on his prey, an owl in the pines hoots – eight times.

He's pushed hard to get here. After Birchville he tracks of the five riders keeping out of sight through the pines. He's al-most discovered as seven warriors rush through the forest. He arrives at the canyon in time to see two riders descend to the Gila River. Quickly dismounting, he eased his way down the canyon wall. While climbing down through the brush and rocks, he spots the last rider prepare to cross the river. Quickly, notching an arrow he lets it fly. Because the rider's horse stumbles, he watches his shot miss and his intend-ed target flees up the other side of the canyon into the forest. Climbing the hillside to his horse, he mounts, swings in a cir-cle back to the trail, and carefully continues to the canyon. Gently, he guides his horse down the steep trail to the river. Crosses, climbs the trail out of the canyon, and finds where those he follows left the trail. They crash through the forest with no effort to obliterate or disguise their travel as if they want to be followed. He notices another set of horse tracks ap-parently follows the five riders.

This white man I've followed has been so careful up to this point, he thinks. *Why does he change his ways now? Where did the new rider come from?*

Quickening his pace, Alchesay follows their journey through the pine forest. He comes to an area where the moun-tains begin to tower above him. The white men continue to travel along the base of the mountain and then the tracks change. The horses no longer step as heavy into the soil. *They are riderless. Where have they gone? Yet, one rider continues.* Turning around he stares at the cliff dwelling.

At dusk, he slowly approaches the cliff house, and rides through an area of rocky outcroppings and large boulders.

No. This white man must be Apache, thinks Alchesay. *He let the riders off on rocks and led the horses away. An old Apache trick to throw off trackers and rest the animals. Once again, this white man insults me. I will not forget.* Alchesay chides him-self for his shortcoming. *I will not pursue the one who leads the horses. My white man stays with the rest. It's what I would do. I stay with my enemy.*

Riding into the woods he moves in front of the cliff dwell-ing. He dismounts and ties his horse to a branch and watches.

Brody follows the tracks of the riders and the mule. It's not difficult. They are on the trail and traveling fast. Their tracks are very visible and the way the horse hooves dig up the soil shows the speed of their travel. Given an hour or less he should catch up with them. He spots a shimmer of reflection well ahead of him.

"Someone's watchin," he mutters. "No matter, its just as well they know I'm after them. Need to pick up my pace; don't want to lose them."

Increasing his speed, intent on his pursuit, Brody begins to hear the Gila River ahead. He knows the canyon is a perfect place to bushwhack someone. He's done it himself a time or two.

Got to ease up and take a close look before I head down the trail, he thinks.

He dismounts at the edge of the steep trail into the canyon, and slowly surveys both sides to make sure it is all clear.

Something or someone moves along the canyon wall. Standing still, he watches. Nothing materializes. He shrugs.

"Starting to get jumpy out here," he mutters. "Beginning to see Injuns behind every bush. Should have brung some who-hit-John with me. Whiskey would steady my nerves."

Remounting, he nudges his horse into a quick and foolish pace down the steep trail. He makes it safely to the bottom, rushes across the ford, and dashes up the trail out of the canyon. Behind him, he thinks he hears another horse. Not waiting to confirm, he rushes along.

When he comes to the spot where the riders left the trail and cut into the forest, he plows in after them.

Brody stays hot on the trail before him. As he approaches the cliffs he spots a dwelling high above the trail.

"Now, if I wanted some place to hole up, that'd be it," he grumbles.

Riding past the structure he stops, dismounts, and moves into the woods. Ground tying his horse, he slowly starts to walk back toward the cliff dwelling.

The owl calls send shivers down Alchesay's back. What now? What is it? Is it Big Owl the malevolent spirit that wreaks disaster on Apaches? It can take animal or human form; where is it at? Suddenly, he hears movement in the bush off to his right.

"Big Owl prowls?" Alchesay mutters. "It's here because of the house of the dead above me? Now is not the time to confront a spirit like this."

Alchesay silently makes his way deeper into the pine forest away from the approaching sounds. Taking his horse, he mounts and rides back along the trail, finds a concealed spot, and settles in for the night. It will be a night of discomfort and worry as the Apache warrior wonders what the spirits have in store for him.

Brody stops and listens.

"I swear I hear a horse again," he whispers. "I got to get back and make camp. Some sleep, yeah, some sleep, that's what I need. A man can go plumb crazy out here in these woods, especially around a spooky old Injun rock house."

He returns to his horse and moves deeper into the forest. In a pile of lightning struck pine trees he finds shelter for his horse and himself.

Bacon, *tortillas*, and *frijoles* are the supper menu for Zep, Alassandra, Manolito, and Miguel. Night drops around the cliff dwelling like a dark cape. Zep and Alassandra leave the campfire and enter the next room. It is roofless, and the sky above it is lit up by millions of stars. They stand there gazing up in awe.

"You know, you won't be able to see sights like this in those cities," says Zep.

"Yes, Zep, I know." Allie reaches over and takes him by the arm. "It is something I have to do. I have thoughts now that make me think it is not so important, but I know I must."

"Yep, I know you must. It's just, I been thinking about what if we could make things work for us." Zep couldn't believe the words that tumble out of his mouth. "You are the most beautiful woman I've ever seen, and the smartest. I know I could spend the rest of my life with you, if possible." *I know this outspoken driven woman is the one I need in my life,* thinks Zep.

"Why, Zepaniah Bierman, you shock me. Where did all this romantic talk come from? To look at your rough physique, weathered appearance, and hawk-eye stare, one wouldn't think a heart of a romantic was inside."

She throws her arm around Zep's neck and kisses him. Momentarily shocked, he joins in the kiss.

Releasing his neck Allie hugs his arm. "I think about us

often. When all this is past, would you be willing to sit with Papa and discuss our future?"

Zep turns to look at her and out of the corner of his eye he spots a campfire twinkle in the woods below them.

20

HORSES AND A MULE

W*HY DID I SAY YES? MANOLITO OR MIGUEL COULD lead the horses*, thinks Guillo. *Zep asks me to go and I go. Sometimes, I'm loco en la cabeza. I need my head checked.*

The horses and mule string out behind him as he finds a way for them through the woods. Finally, he breaks into open ground and the ride becomes easier. As the horses move along at a quick pace, the rope suddenly jerks from his hand. The *remuda* stops and the jackass brays. Loud.

Guillo turns around, dismounts, and moves along beside each horse to quiet the animals. The mule sits on the ground and heehaws its objections.

If we didn't need this God-awful animal I'd shoot him, thinks Guillo. He waits patiently, knowing he has already covered a long distance and a rest is necessary. So, he lets the mule get everything out of its system.

"*Señor* mule, you have one hell-of-a-way to call rest time," Guillo says to the ornery critter.

He inspects the connecting ropes and horses, picks up the lead, and remounts.

"*Señor* mule, can we go now, *por favor?*" He glares back along the line at the now standing mule, gives a yank on the rope, and the string of animals move forward.

Guillo knows how important the animals are to his friends' survival. He must take care of them and protect them. It is time to find a safe place to bed down for the night. Apaches are one worry, but bears and cougars plague his thoughts as well.

At dusk Guillo approaches a small meadow with a creek that meanders through the middle. "*Gracias a Dios,*" he says. It is a great spot with forage and water. Circling up the animals, he quickly uses the ropes to make hobbles, and turns them loose on the meadow grasses. Guillo moves himself into the woods beside the meadow and eats from the supplies in his saddlebag. He cold camps with no fire, wraps himself in his *serape,* holds his rifle close, and rests with his back against a tree to watch his charges in the meadow. As nighttime surrounds them he nods off and sleeps.

A scream, hiss, and snarl jerk Guillo awake. Cougar. Not good news. He stands and looks into the inky blackness. Somewhere out there a cougar smells horseflesh. It is close enough to mean trouble. Guillo walks into the meadow to check on the horses. As he comes to each horse, he pats the animal on the neck and nuzzles its muzzle to reassure it. He counts all the horses. *The mule. Where is that damn mule.* He wanders in the darkness toward the tree line. There, inside the trees, stands the mule.

"I'm going to shoot him, I'm just going to shoot him and be

done with the trouble," whispers Guillo through clinched teeth.

Grabbing the halter of the mule, he leads it back into the meadow. Another scream, hiss, and snarl stabs into the night, closer this time.

That sounds like one big kitty, thinks Guillo. His pace quickens as he moves the mule to the middle of the meadow with the other animals. "I don't want to mess with an *El Gato* like you. Shoo, go away, scat cat," he says softly.

Guillo sits down in the meadow in the middle of his herd and watches intently to get a glimpse of anything that moves their direction. Another cat scream rips the air.

"*Si, Señor Gato,* now you smell me too don't you," whispers Guillo. "Maybe you think twice before you pay a visit, yes?"

Nighttime stills, heavy eyelids droop as Guillo, sitting upright, lets his head fall forward on his chest and sleeps. His rifle lies on his lap.

Morning creeps silently over the treetops. Heavy dew settles on the meadow, and Guillo wakes up appreciative of the well-constructed serape that keeps him warm and dry. The air smells fresh and clean. The scent of Ponderosa pine sweeps over the meadow and morning birds are singing. It's a sure message everything is okay. Moving around the herd, Guillo removes the hobbles, and once again uses the ropes to tie his string of horses and one mule together. Repacking his saddlebags, he mounts and leads the string out continuing to make a circular route that leads back to the cliff house.

He thinks, *second day begins, one more night out, and then reconnect with mi amigos.* Talking out loud to the horses he says, "Let's take it easy today, make it a good trip, and then tomorrow we will be back together with our *companero.*"

This morning, the ride changes from dense forest and

undergrowth to more open areas with separated groves of trees. The land is still up and down with buttes, cliffs, canyons, and valleys. Guillo winds his way through the landscape, not pushing his animals he takes a leisurely walk to give them plenty of rest.

Noontime finds him on a rim looking into a shallow valley. While taking in the view, a sudden movement to his left captures his full attention. Slowly emerging from a grove of trees six horses with riders enter the valley. They are Apaches dressed in breechcloths, boot-like moccasins, various shirts and jackets, with their long hair held back with bands around their heads. Two carry rifles propped up vertically, with the stock resting on their thighs and the other four have bows in their hands. They ride easy like they are one with the horse. Quietly, swiftly they drift along the trail in the valley. Without any sudden movement, Guillo silently, skillfully eases his herd back from the edge, slides from the saddle, pulls his rifle as he dismounts, and moves to each horse giving reassuring pats. The mule. The damnable mule sits down as the animals stop. He rears back his head just as Guillo steps in front of it. Sucking air in through its nostrils, it prepares to bray. Guillo quickly raises his Colt and places the barrel on the mule's forehead between its eyes.

"*Señor* mule, if you do what you plan to do, it will be the last time you ever do it," Guillo whispers a promise.

The large dark eyes of the mule stare into Guillo's dark eyes. It is a moment of truth, a meeting of minds and wills wait for the first one to blink. This moment feels like forever while Guillo's finger tightens on the trigger. One sound from the mule will be its last forever.

The mule blinks and slowly exhales. Guillo lowers the revolver and sinks to the ground. He looks up and stares again into the mule's eyes.

"*Señor* mule, sometimes you test me fiercely. Sometimes, you remind me of me," Guillo says. He slides up to the edge of the rim in time to see the Apaches quickly depart the valley. Rolling over, a huge sigh escapes him. He smiles.

21

STEALTH

Hustling Allie back to the campfire, Zep instructs Miguel to stay with her and for Manolito to watch the entrance to the dwelling. He is going to check out the campfire in the woods.

"I've got to check that fire in the woods. If I can take the fight to the Indians and surprise them, they may leave us alone, but I'm not sure it's Indians. Never known them to be so careless. Got to be done. Keep Allie protected and guard the entrance. I'll be back," says Zep as the others begin to object.

Ignoring their complaints, he slips out with his pistol and knife and climbs down the rock. In the dark, he carefully threads his way along the rocks and scree into the woods. Not able to easily see all the ground cover, each step he takes is dangerous. Carefully, slowly he eases forward. The fire twinkles in the distance.

Balancing himself against the surrounding trees, Zep closes the distance. With the fire's backlight, he begins to make out a fallen pile of pine trees. It looks like a storm has tossed them together. Behind the screen of trees, the fire burns. If the fire was smaller it wouldn't have been easily seen, but this one is loaded up with wood.

This can't be Indians not unless they set a trap, Zep thinks. The possibility causes him to quickly sit down and reexamine the area. Looking at each tree, staring into every bush. Nope, there's nothing to see. If not Indians, then it's got to be whites, but whom? He waits longer. Night begins to give way to pre-dawn. The briefest amount of light sneaks over the horizon. Zep decides to wait for dawn.

Light travels quickly and quietly across the landscape. It steals into the forest and seeps through the trees illuminating everything that's sealed in darkness. There's a stir behind the fallen pines. A groan, a cough, and a curse welcome daylight. Zep is alert and waits to see who emerges. A man stands up; it's the mudsill, the low life troublemaker from Birchville. Zep sinks down in amazement. *What, why would he chase them this far? Revenge, pure and simple, it has to be. I humiliated him in town and he wants revenge.* A morning breeze blows Zep's direction and the stench almost gags him.

Brody moves around the fire in an attempt to pull together something for breakfast unaware his every move is watched. He scratches his armpits and crotch and stretches.

I don't have time to waste with this low life, Zep thinks. *Miguel saw an Indian and they are much more trouble than this waste of flesh.*

Zep decides to do the unthinkable. He pulls his Colt and steadies it across his left arm as it rests against a tree. *It's hard to stomach bushwhacking anyone, but the needs of the many out-weigh the one,* Zep rationalizes. Brody moves around the fire and unknowingly places himself in an unobstructed position.

"Steady, cock the gun, breathe evenly, sight along the barrel, and squeeze off the shot," Zep whispers to himself. His finger tightens on the trigger. Slowly the tension increases.

Wait. Can't do it. Zep lowers the pistol. *I can't shoot someone down in cold blood. If the low life made a play for a gun, I'd drill him, but I've got to live with myself.*

Returning his pistol to its holster, Zep quietly backs away from the tree-surrounded thicket. Slipping stealthfully back through the woods, he carefully climbs the scree and eases up the handholds to the cliff dwelling. He has second thoughts about putting the mudsill in the ground, but the time is past. Manolito greets him on his return. Stepping inside the dwelling, Allie's radiant smile welcomes him back.

"We didn't hear anything," she says as Zep sits down beside the fire. "We didn't know what was going on."

"What did you see?" asks Miguel.

"Who's there?" asks Manolito.

"How many are there?" She hesitates. "I'm sorry, here's some coffee. I'll wait."

"Thanks for the coffee, let me take a sip and I'll tell you everything." Zep blows on the coffee to cool it and takes a sip. "Good coffee, thanks. The same low life that horned in on us at the saloon in Birchville is down below. I think he wants to get even with me for shaming him."

"Will he go away if he doesn't know we are here?" Allie asks.

"No, I'm pretty sure he knows where we are. I'm not proud of this, but I had my pistol on him and almost killed him in cold blood. Just couldn't bring myself to do it."

Silence fills the room. The only noise is the occasional snap and pop of wood burning in the fire.

Quietly, Allie says, "I'm glad you didn't. If I knew, I don't know how I would react."

Zep sits quietly.

"Right now, you mean so much to me. What we can do together thrills me, and I don't want that to change," Allie says.

Zep nods his head, and contemplates what is said.

"A lesser man would have taken his life. Thank you." Allie sits down.

Zep quietly thinks about what could have happened in the woods and what Allie shares with him. *Character and integrity are heavy responsibilities. Others expect specific actions from me in order to be respected.* Zep knows it all boils down to doing what is right. If he does what is right, then he doesn't have to apologize to anyone for his actions.

"Thank you, Allie. I appreciate knowing," Zep whispers.

Alchesay watches Zep leave the woods and climb back to the dwelling. If he had any doubt before, it is gone now. His "rabbit" is there. He also knows the ancients did not build this village in the rock without a way to escape from prolonged warfare or successful enemies. *There must be a way into this dwelling other than the front, which is surely well guarded.*

Alchesay returns to his horse, rides back along yesterday's trail, and turns toward the cliff to find a way to the top. It may take some time to find the hidden escape route, but his prey is going nowhere.

Brody stands in the woods and surveys the cliff house. To go up the front is sure suicide, but I can spot them if they try to come out, he mulls ideas over in his mind. Of course, I could always wait until early, early morning and creep up the front. I might catch someone asleep. There ain't any good way to go about this.

He makes his decision. Tomorrow morning is the day he'll even the score. *Hard Case, you've got a comeuppance headed your way and it's called Brody.* He smiles and settles down to wait.

"It has to be here," Alchesay mutters under his breath. "I have combed the top of this cliff and cannot find the escape route." Disgusted with himself, he wanders back toward where his horse is picketed. Sitting down, he runs through all the locations he's searched. His horse chews on the bush beside him and vigorously yanks at the branches. Uprooting the bush, it slaps against Alchesay. In surprise and disgust, the Indian reaches over to strike the horse and stops in mid-swing. There where the bush was is a chiseled trail in the stone. Quickly, getting to his knees, Alchesay begins to brush away years of blown dirt. Each swipe reveals another stretch of trail. Hanging over the cliff top, he follows the line of the uncovered stone trail, and begins to make out a four-inch ledge cut into the sandstone face of the cliff. Directly above the ledge he sees handholds cut into the wall. The ledge slopes slightly toward the cliff dwelling. It looks like it traverses the cliff face and enters the back of the cave recess where the structure is built. It runs behind the building and enters at the top level of rooms. Quickly, Alchesay retrieves his quiver and bow. He slings them onto his shoulder and makes certain his knife is firmly lodged in his waistband. Lying on his belly he carefully slides his feet over the top edge of the cliff and scrambles to feel for the four-inch ledge. To miss the ledge means plummeting over a hundred feet to the rubble and rocky scree below. Stretching, reaching, his left toes catch the ledge.

He transfers weight, slides his right foot into position by the left, and gropes for a handhold. He snags one and slides his torso into space. Balanced on the narrow ledge, grasping the hand openings, he inches his way along the cliff face. With no desire to look down, he focuses on the ledge before him and scoots slowly toward the cliff dwelling. Hand by hand, inch by inch, he creeps along the wall. Accidentally, he glances at the drop behind him. The distance causes a momentary shift of equilibrium, he sucks his body into the rock in front of him, pressing tight and gripping the handholds with all of his strength. The moment passes and he continues toward the dwelling. Twenty more feet, fifteen, ten, five, and he tumbles over a wall of the structure into the darkness behind the building and drops six feet onto an ancient rubbish heap. This was the community trash pile behind the house. Alchesay's leg muscles shake and quiver, his arm muscles twitch uncontrollably. He is physically and mentally depleted. Sleep overwhelms him and he slips into unconsciousness. His last thought before passing into darkness is, *if the ancients used that route for escape, maybe it was better to stay put.*

Brody sleeps soundly on a pine needle bed beneath the trees. Had he been awake, he would see Alchesay slide toward the cliff dwelling. In sleep Brody dreams of how he will face the Hard Case and gun him down. At early morning everything will begin. He sleeps unmolested.

Yesterday, Miguel warned of the Indian's presence, but nothing happened today. Manolito is ready for some form of attack as is Miguel. Zep roams the dwelling looking for every possibility of surprise by the Indians.

As Zep steps back to the campfire, Allie says, "Maybe they left."

"No, Allie, they are still here. I don't know what the wait is for, or what they plan to do. Maybe, they don't want to try a frontal attack, but I haven't seen any movement today either. I'm confused."

"I will begin supper and soon it will be ready. If we see no other movement, can we sit down and enjoy a meal?"

"Sure, if they don't try anything soon, it'll be too late for today. Darkness will set in and everything'll wait until tomorrow. I don't know where that mudsill, low life, is at either. He should have made some observable move today. I'm going up to spell Miguel in the tower. Give a shout when supper is ready." Zep walks back into the dwelling and climbs the ladder leading to the tower. Pushing his head and shoulders into the tower room, he sees Miguel with the binoculars pressed to his eyes scanning the landscape in front of the cliff.

"So, signs of movement?" Zep asks, stepping into the room.

"No, *señor* Zep, it is *muy* strange. All day, I expect an attack, but nothing. What are they doing, *por que*?

"I'm as buffaloed as you Miguel. This time my experience has let me down. Why don't you head on down, *Señorita* Alassandra is fixin' some grub. You can eat, can't you?"

Miguel vigorously nods his head in the affirmative and climbs down the ladder.

Zep picks up the binoculars and sweeps the valley below, nothing, absolutely nothing. A random thought shoots through Zep's mind, *is there any other way up here?* He turns around and stares at the huge overhang of sandstone and the shallow cave behind the dwelling. There is nothing to see but rock, solid rock.

22

ATTACK

ALLIE QUICKLY MOVES AROUND THE CAMPFIRE AND makes sure everyone has something to eat. Night closed in wrapping the cliff house in its dark cocoon. Firelight flickers on the corner walls. The four eat in silence, nerves on edge, not knowing what to expect. A nerve shredding, night shattering sound erupts from the valley below the cliff house.

Zep knows the skin tingling yip and yap howl of a coyote concert. Each time the sound reminds him of a wail for something lost. It's strange how sounds can work that way with your mind. He watches as Allie squirms because of the noise.

"Don't worry, Allie, those coyotes are out taking in the scenery. One howls what he thinks about it. If we're lucky others will chime in with their two cents worth." He smiles.

"Zep, I've listened to coyotes many times outside the

hacienda. It's just that tonight, with everything facing us, it sounds so lonesome and lost."

"Well, let's keep busy and they won't bother us." Zep gets up and begins to collect plates and cups used for dinner. A bucket of water is brought to a boil and all the utensils take a dip. Everyone helps with chores.

"Manolito, take the first watch, Miguel get some sleep and spell him at midnight. I'll be up at daybreak to watch in the morning, okay?" Zep looks for agreement. Both *vaqueros* nod and move to their assignments.

"Zep, I don't want to sleep alone tonight, would you mind?" Allie drags her sleeping roll over close to Zep's.

"That's fine, Allie." Lying down, Allie cuddles over next to Zep. *This feels right,* he thinks. He wraps his arms around her; they quickly are asleep.

Alchesay's eyes snap open. Momentarily disoriented, he remembers how he got where he is. He stretches each arm and leg to make sure everything works; he stands and peers into the gloom. There is little to no light behind the cliff dwelling. Only at the top does a sliver of moonlight creep over the structure. He knows his prey is in here somewhere, but it is stupid to start to move before he can see. He sits still and waits. Dawn will come soon; his internal body clock tells him it's almost here.

Brody makes his way carefully from the woods up the

approach to the cliff house. He starts before morning light, and slinks gently forward. The rubble and scree are difficult to negotiate with no noise, but he is fortunate. Light peeks over the horizon, it's now or never; he begins to climb up the hand-holds toward the entrance.

Alchesay sees the light skim along the upper edge of the shallow cave. Dawn is quickly coming and it's time to move. He balances on the loose rubble and rubbish, and steps lightly over and around the debris-covered area behind the dwelling. Some walls have caved in from above and tumbled into the area. While negotiating around part of a deteriorated wall, his shoulder bumps into a long pole that rests against the wall. The pole shifts causing two large rocks to slip off a ledge and fall into the rubbish pile. Their muffled crunch is loud. Alchesay freezes in place and waits for a reaction.

Sitting inside the entrance, Miguel drifts in and out of consciousness. It has been a long night. He watches light edge into the valley. Suddenly, there is a thumping sound. It comes from the back of the house. He makes his way across the room toward a hallway leading to the rear. Zep propped up on one elbow watches him.

"I heard it too, *amigo*," he whispers. "Shouldn't have any unwelcome noise back there. Check it out and be careful."

"*Si*, Zep. I will be."

As Miguel steps up and begins around the corner, a bulky

form fills the entrance doorway. The doorway is a low entrance that requires a person to stoop. As the figure steps in and rises Zep instantly recognizes the mudsill from Birchville. The figure raises his right hand with a revolver clutched in it.

"You got this comin', Hard Case. Ain't no Mex lover ever goin' to get the best of Brody Johnson and shame me in my own town. Kiss this life goodbye."

The moment seems to pass in slow motion. Brody's arm straightens out. Manolito jerks awake and stands immediately. Zep falls over Allie to shield her from being shot as Miguel rushes back into the room. Manolito springs between the gun and Zep as Brody's Colt sounds like a cannon in the close confines of the room. Manolito clutches his chest. Miguel rapidly fires two shots toward the entrance. Allie pushes Zep away to see what is happening. Gun smoke fills the room hiding everything in its dense cloud.

Zep shouts over the sounds, "Manolito, where are you? Miguel, did you hit him? Stand still everyone; don't shoot any more until the smoke thins."

In a few seconds the smoke dissipates. Manolito is on the floor clutching his chest as blood gushes between his fingers. The doorway is empty. Screaming, Allie reaches for Manolito. Miguel stumbles toward the doorway. Zep stands surveying all entrances to the room with his Colt in his hand.

"Miguel, take care of Manolito. Allie, grab some clothes from my saddlebag to staunch the blood." Zep charges through the doorway and swings his Colt left then right seeking an enemy. He hears scrambling beyond the debris pile to his right. He peers over the pile seeking the source of the noise as it continues to climb higher hidden by other rubbish and debris.

Alchesay hears the gunfire and leans on the wall preparing for someone to enter the space behind the dwelling. His bow is primed and ready to let loose an arrow. He's sure it is the demon Big Owl that causes him to stumble. He knows only bad comes from the hoot of that evil being. *He can be animal or human but now he causes my clumsiness,* thinks Alchesay. Scrambling and digging noises quickly approach the wall he fell over when he dropped behind the house. The noise gets closer and comes faster. Turning around, he is prepared for whatever comes over the wall. Suddenly, a huge, bulky figure climbs up and stands silhouetted on the top of the wall. It peers down into the dark area where Alchesay stands. Without any hesitation, he pulls his bowstring taut and releases the arrow. It strikes the figure in the middle of its chest and buries the head deeply into the body.

I've killed Big Owl. Alchesay sits down on the pile of rubble.

Brody knows he missed the Hard Case when that damned Mex jumps in front of his perfectly good shot. Then another Mex throws lead at him. It's time to vamoose. Going down takes too much time. Going up is the only option. So, he scrambles up and over debris piles beside the house. Up one, climb another, heading for the top floor, he spies a wall he can climb over and lose the Hard Case. Climbing the last pile, he glances back and sees Zep stand outside the door and swing his pistol around. Brody grabs the top of the wall and heaves himself up. He stands upright and instantly feels like a horse kicks him in his chest. Everything starts to swirl around. His arms lose their feeling and he senses he falls backward. *Oh, the damn pain in his chest; it has to stop.* Brody feels himself leave the wall and fall through space. The one hundred foot drop to the bottom of the cliff takes only seconds. Brody is dead before impact.

In the dark area behind the cliff house, Alchesay shivers. *What happens when you kill a spirit? Do more come to avenge it? Will I never have peace? Shall I run? Where to? How do I fight against spirits?*

He decides to wait. Wait for whatever comes his direction.

23

AFTERMATH

ZEP FURIOUSLY CLIMBS THE DEBRIS PILE, STUMBLES, falls, and scrambles up as he rushes to catch up with the mudsill. He looks up to see the killer's body tumble backwards from the top wall and down the cliff face. Mesmerized, he stares as the body slices through the air to its final impact. Dumbfounded, he yanks himself back to reality and hurries back to the dwelling entrance. Ducking through the doorway, he finds Allie in the middle of the room with Manolito's head cradled in her lap. Miguel stands over Manolito with his sombrero in his hands. Both wear expressions of devastation as tears flood down their faces and slowly drip from their chins. Ragged gasps of breath indicate that Manolito still lives.

"*Mi señorita*, don't cry for me," Manolito struggles to gasp out each word spoken. "We have had much good times together, no? It does not hurt so bad. I will miss your smiles and laughs." He pauses and coughs up globs of blood. "Miguel, take care of our *pequeno señorita; adios amigo*." Looking into Allie's eyes he flashes a sparkling "pearly white" smile from beneath his drooping mustache as his breathing stops.

"No, Manolito, No, NO, NO." screams Allie as she strokes his face and parts his hair. Tears roll down her face. "Why, Manolito, why you, why here, why now?" She stares at Zep with anguished and begging eyes.

Zep moves carefully to her and takes her hands. Gently laying Manolito's head on the ground, he lifts Allie to her feet and motions for Miguel to cover the body with a blanket. After a moment, Miguel responds, he picks up a blanket, and spreads it over Manolito.

"I don't rightly know 'Why' Allie. I simply accept when it's time to go, it's time to go. It doesn't make it any easier for us left here, but that's not in our control. There is someone bigger than us in charge."

"I hate it." Allie screams vehemently. "Manolito didn't have to die. I hate this trip."

Gently shushing her, Zep says, "My Mam used to read to us from the Good Book when I was little. She read one time something about there being no greater love than laying down your life for your friend. I believe Manolito did that."

"We grew up together. He is not just a friend he's like my brother. It seems that way. We did everything together - all three of us, Manolito, Miguel, and me."

"*Si, señorita*, we all grew up together. We learned to walk, run, ride, and play together as *ninos*. Later, Manolito and me, we learn to watch over you. *Si*, it's our job, but also what we want to do. You're our *pequeno señorita*, little miss." Miguel sits down and hangs his head as he cries.

Zep holds Allie in a firm embrace as she continues to sob. The silence of the valley is broken only by the sound of weeping.

As Allie tires, Zep guides her to the bedroll and lays her down. She rolls over and closes her eyes. He moves to Miguel, and motions him outside the dwelling.

"You know we have to bury Manolito here, right? What do you think is best, in the woods or up here? It's hard, but we have to decide and push on. You understand that, right"

"*Si, Señor* Zep. I understand. Do what you think is best."

"We'll bury him here, in the dwelling. Can you help Allie to accept that?"

"*Si*, I'll make sure she understands."

"Good. I'm sorry, my friend. Manolito was a good man, a brother, and a good friend. I'll miss him also." Zep turns and goes inside followed by Miguel.

The rest of the day, Zep prepares the body for burial. He goes into the next room, finds a corner of level stone, and assembles stones to form a crypt of sorts. He returns, picks up the body, and carries it to the newly built burial place. Miguel helps arrange stones over the crypt so nothing can disturb it.

In the evening, Allie revives from her sleep. Zep and Miguel take her to where Manolito is buried. Collapsing by the crypt, she begins crying. After a few minutes Miguel slowly lifts Allie to her feet and whispers to her about leaving Manolito. Reluctantly, she agrees with the arrangement and they return to their campfire for their meal. Suddenly, the evening's quiet is broken with a "halloo" from the valley. Rushing outside they see Guillo climbing up the handholds to the dwelling.

"Where are the horses," asks Zep looking past Guillo.

"Do not worry, *companero,* they are picketed and securely

hidden just inside the trees. They will be fine where I have left them."

"Well, you've taken care of them so far. I trust your judgment," says Zep.

"I checked for *indio* sign and did not find any around the cliff," says Guillo as he climbs. "It appears you didn't have much company after all, *si?*"

"No, we had very unwelcome company. It cost us a bunch," says Zep. "I'm glad to see you made it in one piece." Guillo reaches the top and Zep clasps him in a bear hug. Breaking free, Guillo steps back and eyes Zep carefully.

"*Mi companero*, I know I have been gone a few days, but you have never welcomed me like this before. Are you okay?"

Allie says, "Manolito is dead. The *hombre* from Birchville followed us and killed him."

"That *hombre* fell down the cliff from the top of the house," Zep adds.

"That's the stinking mess I saw at the bottom of the cliff when I was checking for signs," Guillo says.

Miguel and Allie look questioningly at Zep and he nods. "Yep, he took a dive off the top. Good riddance."

Guillo joins the others at the campfire for coffee and a meal.

"We need to move out in the morning," says Zep.

"I'm not sure I want to continue this trip." Allie's comment surprises the men. "It is not worth anyone else's life."

"Señorita, Manolito and I have watched over you for many years. We know you have a purpose and goal to learn about *Americanos* so you can help the *familias* at our *hacienda*. If you don't complete this trip, then Manolito died for nothing. I don't think that is what you want. *Señor* Zep and Guillo will make sure we get to Santa Fe, and I'll stay with you all the way. Where you travel, I travel. I owe that to you and to Manolito. When you are ready to return, I'll see you return safely. *Bueno*?"

"*Si, muchas gracias con mucho gusto*, Miguel. I appreciate your reminding me. I must not let my personal pains overshadow the importance of this trip. We will continue, and I welcome your company, Miguel."

"It's settled then; we leave in the morning." They all turn in for the night. Allie again cradles herself against Zep. Guillo rises up on one elbow, catches Zep's attention, and throws him a kiss and a wink. Zep smiles and tosses a blanket at him.

Uneasiness nags at Zep as he thinks about the road before them. There is still too much uncertainty that might derail the best of intentions.

24

SOCORRO

MORNING DAWNS CRISP AND CLEAR. EVERYONE gathers equipment, what remains of their supplies, and transports everything to the horses and mule. All mount and prepare to ride. Zep motions forward. He takes the lead followed by Miguel, Allie, and Guillo who leads the extra horse and mule.

Where are the Indians? I led the group to this place because of Indians, why are they waiting? Zep feels a 'twinge' on the back of his neck like someone or something watches their departure. It is not an easy feeling.

Miguel and Allie turn in their saddles and sadly take a last look at the cliff dwelling. A large part of their lives lies buried in its stones. Turning back they square their shoulders for the trip ahead.

Zep sets the pace and leads his group up the east branch

of the Gila River paralleling the Black Range Mountains. They travel over and out of the Mogollon Mountains and around the north side of South Baldy Peak. They ride through forest, mountain valleys, open plains, and lush hidden meadows. Wildlife is abundant, easily seen, and startled at times by their appearance. Days are warm and nights chilly. Supplies are almost exhausted. After Baldy Peak, they leave the Ponderosa pine forests behind. The landscape changes and occasional clumps of piñon pine mixed with leafy hardwood trees are scattered across open spaces, undergrowth now becomes grass-covered slopes, and the land undulates with graceful hills. Only a short range of slopes separate them from their destination. Socorro. As they crest the hills, the view forward is similar to the desert vegetation around the *hacienda*.

After a hard day's ride, Zep stops the group in the open area overlooking Socorro. Pulling binoculars from his saddlebag, he shares them for the others to view the distant dots on the horizon. There is a line of green stretching to the north and a little ways south of what appears to be the town.

"That's the Rio Grande River on the far side of Socorro. Cottonwood trees cover the banks of the river and farms follow right along with the river. You see where the green goes north and only a little ways south? The *Jornada del Muerto* comes up to town from the south and is hell on earth to cross. Socorro is the first major stop out of the *Jornada* for northbound travel and really appreciated," Zep shares the view with his travelers. They dismount and make camp.

The horses are unsaddled, hobbled and turned loose to forage. A nearby creek provides for much needed bathing and clothes washing. Supper is prepared and shared. Thinking they are in the open and out of Apache contact, Zep allows everyone to sleep. In the early dawn hours, he snaps awake, grabs his rifle and heads toward the horses. Someone moves among the animals. Quickly, two figures mount horses and gallop away. Zep throws the rifle to his shoulder preparing to shoot, but realizes there's not enough light for a clear shot. Guillo joins him, and together they round up the remaining animals.

Guillo says, "*Ay, caramba*, those *indios* steals my *caballo*." He stomps around the meadow venting his anger.

"*Companero*, take it easy. Looks like it was a couple of young bucks looking to make their mark by stealing horseflesh. They got Manolito's horse as well."

Standing and looking over the *remuda,* reality crashes in on Guillo. "No, NO, *mi companero,* I am not going to ride that mule."

"It's the only other four legged critter we got left," says Zep. "It appears it's the mule or you walk. Sorry, *companero.*"

"*Ay, yi-yi.* You don't understand. I hate that mule and it hates me. We both agree about that. Now, you expect me to ride that miserable beast? NO. This cannot be."

"Take your choice, *mi amigo,* we'll leave shortly. Maybe you better come to terms with your new mount." Zep grins broadly as he walks back to the camp. He leaves Guillo fuming, stomping, and muttering to himself in the meadow.

Miguel stands beside Allie with his gun drawn as Zep walks toward them. "It's as good as it can be," he says. "A couple of young Apaches slipped up on us and stole Manolito and Guillo's horses. They're long gone. While I really hate to lose the mounts, it's better them than us." Zep chides himself, "Just shows Apaches will walk right into your house and take your dishes if you're not always on your guard. My mistake."

Allie immediately grasps the situation. "So, you mean Guillo has to ride the mule?" She smiles broadly.

Zep, laughs out loud, "Yep, he's become a regular "*John Mule Man*" and I know it has to be a love and hate relationship. He loves to ride, and hates the mule. I have no idea what the mule thinks."

Guillo walks up on the group. He has a big smile on his face. "I am now the proud *vaquero* of a big, ugly mule, and I will make that animal like me if it *kills him*."

Everyone has a good laugh at Guillo's plight, gather belongings, saddle up, and prepare to ride.

Zep leads them down towards Socorro and the Rio Grande.

"The town don't look like much," he says, as they get closer. "It's been beat up a mite."

"What's happened to it," asks Alassandra.

"Well, pueblo Indians built it way back, Spaniards moved in, Apaches burned it down a time or two, Mexicans took over, and Americans took it from them. The army built Fort Craig down south of town."

"*Si*, so *Americanos* have the fort, no?"

"Yep, and the road that runs down the middle of town starts way down in Mexico somewhere around Mexico City, and goes all the way to Santa Fe. The Spaniards called it *El Camino Real de Tierra Adentro*, the royal road to the interior land. The name *Camino Real* stuck. It's a glorified name for a rutted, dusty, dirt road."

"So, what is the land called south of town?"

"It's the *Jornada del Muerto*. A more desolate hateful place doesn't exist. If you survive coming north through that land this village is a great sight to see. Ain't all that bad for us either." Zep views the town as they draw closer. It appears to be a gathering of single story *casas*, a few larger multistoried wooden buildings, a mission church, and in the distance is an old dilapidated *pueblo* structure. By midday, they arrive at the outskirts of Socorro.

"Best find a place to stay and stable the horses and mule. Miguel, you'll take the stock to the livery; Allie, come with me; and Guillo, find a place to stock up on supplies. We'll meet back at the large building over there." Zep points out a substantial structure hoping it's a hotel. Everyone moves to his or her assigned task.

Zep, Allie, and Miguel approach the large building and after closer inspection sees it's a hotel, a saloon, a couple of shops, and a dentist office all together. They dismount, hand Miguel their horses' reins, and grab their saddlebags. Zep pulls his rifle; they knock the trail dust off their clothes, and enter the hotel.

"*Buenas dias,*" says the clerk from behind his registration desk. "One or two rooms?"

Zep looks left through a large open doorway into a dining room. "Are you open in there?" he asks.

"Oh, yes. How many rooms?"

"Make it two on the second floor, close by the stairway. Okay?"

"*Si,* sign here. That will be two bits for both rooms. It includes a bath at the end of the hall. If you're first, you get the clean water. Oh, ladies have a separate room and always get clean water," he smiles at Allie. "Here are your keys."

Zep pays, takes the offered keys, asks the clerk to hold on to their saddlebags and rifle, and leads Allie by the arm into the dining room. He spots an empty table by the front window. Pulling the chair out for Allie, he sits across from her and they both watch the street.

"Kind of thought this would be more comfortable than

around a campfire." Zep takes off his hat and hangs it from the chair back.

"Yes, it is good to feel furniture again. It has been a long ride, lots has happened, and I still have a long way to go." Allie looks around, taking in the entire dining room. Her gaze takes in five large tables and a sideboard service area. The floor is hardwood, polished to a shine, and swept clean.

"We will stay the night, resupply, and head for Albuquerque tomorrow. Giving our horses some time in the livery and getting them grained up will help. Do you know yet what your final plans are once you get to St. Louis?"

"Not fully. I know I want to meet my mother's family. See all the innovative things in St. Louis. Learn everything I can about how Americans think, work, negotiate, talk, walk - you know, everything. There is no telling when one or more things I learn will be useful at the *hacienda*. In reality, I am an American; I better act like one."

"Well, I can appreciate all of that, but never lose sight of one big thing. You are a westerner, a New Mexican. You belong to this land; it may enchant or terrify you, but it's yours by birthright. Back there, they see us as different out here. Don't let their opinion change the lovely way you are now."

"Zep Bierman, if you go romantic on me, I'll positively blush. So, shush."

Miguel stands in the doorway and slowly comes into the dining room to join them at the table. He gawks at the surroundings.

"*Señor* Zep, is it okay for me to be in a place like this?" Miguel looks intently at Zep.

"Yep, we're okay here. We'll stay the night and leave with first light. Horses taken care of?"

Miguel nods in the affirmative.

Zep looks back at the doorway and out into the street. "Miguel, did you see Guillo on your way over here?"

"No, *señor* Zep. I left the horses and mule at the livery as instructed. I told the stableman to feed them well. I believe he will give them good care. I have not seen Guillo."

"Well, we'll get some food ordered and let Guillo catch up when he gets here."

Zep motions for a waiter. When he approaches, Zep says, "Bring us whatever your special is today. We're almost hungry enough to eat horny toads."

The waiter smirks. "I promise we won't serve horny toads, but we do have a beef roast with fixings. Will that do?"

"Bring it on, and thanks." Zep nods.

The three travelers finish a terrific meal of beef, vegetables, fresh baked bread, butter, cold buttermilk, and *dulce de leche* when Guillo finally arrives at the dining room.

"*Companero*, you about missed the whole shebang," says Zep motioning for the waiter to bring more food. "What held you up? Did you find a mercantile? Will our supplies be ready in the morning?"

Guillo quickly sits at the table, accepts a plate of food from the waiter, looks up at Zep as he eats, and gives him a sheepish grin. "*Si*, Zep, everything will be ready. I did find a store, and in there I saw a gift from heaven. A lovely *señorita* looks at me and takes the time to talk with me. Her *la chaperon* watches us as we talk about our trip and she smiles, laughs, and likes what I am saying. *Señor* Zep, I must see her again. I can't leave this *pueblo* without seeing her. Do you understand how I feel? Do you? Tell me what to do. I am a man who is lost in this vision of loveliness that steals my heart." He collapses back in his chair.

146

Zep runs his hand through his hair. "Whooeee. You've got it bad, *companero*. We're fixin' to leave in the morning, but if I have to drag you along moping every step we'll never get anywhere."

"*Si, companero*, I was thinking the same thing." Guillo grins. "How about if I wait here until you return from Santa Fe? It will give me time to convince the *señorita* to leave with me. I know I can win her over. After all, look what a great catch I am." Guillo jumps up from the table, places his hands on his hips, throws his head back, and flashes a huge smile. Allie bursts into a fit of giggles. Zep and Miguel hide smiles behind their hands.

"Well, Guillo, since you put it that way, all I can do is wish you 'good huntin'' and I will see you when I return." The travelers rise from the table, leave the dining room and head upstairs to their rooms.

Unlocking Allie's door, Zep hands her saddlebags over. "We're next door; any trouble, shout. Lock the door and rest well." She goes in and locks the door.

"*Companeros,* we're there." He points next door for Miguel and Guillo.

Zep leads the way into the room. Sparsely furnished, the room has a brass bed, flowered wallpapered walls, a lumpy well-used mattress with a tattered bedcover, a small dresser, one washstand, and two chairs. There is a well-worn rug on the floor and a dirty, flyspecked window looks over the street.

Guillo sits on the bed and bounces.

"This is fine with me, *companero*. It sure beats riding a mud-ugly mule."

Miguel walks around looking everything over like a child in a candy store.

"Is this where we stay?" His question echoes with incredulity.

"Yep," says Zep. "Kick off your boots and stretch out on the bed. See if it fits you."

Miguel knocks some trail dust off his clothes and slips out of his boots. A huge grin explodes under his mustache as he lies down.

"This feels *bueno*. I could get use to this, *señor* Zep."

"Well, don't you get too comfortable, we're only here tonight. It's the hard ground again tomorrow." Zep pulls the two chairs together and makes a spot for himself to lie. He grabs a towel from the washstand and heads out the door for the bathtub and shouts over his shoulder, "Get some rest. We ride hard in the morning."

25

QUESTS

I T'S BEEN TWO DAYS. ALCHESAY SITS IN THE DARK, HEAD down on his chest. He mumbles and mutters unintelligibly to himself consumed by a spiritual collapse that has him almost catatonic.

The sun washes over the top of the cliff dwelling and slips down the back wall until it illuminates Alchesay. With the sun comes an awakening. His head rises and his eyesight clears. He remembers the numerous owl calls precipitating the appear-ance of the spirit being, Big Owl. He recalls it's his arrow that strikes the spirit forcing it off the wall, dead. For the past days, he has been waited for the repercussions of his actions. None has come.

He thinks to himself. *Do the spirits not take care of each other? Do they not vent anger on one who harms a spirit? Yet, I am whole and not accosted by them. Was it a spirit I slew or something else?*

I must move, I cannot remain in this house of spirits any longer.

During his stupor, Alchesay recalls activity in other rooms, people talking, rocks being moved, and dropped. While these things connected with his consciousness, he was unable to do anything about them. Now, he is recovered, thirsty, hungry, and driven to leave.

He finds where those he tracks stayed and the doorway out. He exits and climbs down from the cliff dwelling. He decides on a way to get back up to the top of the cliff. Hopefully, his horse is still there. Following the base of the mountain, he smells something before coming upon it. It is a body, crushed and in a heap. His arrow protrudes from the gore. A human, he shot a human, not a spirit. Overcome with relief and rejuvenation, he runs, almost flying over the ground, to the top of the cliff. His horse waits impatiently for his return. Grabbing his supplies from a saddlebag he devours the food and drinks from the canteen. Refreshed, he mounts and rides down to the valley and finds the trail of those he seeks. Alchesay turns his horse and the hunt is underway again.

An open meadow with a stream flowing through it allows Alchesay to hobble his horse and turn it loose to forage on meadow grasses. Walking to a nearby pine tree, he arranges a soft seat from pine needles and rests his back against the tree with his bow across his lap.

I have much to consider, he thinks. *My purpose is to track down and kill the white men I've followed from Mexico. Every time I get close, they slip away. Is this the omen the owl intends? Should I go on with this hunt? I have spent much time and attention on something that may come to nothing.* Shaking his head for clarity, he verbalizes his thoughts, "Why don't I return to my people and give up this chase? I do not have people to return to. The white men enter my land, kill my people, take women and children, and only want more. There is less and less space for *The People*, Apaches. What I'm doing may not make any difference, but it's something I can do. My band's blood cries for revenge. I have come too far to turn away now. Continuing is the only thing I can do; it's the right thing to do. I will find them and put them down." With this decision, Alchesay stretches out on the ground, the warm sun makes him feel drowsy and he begins to sleep.

Midafternoon he awakes and listens to the birds in the forest trees. It is a good sign all is well. Rising, he moves across the meadow and finds his horse. Unhobbling it, he mounts and returns to follow the trail of those he seeks. For the next four days he rides, eats, sleeps, and rides again. He leaves the Mogollon Mountains and goes around the north side of Baldy Peak. Soon enough, he sees the white man's village of Socorro.

Many times the Apaches had dealings with the Mexican and Americans who inhabit this pueblo, he thinks. *I will need to find out where those I pursue have gone from this place or if they are still in this village. It will take time, and time may put them further away from me. Maybe they are already too far for me to ever catch them. The omen of the Owl is strong and plots my failure. I will try to find them or wait for them.*

Alchesay turns upriver and stealthily moves across the open plains to avoid discovery. He sets up surveillance in a concealed vantage point and watches those entering and leaving the village. Waiting is the hard part, but Alchesay has the patience of a rock.

Guillo waits in front of the mercantile store with two canvas bags of supplies. Because he is not accompanying Zep, Allie, and Miguel, his mule is not loaded to leave. The three travelers ride up to the store and Guillo assists in tying a bag of supplies to Zep and Miguel's saddles. He stands back from the horses, and sweeps the sombrero from his head. Holds it in his hands, and gets their attention.

"*Mi amigos*, ride well and be safe. *Señorita* Alassandra, I wish you safe travel to St. Louis and hope all you want to find is there. It has been my pleasure to know you. Miguel, our ride has been one to tell stories about, yes? We have lost a good friend, but have made others, yes? Should you need me, for whatever reason, I will always ride with you. Zep, *mi companero*, I know you will see our *señorita* on her way to St. Louis. When you are done, please come back through here. I will be right here, in this spot, to ride to Mesilla with you. We have a *rancho* to rebuild, yes? Now, *vamonos* and *via con Dios*." He turns quickly to his mule to hide his moist eyes. Slapping his *sombrero* back on his head, he steps into the saddle and rides toward the livery stable. Guillo waves over his shoulder.

Allie's eyes tear; she will miss Guillo's happiness and humor. Miguel's moustache droops a little lower, he will miss *Señor* Guillo. Zep watches his friend ride away, and knows he will come back to Socorro. Turning north he motions the other two to follow. They head for Albuquerque en route to Santa Fe.

Guillo rides back to the livery and turns his mule over to the stableman. He walks out of the barn, steps onto the boardwalk, and heads toward a *cantina* close at hand. Tequila might ease the pain of separation a bit. Next, he will find the *señorita* that makes him feel like he can walk on air. He plans to be a very busy *hombre*.

Alchesay, from his vantage point, spots three riders he recognizes moving north along *El Camino Real*, the royal highway, towards Albuquerque. He follows at a distance.

26

ALBUQUERQUE

THE HORSES ARE WELL RESTED, AND ZEP KNOWS traveling the *Camino Real* beside the Rio Grande River is much easier than the trails through the pine forests. The days are warm and the nights cool. Compared to the stress of the early part of their trip, this portion is pleasant. The 'twinge' on the back of his neck continues to bother him. It's a nagging concern something isn't right. He can't see it or hear it, but he knows something or someone watches them. Many times his life has depended on that 'twinge,' and it would be foolish to ignore it now. Zep is not foolish.

He turns to ask Guillo a question, and remembers his *companero* remains behind to deal with an "affair of the heart." Miguel, watches Zep, understands the señor's expression. He, too, misses Guillo and Manolito. The *Camino Real* trail is well marked and traveled. Wagons, riders, groups of travelers, and even army patrols pass by Zep, Allie, and Miguel.

With constant vigilance, Zep daily changes their pattern of travel. He does allow time to refresh, bathe, and wash clothes in the river at the end of each day. But, he still "smarts" from the horse theft outside of Socorro and is determined not to drop his guard again. One day they all ride, the next they walk beside their horses to make them difficult targets, and another they ride single file. No two days are alike. Zep does not want anything routine about how they travel. The same applies at night with one exception; their campfire is always small and minimal. Sleeping arrangements vary from near the fire one night, away from it the next, singly, and together. Both Miguel and Zep are awake, alert, and armed before sunup.

Zep finds time in the evenings to sit with Allie, hold hands, and talk about whatever is on their minds. Their togetherness grows as each day passes, and Zep knows it will be difficult for him to let her go when they reach Santa Fe. *Could I go to St. Louis? Should I go back east with her? Now, we have each other to enjoy, and that is enough.*

They arrive at *Plaza Vieja* in the old *presidio* of Belen, and Zep knows Albuquerque is only a couple of steady-paced days away. His 'twinge' does not decrease.

During the ride north, Zep shares about Albuquerque. "We're going to see more farms as we get closer to town, and sheep. Woolies is a big business around here," Zep says. "The Spanish built another *presidio*, a fort, in Albuquerque a long time ago. Mexicans took it over and stationed troops there. Now, the Americans are in control. Like all this part of the world, it changes hands over and over. Interesting though, nobody ever seems to ask the Apaches, Navajos, or Pueblo Indians about the changes. I guess that's why they keep fighting."

"What have the Americans done since they've taken over?" Allie inquires.

"Well, they came here in force after the Mexican-American War. Colonel Stephen Kearney made a proclamation up the road a piece in Las Vegas about New Mexico being independent from Mexico, and the Americans promptly made it a territory of the United States. I heard tell of a British military expert riding with the Americans who called them 'unwashed and unshaven, ragged and dirty, without uniforms and totally lack discipline.' I don't guess we've got any better. Of course mountain men, traders, merchants, and settlers traveled the Santa Fe Trail for years. Government soldiers and a quartermaster's depot established the Post of Albuquerque around 1846. Can't say I've really given this spot a whole lot of consideration since coming into this territory in '56. My time's been spent trying to keep everything I have together, and not let the Indians run away with any of it or put me under."

"You've seen quite a bit haven't you, Zep. I'm glad you share it with me." Allie smiles.

"I'm glad too," grins Zep. "Look up there, ahead, Albuquerque." He waves to dots on the horizon. Pulling binoculars from his saddlebag, he shares them.

"Them mountains to the east are called the *Sandia* range. It means watermelon in Spanish. I got no idea why some fool would name mountains a watermelon, but someone did and it stuck."

The *Camino Real* comes to a crossing of the Rio Grande. A ferry waits on the shore. Beside the landing is a ramshackle hut with an old scrawny man in overalls, no shirt, a beat up black hat, moccasins, smoking a pipe, rocking in a chair on the porch.

"Howdy, Friend. What would you charge to carry us across

156

the river?" Zep asks and smiles.

"Well, Feller, I 'magine I'd charge you the same as I do any-body else. It'll be a nickel per person and a dime for each horse," the old coot responds.

"Can we do it today, or wait until whenever you get ready?"

"Peers you be gettin' mighty pushy, sprout. But, we can go now."

"Amos, yank up that rope and get ready to pull." He shouts toward the ferry where a large black man stands. He'd been asleep on the ferry. Zep looks at the boatman, puts his hand to his head and shoves his hat back. On the ferry stands a six-foot-eight-inch man built like a tall tree trunk. The man's body is solid muscle from the top of his head to his feet. His biceps are knotted and his arms are as large as tree limbs. His leg mus-cles flex and ripple when he moves. They look like tree roots. A round bald-head sits atop squared off well-muscled shoulders.

"Yas sar, Mr. Boss. I ready," comes the deep bass response. The big man steps up to the rail of the ferry and gets a grip on a three-inch diameter rope stretching from bank to bank. The riders dismount and lead their horses up onto the wooden fer-ry. The craft has side rails on the left and right. The front has a pole across the opening and Mr. Boss pulls one across the back after everyone is aboard. He gets a grip on the rope as well.

"Pull, damn you, Amos, pull."

"I pulls, Mr. Boss, I pulls."

The craft shudders and moves from the shore. As the cur-rent catches it broadside, the ferry starts to float downstream and comes to a jerking stop as the rope tightens up. Amos and Mr. Boss pull on the rope threaded through front and back loops on the side rail of the ferry. Nervous, the horses begin to stomp and snort as they feel the shift under their feet. Zep rubs the muzzle of his horse to quiet it and sees the other two do the same. The ferry floats, bounces, and jostles its way across the river as Amos and Mr. Boss apply muscle power. With a thump and bump, the vessel comes to a stop on the opposite bank. Mr. Boss pulls back the pole blocking the exit. Zep pays the fee and all three disembark on solid ground. Remounting, they continue along the road after a wave back at the vessel's crew.

They ride on a flat plain at the base of the imposing mountains. Farms and farming activity multiplies as they approach the outskirts of town. By evening, the travelers enter Albuquerque and Zep views the houses. Numerous adobe casas with walls and arched gateways and small-framed wooden homes line the road. Closer to town center, the buildings become larger, multistoried, some with false fronts, commercial enterprises, fancy balconied houses, and saloons. Finally they reach the central plaza, a square of adobe structures, stores, shops, cafes, and saloons built close together to form a fort around the open plaza that's dotted with large cottonwood trees.

Zep spots a beautiful church, the San Felipe de Neri, on the north side of the square. Allie stops to gaze at the old mission church and while he watches she bows her head. *Prayers for travel and safety are always good,* he thinks. He stops a passerby, and asks directions to a livery and hotel.

Two blocks from the plaza, Allie, Zep, and Miguel arrive at the Alameda Hotel. Allie and Zep dismount and pull their saddlebags. Zep reaches over to grab his rifle out of the scabbard. They give their horses' reins to Miguel.

"Señor Zep, I will sleep at the livery with our horses," says Miguel.

Zep nods and taking Allie by the arm, enters the hotel. Walking to the registration desk, he inquires about rooms.

Miguel leads the horses away.

"That'll be two bits for each room including our tonsorial parlor and showers. You can get clean, shaved, and barbered here at the Alameda. We have a bathtub in your room, Miss, and I will send hot water right up for you."

The clerk smiles at Allie.

"Sounds good," says Zep. "We'll take you up on that." He pays the clerk, signs the register, and hands the pen to Allie for her signature.

The clerk spins the register around and reads their names aloud.

"Mr. Bierman and Miss de la Vieta. Let me know if I can do anything for you during your stay at the Alameda."

Zep notices an immediate reaction from a well-dressed gentlemen sitting on a lobby couch after the registration clerk reads their names. He stands and steps toward Allie.

"I don't mean to intrude, but did I hear the clerk say your name is *de la Vieta?*" the man asks. "I happen to know a *Don Louis de la Vieta*. Are you perhaps any relation to that gentleman?" Zep is immediately defensive.

Allie and Zep's entrance has David Claiborne's attention. He watches them register, and flicks a quick knowing glance at his partner, Sam Blander. He motions to the two new comers with his eyes. He's five years older than Sam. His well-established family has profitable business enterprises in St. Louis and Albuquerque. A number of his local contacts are customers of the family's Santa Fe trading enterprise. David is in Albuquerque directing the family owned bank. His appearance is business-like wearing pinstriped trousers, a winged collar white shirt, a black double-breasted vest, a frock coat, and holding a black flat-topped gambler's hat. Both David and Sam are almost six feet tall with light brown hair and dark eyes. David is weak chinned and Sam has a squared off jawline.

Sam Blander came to Albuquerque from Memphis, Tennessee, via Little Rock, Arkansas. In Memphis he worked for a bank until discrepancies were discovered in account ledgers. His trade is bookkeeping, land speculating, fraud, and swindling. He exited Little Rock one-step ahead of long-term incarceration. Land speculation in New Mexico is lucrative for him. He dresses similar to David.

Both men seem entranced by the attractive young woman who looks at them with deep brown eyes and a questioning expression on her pixie-like face. They see her long auburn hair pulled into a ponytail capped by a *caballero* hat. She wears a short waisted *vaquero* jacket over a checkered shirt tucked into denim trousers, and her stovepipe boots show trail wear and tear. None of this hides the well-sculpted curvaceous figure underneath. Sam and David's captivation is not in her appearance, but her name.

Both men discount Zep as a typical well-worn saddle tramp in dusty denim trousers, black stovepipe boots, linen pullover shirt, fringed *serape*, and soft slouch hat.

"*Si*, Gentlemen, *mi padre*, rather, my father is *Don Louis de la Vieta*." Allie acknowledges. "So, how do you know him?"

"*Señorita*, it is an honor to meet you," says David. "I am acquainted with your father through correspondence. In the past there have been transactions involving livestock which utilized my bank."

As if on cue, Sam adds, "I know of your father from acquaintances at *Rancho de San José de la Concordia-El Paso*. They've mentioned your family's *hacienda*."

"*Bueno*, Gentlemen, it is nice to meet you. However, you

must excuse me now, it has been a long trip and I need to retire. Perhaps, we shall meet again." Allie turns toward the stairs waiting for Zep.

Both Sam and David make their excuses and move toward the hotel's front door.

Turning, David asks, "Would it be possible for you to join us for dinner at the Maxwell House, to celebrate your arrival in Albuquerque? It's the least the bank can do for a special client, and it is something we, Sam and I, would appreciate. Will you join us?"

"I will consider your offer, *señores*. Now, please excuse me."

As they exit, she whispers so only Zep can hear her, "They seem like nice, trustworthy Americans, yes?"

Walking rapidly up the stairs beside Allie, Zep's 'twinge' has been quivering since the men spoke their first word.

27

GREED

ONCE OUTSIDE THE CLOSED DOORS OF THE HOTEL, David grabs Sam by the arm and hustles him along the sidewalk towards the bank. Sputtering, Sam stumbles along.

"All right, all right, what's the rush? Slow down. Whatever it is will wait." David continues to walk rapidly and they arrive at the bank. They hurry past the tellers to David's office. Stopping to look around, he quickly opens the door and ushers Sam inside and firmly shuts the door.

"Do you realize what we have here? It has to be her." He looks directly at Sam. "This is *Don Louis de la Vieta's* daughter. We know he has an only child, and this girl is she. This gives us all the leverage we need to take land from the old goat's land grant for railroad right of way, and with lawyers it will be done legal. No dispute, no court delays, and no daughter for him if he doesn't cooperate. Do you understand the significance of meeting *señorita de la Vieta* at the hotel? Do I have to spell everything out for you?" David agitatedly moves around the room.

"Yeah, sure, spell it out for me," Sam responds.

"*Louis de la Vieta* is that old land baron with acres of land in southern New Mexico. His daughter is our meal ticket to providing leverage to acquire land for railroads. Does any of this begin to ring a bell for you?"

David has information from St. Louis contacts that confirms Colonel Cyrus K. Holliday of Topeka is seriously proposing to connect Kansas, Colorado, and New Mexico with a railroad. Its just talk, right now, but the plan is to follow the Old Santa Fe Trail through Raton Pass into New Mexico, and arrive in Albuquerque.

David thinks, *railroad expansion and construction into New Mexico and Arizona territories means wealth. My partnership with Sam is based on being ready to capitalize on the opportunity of railroad growth by purchasing or seizing land to sell for railroad right of way. A fortune stands to be made, if I act first. Legally or illegally this is too big a game to miss.*

"Okay, so we have the girl persuade the old man to give up his land? Then we get rid of the evidence, the girl?" asks Sam.

"Yes and no. The girl is our leverage. But, and hear me very clearly, the girl is not to be harmed in any way. That old Mexican *Don* will send his *vaqueros* and hunt us to the end of the earth if anything happens to his child. *Comprende*?"

Sam scans the room. A large highly polished oak desk dominates the space with a high backed black leather swivel chair behind it. On the wall, behind the chair, an imposing framed map of New Mexico and Arizona Territory hangs. Two large soft leather chairs sit in front of the desk.

Sam nods his head in reluctant agreement to David's demands. All the while thinking, *if things become difficult I will do, as I want.* He responds, "Okay, we'll do it your way. So, what do we do?"

"So, he asks. So. The 'So' is, we tie up land not just in northern New Mexico but the southern half of the territory as well. This positions us for anything moving east to west or north to south. Do you begin to see the size of this deal?"

"You're telling me, that old man *de la Vieta* stands between us and getting wealthy from railroad growth in New Mexico and Arizona Territories? Well then, his land needs to become ours?"

David nods and continues, "I've got an idea on how to do that. At dinner, I'll make it clear. We've extended an invitation to the *señorita* to join us. I'll make sure it's accepted. After all, it would be inhospitable for her to decline, especially since we told her, and everyone in the lobby, we know her father."

"Yeah, yeah, so why go to all the trouble? All we want is to get her Daddy's signature on a land transfer document. She is simply a means to the end we want."

"Sam, there are times I wonder how you've managed to stay in the game. It's obvious you don't think things through or visualize the big picture. This is not a proposition to be rushed into. It takes planning and legal manipulation. I hesitate to think about how you make the land acquisitions you do. Never mind, I'll make the dinner arrangements, you follow my lead."

"Oh, I'll tell you how I've made my land deals with those who don't cooperate and it ain't pretty. Just because your highfalutin, rich family in St. Louis built their business empire on Santa Fe trade and sent you to keep an eye on things, don't make you the high *cockalorum* over me, *amigo*."

"Spare me your drivel. If I hadn't bailed you out and satisfied those you conned out of their money in Little Rock, you'd rot in jail. So, pay attention and follow my directions. This bank is only interested in results. I want things done like I tell you."

"Okay. But, be very careful. One of these days you'll push me too far and you won't like the consequences."

"Sam, Sam, don't get ruffled up like a scared cat. You know we need each other." David's scheming smile is intended to calm Sam. "We share enough dirt on each other to keep us looking out for one another. Now, go intimidate someone. Our future lies in railroads, and we need land to sell for the right of way. Get out and leave me alone. I'll let you know when I've got things arranged." David opens the door for Sam's exit. Sam walks out and David mutters as he closes the door, "Sometimes, I despair of what I have to work with."

He moves to his desk, sits down, and writes a note, which he finishes with a flourish. Picking up a small bell from the desktop, he rings it, and sits it down; he seals the note. A clerk opens the door and rushes in. He stops in front of the desk.

"Yes, Sir, you rang."

"Take this note to the Alameda Hotel. Give it to the clerk and tell him to deliver it to Miss *de la Vieta*. Got it?"

"Yes, Sir. Alameda Hotel, give to clerk, make sure he delivers to Miss *de la Vieta*."

"Good, get out and deliver the note."

The clerk exits quickly and softly closes the door.

For Alchesay, the pursuit becomes much more difficult. In his mind, he knows the white man he chases must be part Apache.

The constant change of routine keeps Alchesay off balance. When he plans one thing the white man does something else. It is almost like his mind is being read, and the frustration takes a toll on him. He is not as careful, taking more risks in order to deal with his adversary. Today, his lack of focus almost has him stumble into an army patrol. At the last moment he finds cover and hides.

"This 'rabbit' may get away from the fox, but I know where my other 'rabbit' is," he mumbles. Turning his horse, he heads south towards Socorro.

28

KIDNAPPED

FRESHLY SHAVED, HAIR TRIMMED, STANDING IN THE wooden stall under the suspended perforated bucket, makes Zep feel like a new person. A Pueblo Indian climbs down the ladder beside the stall to retrieve another bucket of warm water from the fireplace in the corner. He climbs back up, fills the hanging bucket, and water drops through the holes showering down on Zep. Allie left a note for him at the desk that he picks up as he heads to the tonsorial parlor. It says we have an invitation to a dinner this evening from the banker. We are to meet them at Maxwell House promptly at 7:00 o'clock. Zep's 'twinge' begins to work overtime.

Zep sends word to Miguel to clean up and join them for the dinner. From his saddlebag, Zep takes out denim pants, a plaid shirt, and a black neckerchief. They are wrinkled from the saddlebag but clean, and they will have to do for the night.

Sitting on the side of his bed, buffing his boots, Zep's concentration is broken by a knock at the door. He opens it to find Allie in the doorway. She is beautiful. Her long hair freshly washed and combed hangs down her back. A plain linen shift with an accompanying short jacket is simple and elegant. She wears a single Amethyst necklace that shimmers with each flicker of light it reflects. Momentarily, Zep is lost in the sparkle of gold flakes in her deep brown eyes.

"Zep, I hope you are ready. The note said to be prompt," she says.

"Let me slip on my boots and I am good to go," he says as he sits on the bed and hammers each foot into a boot. "I will stop and ask the desk clerk directions."

"Not necessary, I already have and the Maxwell House is only three doors down from the hotel. The clerk assures me it is the best place in Albuquerque. It is owned by Mr. Claiborne's bank."

Zep at once feels uncomfortable, but hesitates to tell Allie. *No reason yet to spoil a good meal.*

Standing up, he extends his elbow, "Are you ready to go?" She takes his arm and they walk down the hall and descend the stairs. In the lobby, Miguel waits for them. His trail clothes are cleaned up and his boots shine.

"I am to go with you, *si*?"

"Yep, you're part of this shindig, so, plan on enjoying yourself on the other fellas nickel tonight, *amigo*." Zep smiles at him, and Miguel gives a big white-toothed grin from under his mustache.

Together, they walk towards their appointment.

"MMMM, you smell wonderful," she says as they walk along the sidewalk.

"Oh, well, it's something the barber splashed on my face after my shave. He said he just got it from New Orleans. It is a special tonic called Bay Rum. It's going to take me some gettin' used to. It's right potent."

"Well, I think it's delightful. You should get some to take with you. Looks like we are here."

Zep holds the door for Allie and Miguel. Other customers enter and leave as they dodge their way into a busy Maxwell House. Fourteen tables with white tablecloths are arranged about a large open room. A constant rattle of glassware fills the air. Waiters in white shirts and black vests with aprons wrapped about their waists shuttle around delivering entrees to the diners and removing plates. Other waiters carry bottles of wine and drinks to patrons from a bar located along one wall. Heads turn as they enter, and Zep knows it's not him people look at. He is sure Allie is the topic of whispered conversation at the nearby tables. She is beautiful tonight. He spies David Claiborne standing at the back inside an open doorway waving them forward. Taking the lead, he moves toward the back with Allie and Miguel.

"Your timing is impeccable," says David. He ushers them into a special dining room much quieter than the clatter and chatter of the open dining area. David motions Allie, Zep, and Miguel to take a seat at the only cloth covered table in the room. The door behind them quietly closes. Sam Blander is already seated. Zep inspects the square room with a suspicious eye. A small bar on his right side holds six bottles and eight glasses; across from him is a second door, to the left is a service station cabinet with napkins, plates, and silverware; the walls hold framed landscape pictures.

David steps to the bar, picks up a bottle of wine, and a tray of glasses; he sits everything on the table. Picking up an opener from the tray, he uncorks the bottle.

"How about some champagne to celebrate your arrival in Albuquerque?"

He pours the wine and distributes glasses around the table.

"I'd rather have whiskey," says Zep as he moves to stand up and help himself from the bar.

"Sit down, huckleberry. Put your hands on the table and shut up." Sam places his pistol on the table pointed at him. Glaring at Sam, Zep clenches and unclenches his fist as he places his hands on the table.

Both doors open and close quickly, two men wearing white waiter jackets step through the doors, and stand with drawn revolvers. Sam stands up and moves quickly towards David. Zep jumps up to block him and sees Miguel lunge for Allie at the same time. A vicious blow crashes on the back of his head and the world goes black. His last conscious thought is of Allie's scream.

"Why, why are you doing this?" shouts David. "This was supposed to be a respectable dinner. Why are your men here with guns?"

Sam is already out of his chair and moves quickly toward David. "I've had a belly full of listening to your pie-in-the-sky schemes. This is my way to do things, no respectability, just get things done, *amigo*." From the corner of his eye he sees Zep make a lunge for him.

"So much is at stake and you decide to ruin it? I always knew you would take us both down," says David.

Disregarding Zep sprawled on the table, Sam steps up close to the flush faced irate David who stares at Zep's inert body. His hand reaches under his frock coat.

"Not both, *amigo*. By the way, this partnership is dissolved," he whispers in David's ear. A bowie knife flashes in Sam`s hand as he plunges it into David`s abdomen and yanks it upward. He pulls the knife out and wipes the blood off on David`s coat and picks up a napkin to wipe blood from his hand.

"You, bastard. We stood to make millions." David gasps and collapses into his chair clutching his abdomen as blood gushes between his fingers. Falling forward, his head slams onto the table. He dies.

"Good riddance," mutters Sam. He moves to Zep and places the knife and bloody napkin in his outstretched hand. Now, they'll blame this jasper. He smiles at his idea.

Miguel wonders why Zep asks him to go to supper with Allie and him. His discomfort goes sky high when he steps through the restaurant door and sees a room full of Anglos. He is extremely self-conscious of his appearance and thinks seriously of turning around to leave. Zep and Allie move toward a man waving at them; he follows.

The square room feels like stepping into a trap, he pauses, and sits beside Allie. When one *Americano* brings out a bottle, the second one shouts at *señor* Zep. In his peripheral vision he sees an *hombre* step through the opened door with a drawn pistol. He watches the *gringo* that shouts at Zep move to stand by the man who serves the wine. *Señor* Zep lunges at the shouting man and is clubbed with a pistol. A knife flashes. Fearing for

Allie, Miguel grabs her arm, stands up and rushes for the door. He must protect his *señorita*. With his free hand, he shoves the *hombre* that blocks their exit; a pistol sweeps around and strikes him on the side of his head. His knees buckle as he collapses unconscious to the floor.

Sam motions his two men to bring Allie and they exit through the back door.

29

RUN

IN A FOGGY HAZE, ZEP HEARS POUNDING. HE THINKS IT'S his head aching until he realizes someone is beating on the door. He looks around, sees the knife, napkin, and David. It doesn't take but a moment to see the set up. Holding the lump on the back of his head, he sees Miguel on the floor. There is no Allie. Quickly, he stoops down, rouses Miguel, and almost passes out. Steadying each other, they rapidly stand up and weakly walk out the door located behind David.

"*Señor* Zep, my head is broken," croaks Miguel. "My eyes, they don't focus so good."

"That's not going to be your number one problem if we don't move faster. The door to the dining room won't hold people out for long and we need to be away from here."

"I am trying, *señor*. Keep me steady."

They find themselves in the alley behind the restaurant

and quickly navigate back to the Alameda. Zep is driven by the overwhelming need to find Allie, and quickly. The clerk is not at the desk. As Zep and Miguel support each other, they take the stairs two at a time. Zep gathers up his gear, throws his saddlebags over his shoulder, and grabs his rifle. Miguel makes sure the way is clear and they rapidly flee down the back stairs. Turning the corner, both hustle to the livery. Miguel gathers his belongings, and they saddle their horses. Zep leads the way out the back of the livery and onto a side street. Rapidly, he and Miguel ride north out of town. Stopping, they carefully listen for any pursuit.

"*Señor* Zep, they will follow, no?"

"Yep. They will look for us. I'm sure David Claiborne's a powerful man in Albuquerque, so people will want some retribution for his death. The vigilantes are probably prowling the streets and joints in town right now. Only, they will look for all of us, Sam Blander and his boys as well."

"Why they no shoot us in the room?"

"Too noisy I imagine. Folks saw us go into that dining room and shots would have attracted too much attention. Sam wanted things nice and quiet like. Do you have any idea what happened to Allie? When my lights went out, I don't remember anything after that."

"No, *señor* Zep. The pistol hits me just after you. I tried to get *mi señorita* out."

"I didn't see her in the room, so my hope is Sam has her, and we have to find out where. I need to borrow some of your duds, Miguel. Is that alright?"

"*Si, señor*, but why?"

"I'm headed back into town to listen to everything being said. I may pick up on something that can lead us to Allie."

"Can I do that also? The *cantinas* have many loose tongues."

"Yep. We'll both gather information. Someone has to slip us something useful."

Zep and Miguel disguise themselves with what they have available. Miguel wears his dusty, dirty, and smelly trail clothes. There is nothing of the cleaned up *vaquero* who walked into the restaurant recognizable. Zep, wears dirty trail clothes as well, a serape over his body, and Miguel's *sombrero*. They ride back into town and arrange to meet at the outskirts at daybreak. At the first intersection, they part company. Each one knows the assignment: find out about Allie.

Zep figures he can't drop in on the best saloons in Albuquerque in his present appearance without causing questions or interest. That's not what he wants. So, some of the seamier ones are a better choice and probably have more news floating around.

It's his seventh saloon. The night has given Zep nothing. He feels woozy from the beers he's consumed. This bar is close to the edge of town; he guides his horse up to the hitching rail, slides off, ties up, and steps up onto the porch. Hanging onto the batwing doors, he looks over at the patrons and action. The fragrant smell of rancid beer, vomit, and body odor floats over him and a low cloud of smoke hovers about the ceiling in the room. Zep thinks, "Yep. Looks a whole lot like the others I've seen tonight." Along the entire left hand side stretches a stout wooden bar with carved animals on the front, a brass foot rail is along the bottom with spittoons behind the rail spaced evenly the length of the bar. The back bar has a large mirror in the middle and bottles of liquor sit on the shelves. A tall bearded tough looking bartender doesn't look like he takes guff from anyone. There are tables with chairs scattered about the rest of the saloon. Customers mill around the tables and back and forth across the room. In the far corner a couple of poker games are humming. A Faro table is busy close to the door. Along the right side, suckers throw their money away on a roulette table. A stairway in the back right corner leads upstairs to where soiled doves practice their trade. Zep steps into the place and up to the bar.

"You're takin' space, *amigo*. What'll you have?" the bartender asks.

"A beer sounds good, set one up, friend," Zep answers. "You seen Sam Blander or any of his boys around here tonight?"

"Don't keep track of comin's and goin's, but Sam is such an asshole I would know if he stopped by. Ain't seen him."

"Don't think much of him, huh?"

"Try to not think anything of him. He's plain mean and when drunk, a mean drunk is the worst. I've seen him knife folks for no reason a'tall, just because they walk past him. His partner, the banker Claiborne, tries to keep him in line, but when Sam breaks loose, look out."

"Does he stop here regularly?"

"*Amigo*, I dun told you I don't keep track of comin's and goin's. Why the powerful interest?"

"No reason in particular. There's a land deal he might be interested in, that's all."

"Land stealin' is right down that mudsill's alley. Say, over there by the big window. That fellar just got took in by one of Sam's land swindles. Ya might want to talk at him."

Zep, shuffles through the crowd to the identified table. A Mexican in a nice short waisted jacket and tapered trousers with conchos down the legs sits in the chair with his face on the table. His detailed and expensive sombrero lies beside his head.

"*Perdóname, Señor*, may I sit with you," asks Zep.

"It is a free saloon," mumbles a reply. "Sit where you like."

"*Señor*, I understand you know Sam Blander, *si*?"

The man rapidly raises his head up off the table; his hand pulls a pistol from its holster and points the barrel at Zep. His blood-shot eyes don't waver as his gaze locks on Zep. The room noises stop immediately.

"If you are an *amigo* of Blander, this is your last night to draw breath, *señor*."

"Zep smiles, and slowly pushes the barrel away. No, *señor*, he is no *amigo* of mine. May I ask you some questions about him?"

"He is a dead man when I see him. That *hijo de la perra*, stole my land. My land, the land of my fathers. He will pay with his life."

Zep treads gingerly, "How did he steal your land?" The noise level of the saloon cranks back up to full volume.

"He brought an *Americano* lawyer to my *rancho* to show me the land grant of my father's father was no good. He paid me *pesetas*, pennies, for what the land is worth. The lawyer sat there and made me sign the paper while Blander's man held my wife and daughter at gunpoint. He said he would take them to the *pueblo* if I didn't sign. I would have died, but I could not let him kill them, *amigo*."

"*Si, caballero*, I understand you did what you had to do. You said *pueblo*, where is that?"

"It is the Sandia Pueblo *norte* of Albuquerque. Blander has used it since he came here. It is where he operates from."

"*Muchas gracias, amigo*. Go home, be with your family, it is no good to stay here, there are no friends in this place."

"*Si, señor*, I know there are no friends here, but I am so ashamed. I should have died before I gave up my land. I didn't. Now I will have to live with it. Every time I look at *mi esposa*, seeing her will remind me I failed. Do not fail *amigo*, it is too hard to live with."

Zep stands up and moves to the saloon door. He looks back and whispers, "I will not fail, *amigo*."

Sam storms out of the restaurant into the alley where a buggy waits. The two hombres drag and carry Allie out and lift her onto the seat beside Sam. Both wait for orders.

"I'll take her to the *pueblo* north of town. You," he points at the nearest hombre, "Ride to my ranch outside of Las Vegas and tell the boys I will be there directly. You," pointing at the other *hombre*, "Hang around town, circulate and listen for what is said about the mess at the Maxwell House. Get any news back to me. Let's go." With that, he snaps the reins over the horse's back and sets off at a trot. The *pueblo* is ten miles away and he wants to get there before sunup.

As the buggy bounces and lurches along the *Camino Real*, Allie awakens. Wide-eyed and frightened, she looks around trying to recognize anything to give her assurance what happened didn't really occur. Reality grabs her and she knows she is in danger. She looks at Sam. His facial features are grim, eyes fixated on the road ahead, jaw line taut and clamped, hands methodically work the reins, and body rigid. He glances over and sees Allie is alert.

"Well, good to see you are awake. Taking a little moonlight, early morning ride. You'll like where we're headed. It's real native-like. You really queered the deal for me. Snatching you was David's idea. He saw it as a way to get land from your Pa. He had real highfalutin ideas, but no brass to make the hard decisions. Now, me, I make the decisions and get things moving."

Sam gets lost in his thought process, ignoring Allie completely and begins to mumble quietly to himself, "Why did I gut David? He has the connections and money. That cowboy just rankled me, and David lords over me something fierce. Well, what's done is done. Damn, people saw me go into the room and know I was there. No way to get around that. Those ignorant vigilantes won't give a hoot in hell for any kind of explanation. Got to leave Albuquerque and hightail it for Las Vegas. Nobody will look for me there, and if they do, I've got enough gun power at my ranch to change their minds. What to do with this girl? David had the idea to use her as leverage, but I can't wait around to get word to her Pap and see what he's liable to do. I'll stash her at the *pueblo* and decide later. If nothing else, she'll probably be a good roll in the hay. I can sell her to one of the whorehouses in Las Vegas for a bundle. That's it, no waiting around for long answers, make the quick money and unload this liability. Sounds like I'll make another deal." He smiles about his decision.

A dark shape looms ahead out of the night. A multistoried adobe *pueblo* begins taking shape the nearer they get. Allie can make out lights from windows high up on the walls and fire pits burning in front of the structure. The buggy slows down as Sam navigates small arroyos and washes nearer the building. A low adobe wall surrounds the *pueblo* with an arched adobe gateway. The gate is opened as they approach. Three *pueblo* Indians wait as Sam pulls the buggy to a stop.

"Tiwa, I need to you keep this Mexican girl with you for a while. Don't ask me no questions; hang on to her. Oh, no harm comes to her; understand? I have plans for this one and don't need the merchandise messed with or damaged. You know you owe me for all the times I saved your ragged butts from troubles in town. Now I'm here to collect. Any questions?"

Allie looks at the scruffy Indians before her. They all have short greasy black hair held back by headbands, they wear dirty white trousers with long sleeve pull over white shirts, and have some kind of woven fiber sandals on their feet. The tallest of the three answers Sam.

"We know what you do for us. You want girl looked after, we do it. Then we done. We no more want you to use our *pueblo*. How long you want we hide her?"

"Just so you understand, I'll use this run down glob of crumbling adobe until I get damned good and well tired of using it. See that you understand that, Tiwa. As the headman of this *pueblo*, I expect you to take care of this girl. No one is to know she is here. Nobody messes with her or harms her. You got it? I'll be back."

"Me get it." His stony expression reveals none of the emotional hatred he feels for this white man. Tiwa knows given half a chance, he would slit the white eye's throat and laugh while doing it. He motions for the other two Indians to get Allie out of the buggy.

Allie hears the conversation and wonders how long she is to be left with these Indians? *What are the plans Sam meant? Why hidden? Did she hear hatred in the Indians voice? Is Zep okay? How hurt is Miguel? Why am I here?*

When Allie is taken from the buggy, Sam clicks the horse

around and heads back down the rutted trail into the early morning sunrise.

Zep sits on his horse in an alleyway at the edge of town where he agreed to meet Miguel. It's been a long night, but successful. He has a fair idea of where Allie was taken. He hopes Miguel is able to get some confirming information. He sits dozing in the saddle when he hears a voice.

"*Señor* Zep, if I was an Apache your scalp would be mine, *amigo.*"

Smiling, he raises his head and looks at Miguel on his horse close by. Zep slowly pulls back his serape to expose his revolver lying across his saddle horn.

"If you were an Apache, I would have plugged you the moment your horse rounded the corner of the alley, *amigo.*" He grins at Miguel.

"*Ay, yi-yi*, do you never really sleep, *amigo*? It is like you have eyes in the back of your head to watch when your other eyes are closed."

"Learned how to do that a long time ago. Has kept me alive. Did you find out anything tonight?"

"Si, si, a *gringo* stumbles into the cantina early this morning. He has a couple of *señoritas* under each arm and brags about a *muy machismo hombre* being killed. He is drunk. The more he drinks the more he talks, *es estupido, Si*? He says a *señorita* is taken to *indio pueblo norte* Albuquerque, maybe ten miles away. Is good, *señor* Zep?"

"I hoped you'd hear something like that, Miguel. It is *muy bueno*. Allie is there. Do you know the trail to the *pueblo*?"

"*Si, mi amigos* in the cantina tell me how to get there."

"It's time to get her back, lead the way, I'm right behind you."

They turn their horses north and ride out of Albuquerque. Sunrise throws out its first rays of sunshine.

30

RESCUE

THE TWO INDIANS UNTIE ALLIE AND MOVE HER QUICKLY down darkened corridors, past square rooms with low door openings on the left and right side. It feels like entering a cave. At the end of a hallway, they open a door and shove the captive inside; Allie falls onto baskets of shelled corn and sees she is in a storage room of some sort. The room is similar to those she passed in the hallway. A square room, six feet tall, all adobe finished walls; the only difference is this space has no furniture; only woven baskets of shelled corn fill half of the room. A candle burns in a bracket on the wall beside the door. It casts a feeble light at the best. Alone, frightened, and unsure of what to expect, she finds some comfort leaning against the baskets. She still feels the effects of shock, but manages to doze off. Her attempt to rest is interrupted when the door is yanked open and a torch floods light into the room.

Zep and Miguel are on the trail to the *pueblo* north of Albuquerque. The directions Miguel received from *amigos* in the cantina put them on the right route and they make good time.

"There up ahead, *señor* Zep. Do you see the *pueblo*? Is a big one, no? How will we find our *señorita*?" Miguel's facial expression is full of questions.

"One thing at a time, *amigo*. Let's get there first; we still have a ways to ride. Let me think about the next steps." Zep looks at the large multistoried *pueblo* as they get closer. It seems to be built block upon block stacked on top of each other. The Rio Grande flows to their west near the *pueblo*. It sits on a flat plain farmed by the Indians using ditches to irrigate the crops.

Soon, the two riders approach the tall, large structure. The wall around the building has a main gate opening as they arrive. Two Indians stand outside the gate. They don't look like they appreciate any company.

"Stop. You must leave. You are not welcome here. Go." The tallest Indian addresses Miguel and Zep as they stop in front of the two men.

"We follow a man and young woman who probably stopped here before sunrise. The woman was kidnapped and carried away. We've come to get her back." Zep tries to reason with the man.

"We know not of what you talk about. Leave."

Miguel speaks up, "It is a *muy malo hombre* we follow. He killed a *muy importante hombre* in Albuquerque last night. It was the *banko el presidente*. He steals *mi señorita*."

"Yep. This is a bad man. He killed David Claiborne the bank

president. The man is Sam Blander. Did he stop here?" Zep adds.

Tiwa considers what the Mexican and White Man say. *I know of Claiborne. This man has treated the Indians of his pueblo well. Often, he brought the pueblo items for our families. Blander, I hate with a passion. He abuses the Indians, has had his way with some girls in the past, and threatens others with death. I no longer want to see him at the pueblo but am powerless to stop him. The Mexicans put down the last uprising of pueblo peoples with such brutal force, killing hundreds, the people no longer consider attacking the white man. But, this time, maybe we have a way to get back at muy malo Blander. I can always claim she escaped and drowned in the river. Bueno, I will help these two.*

"What if *señorita* you seek is here? What can you do for this *pueblo*? Why should we give her to you, if she is here?"

Zep responds, "My friend, we don't have anything to give, but the *señorita*, if she is here, has a father who very much wants her back. My *amigo* and I are charged to watch over her. We did not do a good job of it. I do not want to see what could happen to her if Blander keeps her. Have you had good experiences with Blander?"

Tiwa recalls all the abuses heaped upon his people by Blander. He shrugs.

"We have her. Wait here." He turns and goes through the gate. Both Zep and Miguel dismount and stand impatiently.

Going into the *pueblo*, Tiwa grabs a torch from a wall bracket and motions for two Indians to follow him down the hallway to the storage room. Opening the door, he thrusts a torch into the room and motions for Allie to come out. She stands and reluctantly edges up to and through the doorway. The two Indians grab her by the arms and usher her down the hallway.

She has been this way before. They step out into the daylight and move across the clean swept ground to the gateway. They open the gate and she sees Zep and Miguel standing beside their horses. She yanks free of the Indians and rushes into Zep's outstretched arms.

"I knew you'd come, I knew it; I knew you would not leave me." She cries and tears cascade down her cheeks. All the emotions from last night turn loose and she cries uncontrollably; her shoulders shake as she weeps. Zep hangs on tight and let's her wail.

"She is glad to see you," says Tiwa. "That is good. Now, leave, ride quickly, no one must know you were here. My people are at risk. I do not want to find out I have made a huge mistake."

"You've not made a mistake my friend. I thank you for your wisdom and honesty. Take this as a token of my respect for you." Zep hands Allie to Miguel who hugs her tightly. He reaches over his saddle and pulls his Paterson carbine from the scabbard. He holds the rifle out to Tiwa.

"It is a fair trade. I accept," Tiwa says. "I will use this on the white eye Blander the next time he comes here. Or, you can help us by making sure he never shows up again." They both know what is meant.

"If I see the man, he will never be here again," says Zep. He helps Allie onto his horse, and taking the reins, walks back along the trail. Miguel quickly mounts and follows.

Sam bounces along in the buggy as he threads his way from the *pueblo* to the *Camino Real*. Leaving the Indians, in the early morning darkness, he managed to get onto a less traveled trail that runs up and over a number of ditches and ridges. As he drops into a shallow arroyo, a back buggy wheel slips off the axle and the carriage drops to the ground dragging to a stop.

"Damned livery stable," Sam mutters. "Can't get nothin' that works worth a damn anymore." He doesn't want to linger close to the *pueblo*, and doesn't trust Tiwa any farther than he can see him. He unbuckles the horse from the rig, removes the harness, jumps on to ride bareback, grabs a handful of mane, points the horse towards Albuquerque, and kicks its sides.

Don't want to go back to town, but have to now. I'll try to slip in and out, should be able to do that, he thinks to himself. The horse heads towards its stall at the livery in town.

Zep follows the set of buggy tracks leaving the *pueblo*. Allie tells him she arrived in a buggy and it might be the same one. After tracking over a number of ditches and wash outs, he spots a buggy in an arroyo tilted at an angle and horseless. A wheel is missing. Zep points it out to Miguel and motions for him to take a look around. Miguel quickly locates the wheel and brings it back to the buggy. Zep and Miguel see the pin that holds a retainer ring sheared off and allowed the wheel to slip off. A search of the trail to the arroyo turns up the retainer ring. Zep hoists the buggy up and Miguel slides the wheel on. Spinning on the retainer ring, Miguel pulls a horse shoe nail out of his saddlebag and with the butt of Zep's revolver drives the nail into the pin hole, making the buggy useful again.

"I know your saddlebags and duds are in Albuquerque at the Alameda," Zep says to Allie, "It might be best if we just go north to Santa Fe. You tell me if there is anything at the hotel worth going back for. If we go back, we may not leave."

Recovered from her ordeal with Sam and the Indians, Allie responds, "I have nothing there worth any of our lives. Let's go to Santa Fe, *por favor.*"

Miguel takes his horse and arranges the harness to it. He climbs into the buggy. Zep helps Allie aboard, and they turn toward Santa Fe.

31

SANTA FE

Zep knows Santa Fe is near; it's been four days on the *Camino Real*. Looking over his shoulder at the buggy, he sees they've climbed into rolling hills with groves of trees. In the valleys between the hills, *vegas* of grass thrive; the meadows cover acres of land. Leaving the stark desert behind, he points to the purple shaded Sangre de Christo Mountains with tall peaks stretched upwards.

"Top of the next rise, we should be able to see Santa Fe," says Zep to Allie and Miguel.

Stopping their horses at the top of the hill, Zep views the town of Santa Fe. It has the some of the appearance of Albuquerque but feels nicer and has more appeal. The same type of adobe *casas* are scattered around town, and roads lined with houses flow toward a center of clustered buildings. It appears to him some are business structures, a few houses are log cabins, some adobe and wooden homes are multistoried, a large church dominates the city center, and a forest surrounds the town. This village is situated on a hilltop with a commanding view. Zep pulls binoc-ulars from his saddlebag and looks at the town. Handing them to Allie to take a view, he hears pounding of hooves rapidly approaching behind them.

Vigilantes. Could they have followed us sixty miles to Santa Fe? Most townspeople give up after the first five or ten miles. There have been stranger things happen.

Motioning Miguel to pull the buggy into a clump of brush beside the road, Zep dismounts, holds the reins of his horse, and palms his revolver. Miguel pulls his rifle and holds it ready. Allie moves behind the buggy. They wait for whatever is coming.

Shortly, over the hill thunders a detachment of U.S. Army Dragoons. Their blue uniforms are dirt caked from being in the saddle for a long time. Their horses' hooves dig up the trail and dust swirls. The officer leading the troops looks closely at the travelers and snaps a salute as the horsemen dash past. Zep salutes back and Allie waves. In a few minutes the unit is gone and the dust cloud settles.

The buggy bounces down the rough rutted road as they con-tinue into Santa Fe well behind the rapidly disappearing col-umn of soldiers. Zep sees adobe walls surround the *casas*, vines and ivy wind up the walls and over the adobe archways; flowers hang in baskets from windows and sit in pots on walls. Strings of red chilies suspend from many porches. He admires that some *casas* are painted in soft pastels, others are shades of rust, giving the village a unique appearance. Each *casa* has a covered front porch. Among the adobes, he sees single and two story wooden houses. There are balconies on multistoried homes. The dirt roadway leads to a large tree-filled central square.

Hotels, businesses, and shops, all crowd together around the four sides of the central square.

Zep pays particular attention to a single-story adobe building stretching the length of one side of the plaza, the Governors Palace. Tree trunks provide support for a roof over the porch that runs the length of the building facing the square. An American flag flutters from a pole in front of the structure.

The travelers watch soldiers enter and leave the building that once housed Spanish, then Mexican, government officials. Now, Americans inhabit the structure.

Circling the plaza in the buggy, they pause to look at the large church on the square. Massive stones support a soaring front. Large wooden double doors provide access for worshippers. Opposite the Governors Palace, they stop the buggy in front of a hotel. Allie climbs down and Zep dismounts, pulling his saddlebags, he ties his horse to the back of the buggy. "I will find a livery," says Miguel, "and a place to bed down."

"Come into the hotel, Miguel," says Allie.

"No, *señorita*, I am uncomfortable there and will like it much better to find a place where I can relax. *Gracias,* for your offer, I will be close by and always keep an eye on you." His big grin, under the drooping mustache, lights up his face.

"Come back for supper, *amigo*, we're bound to find better food than we had on the way here." Zep smiles back.

"*Si, señor* Zep, I will take care of the horses and buggy and return. *Adios*." He pulls away and rounds the corner.

Taking a look at his disreputable appearance, Zep tries to knock off some trail dirt. Allie's white dress from the dinner in Albuquerque is tattered, dirty, and torn from the trail. Yet, she wears it regally. With a big grin, Zep offers his elbow and together they walk into the elaborate lobby of the hotel.

191

Couches and chairs are arranged around a large open area. They are red and gold damask fabric covered. A large kerosene lamp chandelier suspends from the ten-foot tall ceiling, illuminating the large room. The walls are smooth adobe plastered and beige, small nooks in the walls around the room hold statuary. A center circular couch provides luxurious seating. Zep stands momentarily to take in the opulence and thinks, *just the other night I was hunkered down beside a campfire in the Mogollons. Now, this. Wow, Santa Fe is some special place.*

Moving to the ornately carved, highly polished registration desk, he registers Allie and himself. Behind the desk stands an equally polished tall cabinet with pigeonhole shelving holding room keys and mail. The clerk whose white shirt, stiff collar, and frock coat project his aloofness casts a look of appall at them.

"That will be two dollars for both rooms including a bath, which would be advisable in your present condition," says the clerk brusquely, looking down his long hooked nose at them.

"Well, thank you for your recommendation, *señor*," says Allie. "The next time we meet, I would sincerely appreciate it if you keep your snippy opinions to yourself." Grabbing the key from him she heads for the stairway. "Oh, see hot water, not warm, not tepid, but hot is delivered to my room immediately if not sooner." Curtly she turns, looks at Zep and winks as she continues toward the stairway.

"Yeah, what she said," Zep says to the clerk and rapidly follows Allie.

Chuckling to himself as they climb the stairs Zep says, "Remind me never to get on your wrong side, *señorita*, it's not a pleasant place to be."

"Oh, Zep, I am ashamed I did that, but the clerk is

insufferable. My Papa taught me to never put up with puffery no matter where it is. I really must purchase a wardrobe for my trip to St. Louis. After I bathe, I loath to put these trail clothes back on and I will check some of the shops around the square for new garments. Would you want to accompany me?"

"Allie, I certainly want to make sure you are safe, but shopping is something as foreign to me as California. What I'll do is to find me a place and get some new duds, and a few extras to pack in my saddlebags. Then, I'll sit out on the square to keep an eye on you as you flitter from shop to shop. How's that sound?"

"You will watch me from the shaded, cool, square and not slip into a *siesta*, no?"

"No. No *siesta*. I will watch closely and you let me know when you need a hand to lug everything back to the hotel. *Bueno*?

"*Muy bueno*. I am glad Papa made sure I carried funds in a money belt. Without it I would not be able to prepare for my trip. I will watch you take your *siesta* while I shop," she smiles knowingly. "Now, I must get clean, I can hardly stand myself." She goes into her room and a few seconds later a woman approaches with steaming buckets of hot water. Zep enters his room, grabs a towel, turns, closes the door, and heads down to the showers.

Walking out of the mercantile wearing new denim pants, a new bib-front red shirt, and a new wide brimmed low crown felt hat and repacked saddlebags, Zep feels reborn. He looks around the square and spies Miguel following Allie from store to store as he staggers under the load of merchandise stacked in his arms. Zep finds a tree in the center of the square to rest against and sits down to watch the show.

Presently, Allie exits a store and stares across the street spotting Zep under the tree. She waves and points at all the items Miguel juggles. Miguel looks at Zep with an expression screaming he would rather be anywhere than where he is or do what he's doing. Zep folds his arms across his chest and smiles.

As Zep watches Allie, an Army officer wearing an orange braided blue uniform walks up to him. Zep notices it's the leader of the dragoons unit that rode past them on the road.

"Sir, I believe I passed you on the way into Santa Fe today. Am I correct?"

"Yes, sir, that's a fact," says Zep.

"Did you by chance come from Albuquerque?"

Zep's 'twinge' goes on full alert. "Well, we have been on the road a few days. Why do you ask?"

"My troops and I were in Albuquerque when an important citizen was brutally murdered, a Mr. David Claiborne. There is a description posted of a young lady, an outstandingly beautiful woman, which seems to fit your traveling companion. Now, I ask you again, were you in Albuquerque?"

Zep rises from his seat to stand in front of the officer. He is as tall and fit as the soldier. "Well, if we were, what's it to you?"

"Vigilantes captured a Mr. Sam Blander in Albuquerque and, before we could stop them, he was hung from a tree in the plaza. Witnesses confirmed he was with Mr. Claiborne and was in fact his business partner. They said the young lady was present as well. It appears there may have been a falling out. Blander had accumulated quite a list of questionable practices in the Territory, so his hanging may not have been unjustified.

My job is not to judge him. I simply need to confirm happenings with the young woman and wrap up my report. Is that plain enough?"

"I see. What if you join us for supper tonight?" Zep points to the hotel. "We plan to eat about seven o'clock. Might be able to shine some light on things for you. By the way, who are you?"

"My apologies. My name is Captain James Russell, U.S. Army, 2nd Dragoons, Company A. My command is actually stationed at Jefferson Barracks, Missouri; I'm on detached service here in New Mexico Territory. A good hotel meal is hard to turn down; I'd be pleased to join you, mister. I didn't get your name."

"My name is Zep Bierman from Mesilla. We'll see you at seven." The soldier walks away. Zep thinks, Sam, hung. Couldn't happen to a better low life.

He walks across the street to catch up with Allie and Miguel. They come out of another shop and enter one further along the sidewalk. Zep smiles and whistles as he walks.

32

SEPARATION

ZEP WALKS INTO THE HOTEL DINING ROOM TEN MINUTES before seven o'clock. He looks around to see if his friends are in the room. Captain Russell stands by one of the two large windows. There are ten cloth-covered tables around the room; six are occupied with noisy customers. A waiter stands beside the door into the kitchen, a cloth draped over his arm. He wears a white shirt, black vest and trousers, a starched collar and bow tie. He approaches Zep.

"Sir, may I get you something from the bar?"

"Yes, whiskey, please, and whatever the Captain would like." Zep points at Captain Russell.

"I'll have the same," says Russell.

Zep steps beside the Captain. "Glad you could make it. I believe the conversation tonight will interest you."

"I'm hoping for that, and to enjoy the company."

Allie steps into the restaurant wearing a low collared cobalt blue dress with long sleeves and a full skirt. Across her shoulders drapes a white lacey shawl with fringed ends. A necklace of multicolored small stones twinkles in the kerosene chandelier's light. Her long auburn hair sparkles against the bright white shawl and blue dress, and is held back from her face by golden combs to display matching earrings. A dazzling smile captures the attention of both men and Zep's heart.

"Good evening, gentlemen."

Zep steps forward and escorts Allie to the table, pulls out her chair, and seats her. He introduces Allie to Captain Russell. The waiter returns with the men's drinks and Allie orders a glass of wine.

Miguel enters the restaurant in new tapered gray *vaquero* trousers with silver conchos down the sides, a white shirt, a black vest, and his shiny black hair neatly combed. Waving at the others, he moves to the table and takes a seat beside Allie. Zep introduces the two men.

The waiter returns with Allie's wine. Miguel declines anything to drink. Zep orders steaks and trimmings for the table and all nod in agreement.

Zep starts the conversation. "The Captain asked me this afternoon about Albuquerque. He says the vigilantes caught up with Sam Blander and hung him. He wants to know what happened in the dining room at the Maxwell House. People saw us enter the room." He sees relief in both Allie's and Miguel's eyes.

"I'm not the law or any kind of sheriff, but because my troops are expected to maintain some kind of order in this territory, I need to tie up loose ends for my report."

"Why don't you ask your questions and we'll answer what we can," says Zep.

"Okay, were all of you there?"

Zep looks at the others at the table and answers, "We were."

"Did Blander kill Claiborne?"

"He did," says Zep.

"Did it appear to be a fight between partners?"

Zep can't answer the question and looks at Allie.

"It appeared it could have been, Captain," she answers.

"That's what I thought. Folks at the Maxwell House recognized Blander's knife, and my scenario is the partners had a quarrel that led to David Claiborne's demise. Good. Those vigilantes really did me a favor and this investigation is closed. Will one of you stop at Governors Palace and sign a statement to this effect tomorrow morning?" The Captain pauses, "I've completed my questions."

Zep answers, "I'll be there in the morning to sign your paper." He spots the waiter bringing out their dinner. "Now, let's eat."

Following dinner, Captain Russell excuses himself. "I must really return to the post and make sure the document is ready for your signature in the morning. Miss *de la Vieta*, Miguel, and Zep thank you for the meal and your camaraderie. I have enjoyed myself immensely. Good night." He leaves.

"*Señorita y señor* Zep, I, too, need to leave. It is late and I hear my pillow calling me. *Muchas gracias* for such a wonderful dinner." Miguel smiles his sparkling smile, rises from the table, and leaves.

Allie and Zep sit alone as the waiter clears away the tableware.

"Bring us two sherries," Zep asks the waiter who hurries off to comply.

"It was a wonderful dinner, Zep. The Captain makes a great dinner partner. Could you believe his stories of Nebraska and the Brule Sioux Indians? It makes me shiver to think about all that is going on outside our territory." Allie ponders on the topic, and from the corner of her eye sees Zep watch her; she smiles.

"He certainly has a lot of stories to share. That's the military life for you, always on the go, moving from one post to the next. It is an interesting life, but I imagine a hard one too, not to mention dangerous," says Zep.

"We've had our share of danger as well. I'm so thankful you managed to get us safely to Santa Fe. There were times I was terrified I would not see you again or be hurt in unimaginable ways. Thank you, Zep. I thank you with all my heart."

"Tomorrow morning you leave for St Louis and I don't know how I can handle that Allie." Zep stares into her deep brown eyes. They seem to absorb him. The waiter breaks the mood by interrupting with the drinks.

"Miguel has the travel trunk I purchased on the back of the buggy. It is loaded with what is needed for travel to St. Louis. Yes, tomorrow morning Miguel and I travel east on the Santa Fe Trail. It will take us weeks to arrive in St. Louis," she pauses and lightly chews on her lower lip. Looking at Zep she says, "I don't know how to handle our separation either." Allie is lost in his blue eyes.

"I know you have to go, your reasons make sense, my head understands, but my heart doesn't," Zep's voice cracks. "Let's walk a while, it will be a long time before we will do it again. There's a veranda at the back of the hotel."

They finish their sherries and Zep extends his elbow for Allie to grasp. She hangs onto him ferociously. Her head rests against his shoulder. He sees tears fill her eyes and knows this is the woman he never wants to see leave; yet she will in the morning. *How can this be? Why does this have to be so hard?*

Walking out of the dining room, down a hallway, they step out on the back veranda into a cool, moonlit Santa Fe night. Stepping to the side of the doorway, out of the light from the hallway, Zep turns and takes Allie into his arms, kisses her lips, gently yet firmly. She responds to his ardor and clings to his strong arms. Breaking the kiss, they embrace and remain locked in each other's arms.

"You could stay," says Zep.

"I could but I can't," Allie replies.

"I know," Zep sighs. *Would I love her less if she wasn't as independent and dedicated? How do I get our wills to meld?*

Looking down, Zep kisses the top of her head and strokes her auburn hair. He places his cheek against her head. "I am so lost right now. I have always been able to find my way, no matter what, but tonight, considering you gone seems to be more than I can bear."

"I could say it won't be long, but even a day is too long to be away from you, Zep."

They turn towards each other and linger over another kiss. Allie strokes Zep's weather-beaten face and stares into the depths of his blue eyes.

"Zephaniah Bierman, I love you with all my heart. I will come back. Please take care of yourself until I return? I will make it very difficult on you if you don't." She smiles through her tears.

"Alassandra *de la Vieta*, you go with my heart. Take care of it, and bring it back to me soon. I love you."

They walk, arms around each other into the hotel.

Morning comes too soon. Miguel drives the loaded buggy to the front of the hotel. Zep's horse is tied behind the rig. He stops at the steps and patiently waits. Allie steps outside in a long brown travel dress with high collar and long sleeves. Zep wears his clothes from last night. They walk down the steps and he helps her onto the buggy seat. Clasping his hands around hers, he stares into her face as if to engrave it into his brain. The auburn hair, pixie face, brown eyes all absorb into his memory. Allie likewise looks at a weatherworn compassionate face dominated by blue eyes, a face she loves, and a face she wants to see for the rest of her life.

Zep slowly releases Allie's hands, he steps back and goes to the end of the rig, unties his horse, and walks it to Miguel's side of the buggy. Raising his right hand, he grasps Miguel's hand. A powerful, man-to-man handshake transmits all the trust they have between them.

"I know you will be with her and watch over her, *amigo*. Just bring her safely home to me, *bueno*?"

"*Señor* Zep, you know I will. Both of you are *familia* to me."

"*Via con Dios.*" Zep steps back and the buggy jolts away, around the square, and heads out of town. Allie leans forward and looks back over her shoulder at Zep until her view is blocked.

Zep stands in the road, reins in hand, watching Allie depart. Slowly, he moves to his horse, puts his boot in the stirrup and mounts. The weather-beaten face shows no emotion and is unreadable. Inside, his heart is breaking.

"See the Captain, sign the paper, ride south, and find Guillo." He whispers almost incoherently.

He rides across the plaza, dismounts, and enters the Governors Palace where an orderly hands him a packet. He pulls a document from the packet, scans it, signs it, puts it back in the packet, and hands it back. Stepping outside onto the porch of the Governors Palace he looks at Santa Fe's plaza, then steps up into his saddle and slowly walks his horse out of town.

33

SOUTHBOUND

ALCHESAY SITS IMMOBILE ON THE HILL OVERLOOKING the road into Socorro. It has been days, maybe weeks he's waited. *There is nowhere else to go, or nothing else to do,* he thinks. He watches numerous riders, wagons, coaches, and soldiers travel the road. Water and game have sustained him in his vigil. The dust on the road stirs again. Another rider approaches. Straining sun-glazed eyes, he focuses on the lone horseman.

I know this man. My 'rabbit' returns.

Zep plods along the *Camino Real*. It has been weeks since leaving Santa Fe, and he can't remember much of the ride. He knows he skirted Albuquerque to avoid any entanglement.

Days and nights pass by in a blur. His unhealthy mind makes him vulnerable, but it seems he just doesn't care. Everything he values is gone. Behind him, he hears the rumble of a rapidly approaching wagon or carriage. Uninterested, he moves his horse to the side of the trail and stops. A team of greys pulling an enclosed carriage rapidly closes the distance and it also slows to a stop behind Zep.

"Hey, mister, is your name Zep Bierman?" the driver of the team shouts.

Shaken out of his mental fog, Zep looks back. He doesn't recognize the team, carriage, or driver.

"Who wants to know?" he drawls.

The cover on the carriage window quickly yanks back as a head leans out.

"I do. Is that good enough for you?" Allie smiles joyously.

Zep recognizes his love, leaps from his saddle, races to the carriage door, and flings it open. He catches Allie as she jumps into his arms. Together, they tumble to the road, laughing, hugging, and kissing in a frenzy of happiness. Slowly, they stand and try to reassemble some dignity and composure.

"I am very glad to see you again, Miss *de la Vieta.*" Zep says grinning as he holds her hands.

"I, too, am so very glad to see you, Mr. Bierman." Allie chortles fighting to hold back laughter.

"Well, *señorita y señor*, can you finish kissing and hugging, *por favor*, so we can continue on our way?" Miguel says as he leans out of the coach doorway, watching the happy couple. A toothy grin sparkles beneath his drooping mustache.

Zep turns and races to his horse, leads it behind the carriage, ties it on, and runs to assist Allie as she steps back inside; and following her in, closes the door behind him. He takes the seat across from her.

"Why, who, when…I can't believe you're here."

"Believe it, *señor*, we ARE HERE, safe and sound," Miguel says.

Grasping Allie's hands, Zep stares at her face. "So, why are you here, and what happened?"

"Oh, Zephaniah Bierman, I'm here because I love you. That's all you really need to know, but I will let Miguel fill in the details while I look at you."

"*Si*, I feel like I continue to be *señorita's duena*." He watches Allie and Zep closely as they continue to be lost in each other. "But, I think the *Patron's* wishes for me to watch over *mi señorita* will not be much longer."

Allie catches snatches of Miguel's comment and breaking contact with Zep's eyes she responds, "Miguel, you are not my *duena*. Papa never intended for you to watch over me like a chaperone, but like a brother." Pausing, she gazes out the window and then turns her head and blurts out to Miguel. "Miguel, you ARE my brother, *mi hermano*, that is why Papa sent you."

"*Perdóname, señorita. Si*, Manolito and I are both like brothers to you." Miguel's eyes dampen as he silently grieves the loss of Manolito. "We grew up together and you have always been *mi señorita*."

The enclosed carriage begins moving and soon is rocking and bouncing along. Everyone inside becomes accustomed to its movement.

Allie continues as she lays a hand on Miguel's arm. "Before we left the *hacienda*, Papa called me into his study. He told me about my responsibilities and also there was another woman in his life before *mi Madre*. Her name was Isabella; she was beautiful, and he loved her deeply. They met in Chihuahua, married, and traveled north with *vaqueros* and settlers. When their party arrived at the springs by Animas Peak, they stayed. You were born a year later, and your mother died from sickness. The *hacienda* was under construction, and Papa was lost without Isabella; he left instructions for the *hacienda*, your care with the other families, and traveled to St. Louis for business reasons. There he met my mother, she helped him mend his broken heart, and they married."

"*Señorita*, you are telling me you are truly my sister, *mi hermana*?" Miguel's face expresses incredulity and surprise.

"Yes, Miguel, you see Papa didn't send me unescorted on this trip, he sent my brother and best friend with me, along with Zep and Guillo."

"Why are you telling me now, after such a long time?" Miguel shakes his head in amazement.

"Papa told me to keep the secret. He said he would tell you when he wants to, but I cannot. Papa said he hasn't told you because he wants you to grow up independent, strong, and able to make decisions from experience. It is his way, and his decision. I cannot keep the truth from you, I love you too much, and know what you do to watch over me."

"*Ay, yi-yi*, a sister and father, a family. It is almost too much to take in and understand. I know the *patron...mi papa*, is a strong man, very set in his ways. I don't know if I should hate him or love him."

"Miguel, don't hate him. He loves you in his own way, and the *hacienda* is listed in his will in both of our names. I saw the document when he told me. The future is in both of our hands. Can you accept that?"

"It is much to think about...*mi hermana*. I need time to work through everything. I do know this." He looks at Zep.

"She is my sister, and while I've always taken care of her, I will do so even more now. You are my *amigo*, I trust you with my life, and the life of my sister. I am no longer any kind of *duena*. You both love each other; it's plain for anyone to see. If there is any blessing from me, you both have mine. Do not make me sorry, *por favor.*"

Miguel lapses into quiet contemplation about all that just transpired. He is lost in his thoughts.

"Wow. You landed a heavy load on Miguel, Allie," says Zep.

Looking back at Zep, she says, "Yes, it was unfair of Papa to not tell him sooner, and even more unfair to ask me to keep the secret as well. It's a huge message to deliver, but he is *mi hermano*, and I cannot keep it from him any longer. You do understand, *si?*"

"Oh, I understand your dilemma. Let's give him time, okay? Now, what happened to bring you here?"

"Ah, we traveled two days from Santa Fe when the buggy wheel came off, the same wheel that came off before. Miguel said the horseshoe nail that fixed it earlier sheared letting the wheel fall off. This time the wheel broke apart on rocks and was unusable. I knew right then it was a sign going to St. Louis was not as important as being with you. If my mother's family wants to see me, they can come to New Mexico, and I already have a wealth of information about Americans from this trip. Fortunately, freight wagons headed to Santa Fe found us stranded and carried us back to town. We asked about you at the Governors Palace and were told you left town. Miguel arranged for this enclosed carriage and a driver to take us to Socorro, if necessary. I left my bulky, heavy trunk of clothing in Santa Fe so it wouldn't slow us down. We missed you in Albuquerque and find you here, outside of Socorro."

"I'm beginning to feel overwhelmed like Miguel. You being his Sister and how you managed to find me." Sitting back in the seat, Zep raises a hand to shove his hat back on his head. "I'm glad you're here and safe, that's all that matters." A huge grin lights up his face.

"Socorro's ahead, y'all," shouts the driver. "End of the trail for me." The carriage bounces along toward the village on the horizon.

Watching the carriage move along the *Camino Real* toward Socorro, Alchesay thinks, I have not waited too long. I have all of those who escaped me now in one place. They will come out to me. They are mine. His revenge rekindles from the banked coals in his heart and blazes anew.

34

JORNADA DEL MUERTO

ZEP SITS IN A CHAIR ON THE FRONT PORCH OF THE HOTEL thinking about what lies ahead. Probably, no certainly, the worst stretch of the trip so far. Ninety plus miles of stark, treeless, waterless, scorched land; only pronghorn antelope, coyotes, rattlesnakes, prairie dogs, and mule deer can live in; and covered with sand dunes and gravelly flats anchored by scattered bunches of grass, yucca, mesquite and creosote. It's the shortest route home, and worth the risks.

Allie steps out onto the porch and takes the chair next to Zep; she wears trousers, long sleeve shirt, vest, *caballero* hat, gloves and boots for riding.

"You're thinking about the *Jornada* aren't you?"

Zep momentarily remains staring straight ahead, and then realizes Allie asked a question, he turns to her.

"Sorry, was thinking about the *Camino Real* passing through volcanic rocks and how it drops into bottomland flanked by distant mountains, In my mind, I can see the ruts from wagons that have traveled the road."

"It will be difficult, yes?" Allie asks the obvious.

"Water is the issue," says Zep. "If we crossed during the August rainy season we might find water at the *playa, Laguna del Muerto*; but we are crossing at the wrong time of year. This stretch of road was named for a German trader who died from thirst fleeing the inquisition in New Mexico way back in the 1600s. Others making this crossing say there is a grave every 500 feet."

"This is not a journey to look forward to," says Allie.

"No, it is not an easy journey, but it is much shorter than going back the way we came. So, it is a calculated risk," says Zep.

"By the way, where is Guillo?" asks Allie. "He said he would wait in Socorro, no?"

Miguel rides up to the hotel leading another mount. He stops, dismounts, ties the horses to the hitching rail, and steps up onto the porch.

"*Buenos Dias, señorita* and *señor* Zep."

"*Buenos Dias*, Miguel de la Vieta." Zep and Allie smile. "Kind of seems to fit you pretty well, *amigo*. Can you handle the brand?"

"*Si, señor* Zep, I have been thinking about it all night; and while it has been some time coming, now it's here, I can deal with it."

"Looks like you've arranged some horseflesh for our ride instead of the carriage."

"I arrived at an agreement with the stables to trade horses and saddles for a carriage. I think it is a good deal, the stable owner says he is pleased," said Miguel. "That makes me think he got the better deal," he smiles.

"Well, I agree with your decision. A carriage might be a bit more than what you want to wrangle across the *Jornada*. Lots of folks have done it, but on horseback seems the best to me. Looks like we will have seven days of riding to cross the *Jornada*," says Zep. "Water will be at a premium. We'll stop at Fort Craig south of town to tank up canteens and water bags before we start. Ready to ride?"

"What about Guillo?" Allie asks again. "He was to be here and meet us. Have you seen him?"

"No, I spread the word last night in a couple of *cantinas* that we were in town and looking for him. Told others to let him know we are leaving this morning from the hotel. *Cantinas* are the best way to get the word around quickly in a town this size," says Zep. "If and when he gets the word, he can catch up."

"*Señorita...mi hermana*, here is your horse." Miguel leads a horse to Allie to mount. "Old habits take a while to change, sister." His big grin escapes beneath his drooping mustache.

"It is wonderful to hear you call me, sister, brother." Allie returns the smile.

"Family reunion is over y'all. We need to ride," Zep butts into the moment. He turns his horse and begins to ride.

Around the corner of the hotel gallops Guillo. Yanking on his bridle, he pulls his mule to an abrupt halt. The mule begins to bray loudly.

"*Ay, caramba, estupido*. Shut up before I shoots you between your ugly eyes." Guillo stands up in his stirrups and looks at Zep. "You leave without me, *companero*?"

"Nope, just figured you was takin' your time gettin' things settled," Zep replies.

"*Ay*, they are settled. We leave immediately, yes? There are three *hombres* I do not want to see this morning," says Guillo. "That *señorita* I stayed for has *tres grande hermanos*, three big brothers and they do not like Guillo."

"What's not to like about you, *companero*? Oh, by the way, it's good to see you too."

"So sorry, *companero*. It is good to see you and be seen again. Why are Allie and Miguel with you? I thought you were to leave them in Santa Fe."

"Long story, Guillo. We'll have time to fill in the gaps on the way. Say, do any of those *grande hermanos* have pintos and a big roan?"

"*Si*, Zep, two pintos and a roan. How do you know this?"

"Because, they entered the other end of town."

"*Madre Mia*, let's ride, *amigos*." Guillo wheels the mule around and begins riding rapidly through town exiting the opposite end from the *tres hermanos*.

Zep, Allie, and Miguel quickly catch up with Guillo and all ride south toward Fort Craig.

Alchesay has circled Socorro on the chance his white man and Mexicans would exit the other end. The only way from there is through the *Jornada*. If that's where they are headed, it is the perfect spot for him. Deciding to once again risk thinking ahead of the white man, Alchesay decides to ride into the *Jornada*, around the white eyes fort, and set up an ambush of his choosing to take away any advantage his Apache-thinking adversary might have. It is time to end this prolonged chase and put to rest the revenge he feels for his people. It is good.

"So, you mean a murder in Albuquerque, kidnapped by *muy malo hombre*, kept by *indios*, left for St. Louis, broke a buggy, and returns to you, *companero*? That is a story to tell." Guillo looks amazed as their horses walk south on the *Camino Real*.

Looking over his shoulder, Zep watches Allie talking away with Miguel as they ride side by side. Nice to have a brother and sister together, he thinks.

"Now, Guillo, what gives with your amazing *señorita* in Socorro? I thought you'd convince her to go with you when we met again?"

"Oh, *companero*, what starts as an affair of my heart turns into a huge attack on my heart," says Guillo. "My gorgeous, attention giving, living angel, she turns into a griping, uncontrollable, ugly sounding witch. As I pursue her and meet with her when she comes to town, she expects more and more things from me each time we meet. When I cannot provide things she screams at me, says I am not worthy of her, and how she cannot be insulted. It was ugly, *companero*. She tells her brothers about me and they hunt me into the cantina where I live to tell me if I shame their sister, they will whittle me up a little bit. *Companero,* what was I to do? I ran from her, hid from them, and looked for you, hoping to see you soon. I was beginning to be desperate when *amigos* from the *cantina* say you are in town looking for me. *Muchas gracias*, you arrive in time to save Guillo one more time, *companero*."

"Whew, that's one story, Guillo. Good to see you are still here with all your pieces and didn't get whittled on." Zep grins at Guillo who grins back.

"*Si*, your story, it is a good one also. I am glad Allie and

Miguel returned and are with us. What about the *Jornada*? When we face it what should we know?"

"Well, we're fixin' to stop at Fort Craig ahead to find out what's happening, fill up everything able to carry water, and light out across the *Jornada* to Las Cruces. From there it is a smooth trail to Mesilla. Between times, I need to figure out what Allie and Miguel want to do. Look over there, the buildings of Fort Craig." Zep exclaims pointing down the road.

The orderly at headquarters of Fort Craig leans on the hitching post as he talks with Zep and Guillo. Allie and Miguel go to the post mercantile to pick up supplies and extra water bags.

"You gotta watch out for Mescalero Apaches down around the *Laguna*," says the soldier. "The last bunch coming up from the south mixed it up with half a dozen warriors on the prowl for horseflesh. They come down from the mountains to the east to hit the trail regular like. We don't have much trouble with the Chiricahua but them Mescalero are a handful. Old Santana has got them whipped up big time. Just be careful out there, not much we can do to help without being too late."

"Yep. I know that bunch of Apaches pretty well. Been havin' to keep one step ahead of them while mustanging. Thanks for the warning. Any water in the *Laguna*?"

"Nope, the last bunch said it's dry as a bone," the trooper replies. "Carry what you'll need and push straight through to Fort Selden on the south end. Las Cruces ain't far from there."

"Appreciate your information; we'll be pushing off." With that, Zep and Guillo turn their horses and catch up with Allie and Miguel in front of the mercantile.

"Any good words about the *Real*?" Allie inquires.

"Still the meanest stretch of earth the good Lord ever created," says Zep. "Miguel, glad you filled the canteens and water bags, we're liable to need every drop."

"*Si, señor* Zep, it will be a dry ride."

"Miguel, would you do me a big favor and drop the *señor*?"

"Okay…Zep. It may take a while." Miguel smiles and shrugs his shoulders.

"Thanks, I appreciate your trying."

The group rides across the parade grounds following the *Camino Real* south.

Second day into the ride, Allie scans the desert thinking, *it seems so stark and unchanging.* A trail of rutted wagon tracks leads across the open expanse.

They camp each evening under the stars; millions of them seem to be so close you can reach out and touch them.

Early morning Zep rousts everyone up, "We'll ride until mid-day, stop and rest. Then we will ride in the evening until early nighttime before we camp. This is the schedule we will keep each day."

Three days into the crossing, Allie sees a large bowl-like depression in the distance and it reflects light like it is filled with water. "Zep, there is water over there." She points into the distance.

"No, Allie, you see a mirage from *Laguna del Muerto*. The heat waves rise from the dry lake bed wiggle and shake and make your eyes think you see water."

Everyday feels like they travel without going anywhere. Allie falls into an almost hypnotic trance, buffeted by dry hot breezes, riding endlessly under the beating sun, the horse sways, leather creaks, and a land of silence surrounds her.

By the end of the sixth day, Zep points ahead to a tall hill of jumbled rocks thrust from the desert floor.

"Point of Rocks ahead," he says through cracked wind burned lips. "Only one more day and that's good. Horses starting to drag down, three water bags finished, and all the canteens empty. One bag is still full. Looks like we figured it about right. We'll camp tonight at the base of the hill, rise early in the morn-ing and keep on the move. Fort Selden's not far now. Just keep moving. Looks like we'll make it fine." Zep's optimism is almost contagious.

The midday rest passes and dusk finds them close to the Point of Rocks hill.

"Ummm, more *frijoles* tonight," says Guillo. "I am about up to the top with *frijoles* my friends. I think a big steak in Las Cruces looks for me right now." He sighs and grins.

"Make it two, *companero*," says Zep. "Let's move over there toward the flat area this side of that landslide of boulders comin' down the hill. We'll make our camp there tonight."

Zep circles the area checking things and signals everything looks good. The group moves in and unsaddles their mounts, rubs down their horses, and stacks their saddles around a fire pit Guillo pulls together with loose stones. Miguel stomps around the area outside the saddles to flush out any rattlesnakes and chase them away. "Hey, *hermano*, when you see a rattlesnake kill it, I'll cook it, they are good to eat," Guillo tells Miguel. Allie gags. Zep walks toward the hill surveying the rock-strewn slope.

"No Mescalero yet," he mutters. "Could be gone, could be

they wait for the right chance. Not takin' any foolish chances this close to the end."

Zep walks over to Miguel.

"Miguel, I want to string a picket line tonight for the horses. Stretch it over there out of the fire light and away from the hillside. Tie all the horses to the line and let them graze what they can. Also, I want all of us to sleep underneath the picket line tonight. My neck is 'twingeing' again; when it does, I pay attention. Make sure you let everyone know to build up sand piles to throw their blankets over beside the fire tonight. I want it to look like we sleep there. Then one by one slip off and sleep by the horses. Can you see it's handled?"

"*Si*, Zep. I, too, am concerned our ride has been too easy. Better to be ready for trouble." Miguel moves away to tell everyone about the arrangements.

A fire is started with grass, twigs, and any other burnable materials Guillo can scrounge up. Coffee, fried rattlesnake, the last biscuits from Fort Craig, frijoles, and jerky make a gourmet meal. Everyone slowly makes their exit after arranging blankets to appear they sleep under them. Miguel sits at one end of the picket line, Zep at the other, and Guillo with Allie in the middle. All except for Allie are armed and ready. Night's black shroud surrounds them as the stars blaze away in the sky.

Alchesay knows he has the right spot for his ambush. The hill covered with boulders and rocks provides a perfect place to hide. It sits alone with the flat land that surrounds it, and anything approaching is visible for miles from the top. He sits, waits, thinking, *they will come this way to exit the desert; they*

must pass this place. Today, tomorrow, the day after, they will come. Alchesay spends time to become familiar with the hill, paths, drop offs, hidden places; he knows the pile of rocks well in a couple of days.

It's six days' wait. He sips from his canteen, and eats sparingly of snake meat, when he sees four riders approach. The big white man rides forward and searches everything closely making sure no trap awaits them. He does not see Alchesay hidden in the rocks at the top of the hill. He signals for others to make a camp. *This man must be part Apache, a worthy enemy,* thinks Alchesay. He suddenly spots four figures skulking among the boul-ders below him.

A faint whisper of morning breeze slips across the desert as Zep peers into the darkness. He knows Miguel is awake; moments ago he heard him shift his position. Another hour and predawn will seep into the eastern sky over the distant mountains.

"If it's going to happen, it will be soon," Zep whispers. He hears Allie's rhythmic breathing. Guillo is also alert and Zep hears him cock the hammer on his rifle. The fire has burned down to only a few smoldering coals still alive.

Predawn sneaks over the horizon when they hit.

Four warriors, Mescalero Apaches---Zep recognizes their long boots, colored shirts, long breechcloths, and banded hair---run rapidly toward the horses from the cover of rocks at the base of the hill. Miguel's first rifle shot drops the nearest Indian. The other three know it is a fight to the death not just horse stealing. They immediately hug the ground and squirm their way toward the picket line. They use any ground cover for concealment. Guillo spots a warrior slide from one small mesquite bush to another and shoots. A soft moan drifts from the mesquite. Miguel stands up to better see what is on the ground and a third warrior jumps up and tackles him to the ground. Allie screams as both Zep and Guillo swivel around and aim their weapons at the pair on the ground. Miguel and the Apache squirm around, grabbing, gouging, and thrashing about. The warrior manages to reach his waist and pull out his knife. Miguel quickly grabs the Indian's knife hand and it weaves back and forth over him. He is now penned beneath the Indian and the warrior uses all his strength to shove the blade into Miguel. Zep quickly kneels, steadies his aim with both hands and fires his Colt. The bullet strikes the warrior in his side and the force of the slug at close range lifts him up and off Miguel. He quivers once and lies still. The rattle of gravel and breaking of manzanita branches indicate the fourth warrior is escaping.

Suddenly, behind Zep, with a blood-curdling scream a fifth Apache leaps from the ground and violently collides with him. Allie shrieks and covers her mouth. Instinctively, she grabs the picket line to keep the horses from bolting. The force of the Indian's rush causes Zep to drop his revolver and fall backwards. He clutches the Indian to make sure he is unable to pull a knife. As they hit the ground, both are momentarily stunned, but quickly jump up. They begin circling each other. Zep recognizes a Chiricahua, by the length of hair, height of moccasin boot, and type of long breechcloth. Fleetingly, *he wonders why this Chiricahua warrior is with Mescalero horsesthieves?* The Indian quickly yanks out his knife and poises it like a stinger of a scorpion. Zep pulls his knife and they circle, each looks for the right kill opportunity. Stepping in, the Indian slashes downward trying to catch Zep's arm or wrist. Swinging back,

Zep thrusts upward attempting to catch the torso of the Indian. Both have fought too many knife fights to be easily out maneuvered. Another jab by the Indian allows Zep to masterfully trip him up and send him sprawling. Zep steps forward for a quick kill while the Indian's back is vulnerable. Rolling over, the Indian grabs a handful of sand and throws it in Zep's face. Blinded, Zep stumbles backward. The warrior has his moment; it's now or never.

Springing up, he lunges at Zep who is clawing the sand from his eyes. With a downward jab, he buries his knife into Zep's upper left arm. The white man twists away taking the Indian's knife with him.

Alchesay uses this moment to grab Alassandra. He twists her violently around as a shield in front of him. Yanking a handful of hair, he pulls her head toward his. Shoving her arm up behind her, he moves her quickly into a collision with Guillo that sends both of them sprawling. He sprints for the cover of the boulder-strewn hillside.

Alschesay is furious the Mescalero ruin his perfectly set ambush. Their blind rush to steal horses puts everyone at risk. He knows the sleeping arrangements around the fire are false. He knows where each person is at the picket line. He is forced to climb down and follow behind the Mescalero or lose any chance to kill his prey. The white man fights like an Apache. He is strong and agile; moves quickly to dodge each thrust and return the attack. Foolishly, Alchesay goes for a quick kill and trips. He can almost feel the knife bear down on his exposed back when he flips over and throws a handful of sand.

Now, now, now, he thinks as he leaps up jabbing with his knife. Sinking it to the hilt. *No, no,* the knife is yanked out of his hand as the white man twists away.

The woman, he thinks, and lunging toward Allie he grabs her by the hair, twists her arm behind her, and shoves her to-wards the man with the rifle. They both collide and tumble together to the ground. The way is clear to the boulders and Alchesay sprints for cover as darkness shrouds him.

35

LAS CRUCES

GUILLO STRUGGLES UP AND LIFTS ALLIE FROM THE ground. The Indian is gone. She rushes to Zep and starts to yank out the knife.

"Stop. Check to make sure how much I'm bleeding. If the knife cut an artery I'll need a tourniquet to stop the flow," says Zep. "Now, gently, look around the blade, doesn't look too bad. Slowly, pull the knife out; prop my feet up and throw a blanket over me. I'm fixin' to pass out."

Allie quickly responds as Zep instructs.

"Okay, let me rest a bit. Is everyone else okay?"

"*Si*, Zep, we are all okay because you knew something was coming," Allie says through tears.

"Oh, get Miguel for me, *por favor*."

Miguel walks around the horses to make sure there is no longer a threat. He sees Allie motion for him and moves to her.

"*Si, hermana*, what is it?" Miguel asks Allie as Zep speaks up.

"Miguel, you and Guillo drag those Indian's bodies into the rocks. Saddle the horses and let's load up. We have another day's ride to finish."

"Watch for the Indians that got away," says Guillo glancing at the rocky slopes.

"Zep, we have to stay and take care of your arm. We cannot move from here." Miguel objects.

"No, we move now. Two Apaches got away; that may mean nothing and it may mean everything. We're not going to wait around to find out. We've got some morning hours to still ride and every mile puts us closer to Fort Selden. You understand, brother?"

"*Si*, you are right. We ride," says Miguel realizing what Zep means.

Allie works with Zep to get him up, and tearing up a new shirt from his saddlebags, she fashions a bandage and sling for his arm. Guillo helps Zep step into his saddle. Allie and Guillo ride on either side of him, and Miguel takes the lead. They turn south leaving the Point of Rocks behind.

"Allie, I'm liable to start running a fever. You don't know what those knives have been into and what ever it might be has been shoved into my arm," says Zep. "We should be into Fort Selden by tonight. Maybe the Army Doc has something to help, but don't let him even suggest my staying at the post. Them Army doctors are good with saws and cuttin' limbs off. If he can patch me, we'll go on to Las Cruces and find a real doctor there."

"*Si*, Zep, I will make sure your arm is safe," promises Allie.

"Zep, what we do when we get to Las Cruces?" asks Guillo.

"You have a plan?"

"Well, companero, one thing at a time. Right now, I'm a little occupied, but I'll get back to you real quick with a plan," Zep grins at Guillo who grins back.

"*Si*, you think a little stick in the arm is more *muy importante* than what we do next?"

Guillo looks at Allie and winks.

Laughing out loud, Zep shakes his head. "This is some roundup I've been trail boss over; it's just unbelievable."

They ride south heading out of the *Jornada del Muerto*.

The arm still hurts, but nothing near what might have been, thinks Zep as he relaxes in the rocking chair on the front porch of the boarding house in Las Cruces. *Those last miles about got me. The fever came on with the ferocity of a cornered badger. If Allie and Guillo hadn't kept me in the saddle, I'd be out in the Jornada short of the end.* He sits in his chair wearing new denim pants, a white bibbed long sleeved cotton shirt, with his left arm trussed up in a doctor-applied sling. Guillo sits on the steps whittling on a piece of pine.

"The Army doctor, he didn't want to turn loose of you Zep. Allie make a big scene to get a buggy to carry you to Las Cruces, you know?" Guillo says out loud. "She one mean spitfire when she no gets what she thinks you need."

"Can't say I remember a whole lot, Guillo. I kind of drifted in and out at that point." Zep continues to rock. "I do remember a skinny fellar, the city doctor, who kept talking about some guy named Joseph Lister while he wiped the knife wound with something called carbolic acid. Why, I thought he was trying to dissolve my arm away."

"Oh, no, *companero*, that *amigo* is one *muy* smart *hombre*, the young doctor from Philly somewhere back east *Estados Unidos*. Allie, she make sure he can save your arm and not cut it off like the Army doctor wants to do."

"Well, it would sure spoil my mustanger ways to try to do it with one arm. I sure am glad Allie and you held out for me when I couldn't."

"*Da nada*, Zep. It was Allie who stays with you to break the fever and changes bandages for your arm. She no let anyone else take care of you. You know *companero*, I think she likes you a little bit," Guillo looks at Zep, winks and grins.

"Better her taking care of me than some saddle tramp like you," Zep grins back.

Miguel and another rider approach the boarding house. Zep and Guillo look over and both respond, "Joe."

"My golly, look what that there dog drug in, both of you two varmints sittin' here above the snakes takin' life easy as can be. I don't believe it." Joe stops his horse and leans forward on its neck to look at Zep and Guillo. "Miguel comes ridin' up past the livestock pins this mornin' and I sees him right off. He tells me what y'all been mixin' in, shares with me Manolito is gone, and that Allie is with you. Why I don't believe it, says I, got to go see them myself. So, here I am, and here you be."

"You old coot, you're a sight for sore eyes. Good to see you still get around. What's happening at the *hacienda*?" Zep questions.

"Oh, well, Don Louis is keepin' everythin' runnin' like clock-work. He got all the hands together and we drove a herd over here to fatten up and sell to the Army over in El Paso. He's down at Johnson House, the hotel downtown. I'll bet he don't even know y'all is here. He's been frettin' he hasn't heard anythin' from Santa Fe about y'all. Whatcha think; do we go surprise him?"

"That's the thing to do," says Miguel. "I will tell Allie Papa is here; she will be beside herself with excitement." He slides off his horse and goes into the boarding house.

"Did that there boy just say 'Papa'?" asks Joe.

"*Mi amigo,* you have got a big awakening coming, hold on and enjoy the ride," says Guillo.

Allie comes busting through the doorway wearing a blue skirt, white blouse, and her auburn hair pulled back into a ponytail.

Looking at Zep she asks, "Are you well enough to go to the hotel to see Papa? We can bring him here if you aren't."

"We'll go there. Guillo, can you go the the livery and arrange a surrey? Miguel, you and Joe tell Don Louis we are on our way. Allie, you going to go looking like that or do you need to change?" Allie spins around and races inside. "I believe that's a 'I'm going to change move.'" Zep grins.

Guillo heads for the livery, Miguel and Joe head downtown. Zep stands and walks into the boarding house.

Allie, Don Louis, Miguel, Guillo, and Zep sit around a table in the large dining room of the Johnson House. It looks like all other hotel dining rooms with maybe more tables, fifteen of them, cloth covered with glass chimney candles on each table. Waiters stand patiently around the room taking care of customers. Glasses rattle, china pings, conversation rises and falls, all lit by kerosene lamp chandeliers suspended eight feet above the occupants. Multiple framed pictures hang from the pink and green floral wallpapered walls.

Allie glows in her pale green dress with white shawl and her colorful stone necklace and earrings. Zep and Miguel are comfortable in white bib-front cotton shirts with denim trousers. As always, Guillo wears *vaquero* trousers and short waisted vest over his white shirt. It appears dinner is a success from what little remains on the dishes. Don Louis taps his glass with a knife to get everyone's attention around the table.

"*Mi familia*, I'm the most happy man tonight. Everyone I love is here with me and safe. I have missed many nights' sleep wondering about my children. Yes, children, Alassandra and Miguel. We are all aware of the circumstances. Miguel and I took time to talk today. I acknowledge my way may not be perceived as the best, but our outcome is wonderful. Alassandra, you are back safe. I had to let you go and seek your way. I didn't want to, but had to. By your own choice, you are once again with us.

Zep, my dearest friend, you and Guillo have risked your lives many times for my children; you are always welcomed members of *mi familia*.

"Alassandra and I had an in depth conversation this afternoon. She tells me she is not going back to the *Hacienda de la Colina*. I am shocked, stunned, and object vociferously. Then she tells me she is going to marry. How can this be. I am the Papa and no one asked me. Yet, I know the husband to be of my daughter. Zep, I could not be happier. You will take care of her, no? She has driven me crazy many times; now it is your turn. Careful what you ask for, my son."

"*Don* Louis, I apologize for not seeking Alassandra's hand from you first; it was my intention, but it appears she's 'let the cat out of the bag' already," says Zep. With a raised eyebrow he looks at Allie. She smirks and hangs her head.

"It is no problem, Zep." *Don* Louis responds with a smile. "We will have the wedding here in Las Cruces. I will talk to the Padre at the church tomorrow. *Bueno.*"

Allie jumps up, runs and hugs *Don* Louis. "*Muchas gracias,* Papa."

Returning Allie's hug, he motions her back to her seat and continues, "My Miguel will return to the *hacienda* and start running the *rancho* as the *Haciendado* he is entitled to be. Zep and Allie will go to Mesilla and begin a life together and expand their *rancho.* Between the *hacienda* and Mesilla we will build and sell herds of cattle and horses. Both locations will operate together in one family business."

Allie looks across the table at Guillo, and staring into his eyes says, "I left the *hacienda* with *mi hermano,* my best friend, Zep, and you. I lost my best friend, Manolito, on this trip and gained a new best friend." She smiles at Guillo. With moist eyes, he smiles back. Zep and Miguel grin ear-to-ear.

Don Louis nods in agreement then says, "I also have talked with *Americano* lawyers from El Paso, who I trust. They talk about the possibility of railroads. Our lands are in an area the railroads may potentially cross. We must be watchful and plan for this change when it comes. It can mean major changes for our territory and lives. Soon *Nuevo Mexico* will change again."

"They are coming, *Don* Louis. We heard conversations in Albuquerque," Zep says and looks to Miguel for confirmation, who nods his head in agreement.

"There is also a strong possibility a war is on the horizon," says *Don* Louis. "The northern and southern states continue to debate, argue, and fight over every excuse they find. This does not look or feel good."

"Surely, calmer minds will prevail Papa," says Allie.

"*Si, si*. I am sure you are right. Let's not borrow troubles. I want my children on the front of changes here in *Nuevo Mexico*," says *Don* Louis. "The days of the old *Haciendado* pass, our major Indian wars are fewer, land grants may be wiped away, and *Nuevo Mexico* is now part of the *Estados Unidos*. Old ways make room for new; it's the way of the world. My last responsibility is to make certain my children prepare to take their places in what is coming. But, tonight, we *fiesta*. Tomorrow is time for work."

In the stables behind the hotel, Guillo hears the familiar sound of his ornery jackass braying at the moon, and mutters, "That *maldito* mule always has to have the last word. I think someday, I might have to shoots him between the eyes." He grins. "But, not tonight."

36

MESILLA

IS ARMS LAY UPON THE CORRAL RAIL WITH HIS CHIN resting on them. His gaze follows the slow milling horses within the enclosure. It's been three months recuperation from the arm wound Zep received while crossing *Jornada del Muerto. Better a wound than lying out there dead,* he thinks.

"*Hola, companero.*" Guillo walks up to the corral, stands beside Zep, hikes a booted foot up onto a bottom rail, and leans on the top cross member.

"What's your thinking?"

"I been laying around too long," says Zep.

"You're letting your arm heal, no?"

"Yes, but I can only stand so much healing."

"Well, *companero,* let's ride out to chase some horses."

"Thought you'd never get there," smiles Zep. "Got to tell

Allie we're goin.'"

"*Si,* you now have *señora jefe* to answer to," quips Guillo with a smile.

"Quit standin' there grinnin'; go get the gear and horses ready to ride," says Zep as he hustles toward the ranch house.

Walking across the open field he looks at the house. *Those carpenters and workmen Don Louis hired have really shaped things up,* he thinks. *Just a few months ago we arrived to charred timbers and now we have a nearly completed house and bunk-house. The huge barn is under construction.*

Allie steps onto the covered front porch as Zep approaches. She brushes her hands on a white bib-front apron.

"I watched you and Guillo at the corral."

"Yep, we're fixin' on going out after some mustangs."

"Yes, I figured you're itching to get active again. I'm surprised I kept you here this long."

"We shouldn't be gone too long, and there are plenty of *vaqueros* here to keep an eye on things. Are you okay with my going?"

"Yes, go on, get, *fuera,* scram. Go get your horses." She smiles as she waves him away.

"I knew I married the right gal, " says Zep as he turns and hurries toward the barn.

Allie watches Zep catch up to Guillo. Smiling, she thinks, *where have the months gone? I remember Zep standing at the church in Las Cruces looking nervous as a long tail cat in a room full of rocking chairs waiting while Papa and I walk up the aisle. His new boots, denims, and bib-front white shirt shine. My nerves tingle, and my heart pounds in my ears. I want to be all Zep expects me to be. My long white dress and short lacey jacket sparkle in the sunlight that comes through the windows. My billowy veil supported by a beautiful tortoise shell peineta covers my head down to my shoulders. Our future stretches before us. The priest goes on forever and finally we are man and wife.* Leaning against the porch post momentarily caught up in her remembrances, she watches Zep and Guillo ride into the open desert.

Turning, she surveys the progress the ranch has made. Since arriving in Las Cruces, getting married, tending Zep's wound, moving to Mesilla, and establishing married life; she's supervised the building of the ranch. The house is adobe, thick walls for insulation and protection; its almost completed ridge roof is red tile. A covered front porch runs the length of the house. Allie loves it and it is home.

She sees the huge multistalled barn with a sizable hayloft under construction. An eight-bed bunkhouse, still in need of roof tiles, will house to more hands to work the ranch, and multiple corrals for livestock complete the homestead.

The *vaquero jefe* approaches her on the porch. His hat in hand, he addresses Allie.

"*Señora, una momento, por favor.*"

"*Si,* Bernardo, what is it?"

"*Señora,* it has been a few days now my *vaquero* tell me Apaches are around the *rancho.*"

"Why did your not tell *Señor* Zep?"

"I first wanted to be sure, *señora.* Just now I see *señor* ride away and I know I must tell you."

"So, you are sure?"

"*Si, señora,* I have found tracks around the barn, and followed an unshod horse into the desert before I lose the trail."

"Are Apaches still here?"

"Who knows, *señora?*"

"Bernardo, you must know. Double our guards at night, do

not leave anyone unprotected, and let me know when you find other signs."

"*Si, señora.* I will do as you say."

Allie glances past the *vaquero* to watch the dust from Zep and Guillo. *Be careful, my love,* she thinks.

Alchesay sprints into the boulders surrounding the base of Point of Rocks Hill in the *Jornada del Muerto*. Flattening himself on the ground he quickly scrambles and crawls to a spot of concealment under manzanita bushes and fights to control his panting breath.

"So close, the white man was so close to killing me," he mutters. "I know I stabbed him. Was it a mortal wound? I have to know."

Lying under the bushes, Alchesay hears talking and things being dragged around. Soon, the white men mount their horses and quickly ride away.

Alchesay stays hidden until morning is past before he crawls out and climbs up the hill to his vantage point. From there he surveys the area around and finds his prey has once again escaped. This time, he knows one is wounded and, gathering his belongings, he moves down to where his horse is hidden. He begins tracking again and knows he will continue this quest until he or the white man is dead.

Their trail heads toward Las Cruces.

Guillo and Zep leave the ranch traveling northwest. Zep knows wild horses tend to roam in the foothills where water and forage are plentiful.

"We'll ride west a while, then turn north, and work our way back," says Zep.

"*Si,* you are the mustanger," replies Guillo. "Me, I'm just along for the scenery."

"Scenery be darn, you'll work on this outing. So, unlimber your lasso and keep it handy when we come upon some horseflesh."

"*Si,* I will, *companero.*"

"I think we'll ride along the *Rio Mimbres* towards *Cerro Roblado* Mountain."

"That sounds like a good ride. Are we in Apache country going that direction?"

"It's all Apache country out here, *companero,*" says Zep with a grin.

It's been a month since Alchesay followed his 'rabbits' to Las Cruces. From what he's been able to discover, his big white man lost a lot of blood on the trip after their knife fight, but no body was buried along the trail. He assumes his enemy lives. Like an ever-present shadow, Alchesay lurks close enough to learn about his prey, but far enough away to keep from discovery.

Soon his prey leaves Las Cruces; he follows them to rebuild a ranch outside of Mesilla. Day after day he watches his 'rabbits.' His purpose in life is to find the right opportunity to kill this enemy, so he moves stealthfully around the countryside that surrounds the *rancho.*

I have no one left, no clan to return to, Alchesay thinks as he

234

sits behind a screen of bushes on a hillside that overlooks the ranch. *Certainly others would have given up, they may think I am a fool, but these whites must die. Nothing else will avenge my people or quiet my vengeance.* He spends his days living off the land and always watching for an opportunity.

Today, he watches two riders mount. "The two 'rabbits' I have followed from Chihuahua leave the ranch," he mutters as he watches Zep and Guillo head west.

Moving rapidly up the hillside, he slinks over the top and descends the backside to a concealed arroyo where his horse forages. Gathering his belongings, he mounts and rides after the departing riders.

"*Es una* Apache, *señora.*" The *vaquero jefe* stands on the porch reporting to Allie.

"Not a raiding party?"

"No, *señora. Mi vaqueros* found his trail all around the *rancho*. It appears *el indio* watches us *muy dias.*"

"Why would one Indian keep a constant watch on this ranch?" Allie asks aloud. "You are certain there are no other *indios* around? He is not a scout for a raiding party?"

"*Mi vaqueros* have ridden out *muy* miles to make certain *señora.* We can not find any others, just *una indio.*"

"It doesn't make any sense. Why one Indian watching? Unless, there is someone here he wants badly." Allie mutters to herself. Turning, she stares at the *vaquero jefe.*

"Find *el indio,* capture him, rope him, tie him, and bring him to me. *Vamonos.*"

"*Si, señora.*" Spinning around the *jefe* quickly steps from the porch shouting orders to his *vaqueros*. Seven riders mount and head into the hills around the ranch.

The *jefe* wonders, *w hy does the señora want the Apache brought to her...alive.*

As Zep and Guillo ride west, the horizon lights up with a brilliant red and golden sunset. They camp in a deep ravine to conceal their campfire from the surrounding openness. Horses are hobbled and coffee and beans are consumed as they recline against their saddles.

"Tomorrow we strike the *Rio Mimbres* and locate my corral." Zep slowly rolls a cigarette from the fixings spread out on his blanket. He pulls a match from his shirt pocket, lights up, and inhales a long drag.

"You have a corral out here somewhere, *campanero?*"

"Yep. How else do you figure I can round up horses?"

"I don't know. I thought you just chases them around and points them to our *rancho.*"

"Well, Guillo, it ain't that easy."

"How DO you chases horses to our *rancho?*"

"First, we'll gather up a few small herds, chase them to a box canyon corral I've used in the past, pacify the lead mares, and break the stallions. Then we can take the horses to the ranch."

"Can you break a stallion with your arm, *companero?*"

"Not really," Zep stares at Guillo. "Got to do what has to be done."

"*Ay yi-yi.* Again. You are not going to do it again, *amigo,* are you? Here is a little job for you to do, Guillo. This time just climbs up on a big, angry, mean stallion and saddle brokes him, no?"

"No, *companero*, I will take the stallion," says Zep smiling. "You'll work with the lead mare."

"*Ay, muy bueno.* I takes the ladies and you gets the mean things," says Guillo as he rolls up in his blanket. "*Buenos noches, companero.*"

Throwing a few more pieces of dry wood on the fire, Zep gathers his blanket and moves outside of the circle of firelight to keep watch. He knows the next few days will be a lot of hard work. "*Buenos noches,*" he whispers.

It's taken a while, but Alchesay finally locates the camp. A hidden fire in the ravine and kept small is an Apache trick. He continues to appreciate that the white man is a worthy opponent. He locates an arroyo about a mile away to make his camp and settles in for the night. His thoughts turn to, *how can I make these 'rabbits' suffer as I have suffered? What can I do to cause them much pain before I kill them?*

In the middle of the night, he moves quietly over the rough ground around the manzanita and other brush. He stops every few feet, his vision drills into the darkness. Easing into a ravine, he sees a low burning fire with a figure rolled up in a blanket beside it. *Where is the other 'rabbit,'* he wonders?

Suddenly, the glow of a cigarette punches through the darkness. *He's there,* thinks Alchesay. *Does he watch me as well?*

Silently, he backs away down the ravine into a darkened washed out area. Smoothing out a spot along the gully wall, he curls into a fetal position and sleeps.

Zep continues to smoke his cigarette. *He's out there, and close,* he feels the presence of an enemy. *I've felt someone watch me for days at the ranch,* he thinks. *My 'twinge' is going off regular-like, and tonight it gnaws my neck.* Zep slowly reaches up and rubs the knife scar on his arm.

37

RESOLUTION

Morning sun creeps over the eastern horizon as Zep and Guillo load up and get ready to ride. Alchesay is mounted and concealed down the ravine from where both men camped.

"Is a good morning, yes?"

"If we find horses, it will be a good morning," says Zep.

"The *caballos* are out there. Let's ride to collect them."

"Sooner we get started, the sooner we are on our way home. Let's ride."

Mounting, Zep and Guillo head toward the foothills and the box canyon holding the corral Zep is familiar with. Behind them, at a slow walk, follows Alchesay.

About noon, Zep spots a herd of eight horses; a stallion stands apart watching over his dependents. Guillo and Zep lash their horses into a run and begin chasing the herd steering them toward a nearby butte. Zep turns off in pursuit of the stallion and flexs his wounded arm. He unlimbers his lasso preparing its use.

Galloping full speed over the countryside, Guillo closes on the herd and manages to maneuver the lead mare into the valley at the base of the butte. As he shouts and waves his lasso in the air, the small horse herd charges in front of him into the narrow and deep valley. The walls become vertical boundaries and the only open pathway is forward.

Zep charges toward the midnight black stallion as it rears up on his hind legs. He paws the air with his front hooves in a challenge to fight and protect his own. Zep closes the gap and shakes out the lasso prepared to throw. Suddenly, the stallion charges toward him intent to run over his pursuer. At the last moment he breaks away and with mane and tail streaming behind him, charges past. Zep manages to sail the lasso's loop over the stallion's head and ties the lariat to his saddle horn. His horse is almost yanked off of its feet when the rope snaps taut. In a bucking rage, the stallion attempts to throw the rope cinched around its neck. Struggling to free itself, the stallion twists, turns, snaps, yanks, and thrashes. Zep expertly works the lariat to tire the magnificent animal. His wounded arm aches.

Alchesay dismounts and watches the master horseman from behind cover at the rim of the valley. A cloud of dust rising from the valley indicates one rider chases the herd while another cloud near the valley entrance is the white man and stallion engaged in a monumental test of strength and wills. He sits down to watch the outcome.

I want this white man dead, but not while he is distracted. I want him to know when I kill him, thinks Alchesay.

The day wears on; in the cloud of dust both the stallion and Zep are fully engaged. Both are covered in dirt and sweat etches paths down their bodies; muscles fatigue and quiver from exertion. As the stallion tires, Zep takes up the slacked rope. Periodically, the horse rears and races away only to reach the end of the rope once again. For hours the combatants contest and as evening nears, too exhausted to continue, the stallion allows itself to be led down the valley.

Guillo's corralled the milling herd in the box canyon. Zep leads the stallion into a smaller enclosure with a stout pine pole buried upright in the middle of the area. He ties the horse's rope to this snubbing post with enough lead to let the animal move his head but not enough to run.

Zep exits as Guillo closes the gate. Sliding from the saddle, his left arm dangles almost useless at his side; he leans again his horse.

"Been a long day, Guillo."

"*Si, companero.* I don't know who looks worse; you or the stallion."

"Don't know who feels worse, me or the horse," says Zep. "Might have pushed things a little too hard today."

"Come over to the fire. Coffee and *frijoles* are ready. I'll take care of your mount."

Zep stumbles to the fire and pours a cup of coffee. Slowly, he sips from the cup as Guillo returns and dips beans from the pot for both of them.

"Tomorrow we start work on the herd, yes? The sooner the lead mare is won over, the sooner we head home, no?"

"You're right, but now, I'm bushed and going to get some rest. You take first watch and I'll spell you at midnight."

"*Si*, sleep well."

With an audible groan, Zep maneuvers his left arm around to a comfortable position as he drapes his blanket around himself.

The full moon hangs above the canyon and lights up the corrals below. Alchesay sees the Mexican talk quietly to the horses in the corral. He silently moves down the hillside knowing the horses milling and nickering will cover any sounds he might make. He stops beside the stallion's corral and surveys the camp. The white man quietly sleeps, he breaths even and deeply. The Mexican still leans against the corral and whispers to the horses.

Stepping quietly up behind the man, he swings his knife handle solidly against his head knocking him out. He collapses, and Alchesay turns to watch the white man. No movement. Good. He stoops, gathers the Mexican up onto his shoulders, starts carefully to climb the hillside, and grabs a lasso dangling from a corral post. With gentle and firm steps, he traverses the hill. He knows he leaves a trail.

Now, the white man will come to me, to the place I choose with no interference this time.

Guillo groggily wakes up with a sensation of swinging. His arms are stretched over his head with his hands tied together. His feet are bound and he is suspended over a pile of kindling and brush. Wide-eyed, he stares at the fire makings below him and glances around the butte top. Seated on the ground beside the tree is an Apache warrior. He sits cross-legged, hair held back by a wide band around his head, tall leather moccasin-boots, long breechcloth, calico shirt, and crossed bandoleers. He stares at Guillo. Speaking in Spanish, he addresses Guillo.

"Your white man comes soon."

"Who are you?"

"It makes no difference who I am. But, because you are soon to die, I will tell you. I am Alchesay, of the *Chokonan* of the *Chiricahua*. You and your white man have eluded me too long."

"*Ah, si,* you are *señor* Zep's 'twinge,' no?" With sudden insight, Guillo realizes this Indian has been on their trail since Chihuahua.

"You were part of the ambush in Chihuahua, no?"

"Yes, I kill those who kill *The People.*"

"*Si, señor indio,* but *señor* Zep and I have killed none of your peoples. But, you have tried to kill us, no?"

"Your white man will come soon, and it shall be over."

Predawn slips into the valley spreading filtered light. Zep jerks awake.

I slept too long; where is Guillo?

Rising, he searches around the campfire and moves to the corrals. Horses nicker and stir at his approach. The stallion pulls at the rope tied to the snugging post. *Where's Guillo?* Zep grows more alarmed. Footprints litter the ground beside the corral and tell him all he needs to know.

"Indian and Guillo, a struggle, a fall, deeper moccasin prints head up the hill, the Indian has Guillo," mutters Zep to himself. "Got to follow."

He rushes to his horse, saddles, mounts, and follows the trail that leads up the hillside. The broken ground, rocky rubble, and scree make tracking difficult. The trail continues to climb the butte and Zep locates where the Indian picked up his horse. He continues to move around and between boulders and rocky outcroppings ascending the mountain. Zep realizes the Indian follows a game trail to the top. *Probably pooled water attracts animals,* he thinks.

Each step is dangerous. The mountainside is a vertical drop and the trail is on loose ground. Zep is forced to dismount and lead his horse upward, weaving around and through broken rock outcroppings.

He must have taken Guillo early evening and climbed this trail in the dark. Its scary in the light, must have been terrifying in the dark, thinks Zep to himself. *Why would an Indian take Guillo in the first place? Is he still alive? How much farther?*

The trail begins to level out and Zep realizes he's reached the summit. Pausing a moment, he looks around, and the vista before him is inspiring. The valley below sweeps north and south. To the east and west rise mountain ranges. *This butte sits like a silent sentinel.*

Ground tying his horse, Zep pulls his carbine and stealthfully moves into the scattered, shattered, weathered, rock-strewn area in front of him. *Somewhere up here is Guillo.* A few twisted but stout Sycamore trees cling to the mountaintop indicating the presence of water. Zep slides up against a tree trunk and peers around. On the far side of the butte there seems to be something hanging from the limb of a tree. With sudden realization, Zep knows it's Guillo. *Where's the Indian?*

Slipping to the ground onto his belly, Zep inches his way across the butte towards Guillo. Stopping every few minutes, he listens for any sounds and looks for movement among the rocks.

The bait is placed and the trap is set, thinks Alchesay, patiently waiting. His back is toward a tall rock wall and his forward view is unobstructed. *He will come. He may already be here. Patience, patience, I have waited a long time for today; this is no common white man, he is almost Apache.*

A slight noise to his left causes Alchesay to crouch lower. He strains his eyesight to spot movement among the rocks. His bow is upright, string taut, arrow nocked, and breathing quietly; he waits.

He's here. I know he's here. I feel him, thinks Zep. He slowly and quietly twists his neck. *My 'twinge' throbs. The first one to make a mistake…dies.*

Inch by inch, Zep slides quietly across the sandy soil of the butte top. Almost melded with the rocks for cover, and feels like his stomach muscles clutch the ground, his eyes dart rapidly from spot to spot seeking any telltale motion. His ears strain for a sound to betray his enemy's location.

Instinctively, he pulls back. A wooden shafted feather fretted arrow slices silently through the air in front of his face. It strikes a rock and shatters. Every nerve in Zep's body screams run. Slowly exhaling, he eases to his right, the direction the arrow came from. Sliding back and around a large rock he moves to find where his enemy hides.

Alchesay curses under his breath. He anticipated the movement of the sound and it didn't happen. He knows he's discovered and his eyes dart rapidly around seeking his enemy. *I knew he was moving; he should have been there and met the arrow.* Alchesay silently berates himself for acting too soon. *Now, I wait for him to act. He will find where I hide soon.* A rock clatters only a few feet away. Twisting around he fires another arrow. In a blur, a man leaps from the ground and flings himself on top of him.

The arrow flashing in front of Zep betrays his enemy's hiding place. He moves quietly and quickly into position. He knows he must disarm the Indian. Getting him to fire another arrow will provide a fraction of a moment to act. Zep tosses a rock and every muscle in his body tenses up to leap. *I have one chance; it has to be right.* As the second arrow zips past, every coiled muscle releases and he springs.

Zep and Alchesay collide and roll over and over, neither one releases a hold on the other. They roll toward the edge of the butte and before either can slow their momentum, they disappear. Guillo watches the action in horror. Wide-eyed he sees both figures clutched in death grips plummet over the edge of the butte. Frantically, he twists, turns, and yanks until he hears a breaking sound. The limb holding him cracks. He gyrates harder, twists, yanks, and bounces until suddenly the limb snaps and tumbles him to the ground. Guillo scrambles to untie his feet, and uses his teeth to tug at the rope. He manages to untie his hands, and rubs his wrists to restore circulation. Quickly, he scrambles to the edge of the cliff and leans over.

On a ledge, ten feet below, lay two bodies, unmoving, still.

"Zep, *mi companero*, are you alright? Can you hear me? Zep, answer me." shouts Guillo. As he watches, both men awaken and lunge at each other. On the narrow ledge they both grope for their knives and cling to each other to keep from slipping off.

Zep manages to get a foot behind Alchesay's heel and trip him. Out of balance, Alchesay slides off the ledge and frantically grabs the edge. Dropping to his knees, Zep extends both hands grabbing Alchesay by his wrists.

Gazing into each other's eyes the men exchange a split moment of understanding. Alchesay sees help and rescue in Zep's eyes.

Zep, staring into Alchesay's eyes, sees release and acceptance.

Sweaty hands begin slipping apart. Zep's wounded left arm muscles ache. Frantically, regripping for a better hold, both men lose their double grip and now Alchesay dangles by one hand. Zep flattens out on the ledge and desperately grabs with his right hand to get a hold on the Indian's clothing.

They hear an owl hoot in the distance.

Suddenly, sweat soaked hands part and Alchesay's fall accelerates in gravity's death grip.

Zep rolls onto his back, not wanting to watch the consequences. He sees and hears Guillo shout from above and weakly waves.

AFTERWORD

Thank you for purchasing this book. If you enjoyed reading it, please consider leaving a review at your favorite book retailer. For more information about Dr. Wm. A. Burgdorf and his books, please visit the author's website: **www.waburgdorf.com** and email: **DrBilly@waburgdorf.com**.

NEW RELEASE.

The Bierman Saga -- Book 2

COMPANY A
BY
WILLIAM A. BURGDORF

Continue the adventures of Zep Bierman in 1860s New
Mexico Territory.

1

THE BEGINNING

THE SMALL STREAM IN THE VALLEY BUBBLES AND gurgles as it sweeps along. Zep hears it clearly from his hiding place inside the tree line. The grass-covered valley below spreads out on either side of a small creek and is bounded by towering pines. Beside the brook, four men move around a campfire noisily preparing to eat. Their horses are hobbled a short distance away.

They are the bait.

Wait, patience, it can't be long now. Take the bait damn it, Zep thinks. He glances at the three chevrons on the sleeve of his gray shirt that mark him as the leader of the six Arizona Rangers crouching concealed and quiet beside him. The next move belongs to the Apaches.

Shouting from the valley galvanizes his attention in the direction the men are pointing. One of the men by the campfire spins around with an arrow protruding from his shoulder.

From the far side of the valley, mounted Apaches break from the trees charging the men by the campfire.

Screaming, wailing, and shouting, the Apaches fire a volley of arrows. The few carrying rifles fire wildly as they charge. Most have lances ready to ride down the white men.

"Wait," whispers Zep. "Give them time to get into the open."

Impatiently, the rangers stand beside their mounts. Their friends in the valley are being attacked.

"Now. Mount and charge," shouts Zep as he flings himself into his saddle. Yanking his revolver out of its holster, he waves the rangers forward.

The Apaches realize the trap too late, their horses are already charging the men in the open field, and they are too far from the trees. A few yank their mounts around to flee. They are the first targets of the rangers exploding from the forest.

"All of them, get them all, not one escapes." shouts Zep pointing at the rapidly approaching Indians. Pistol fire explodes and echoes around the open valley.

The six rangers spread out to form an encompassing net swallowing the Apache warriors. Indians tumble from their horses spreading pools of crimson where they land, they lie still on the meadow grass.

One warrior leaps bravely from his horse dashing into the grass as he makes his way toward the trees. A ranger by the campfire levels his Sharps rifle and fires. The Apache shrieks and falls silent.

Zep slows his horse to survey the remains of the chaos visited on the quiet mountain valley. Indian horses wander around riderless. Rangers continue to check out Apache bodies on the ground making certain they are dead. The men by the fire gather their gear and mount their horses.

"Report, corporal," shouts Zep.

A young man in a gray flannel uniform quickly rides up.

"Looks like all six savages are dead, sarge."

"Looks like or are?" shouts Zep.

"Sorry, sarge. They is, for certain."

"Our men?"

"McIlhenny took an arrow in the shoulder. Smith caught one in the leg. Other than that, we're okay."

"Good. This is one band won't be raiding again. Gather the troopers, let's head south. Move out, corporal."

"You betcha, sarge." Spinning his horse around the young ranger spurs towards his comrades.

Zep hand signals the troopers to fall into formation.

"Cortez, scout ahead." He motions for a trooper to lead the way.

Turning toward two other troopers, he motions them to the front of the column forming behind him.

"Jones and Seguin, you are point. Don't walk us into an ambush."

The line of eleven gray clad soldiers moves quickly away from the mountain valley disappearing into the woods.

This patrol's successful, thinks Zep. *No more raided ranches or murdered settlers from these Apaches. Need to get home and check on Allie.*

2

GO WEST

RIDING INTO MESILLA, ZEP WATCHES THE INCREASED activity going on and assumes something big is underway. Dismounting at his squad's bivouac area, he ties his horse to the picket line as Corporal Jenkins walks up.

"Sarge, glad you're back."

"Everyone accounted for, anybody in the stockade?"

"Well, Sarge, you see there was this here difficulty and Seguin..."

"For how long?"

"Ah, he'll be out tomorrow. He only busted up some *cantina* tables."

"What's all the activity?"

"Something big is happening. Kind of hoped you'd know about it."

"If there's nothing else happening here, I'll hike over to

headquarters and see what I can find out."

"We're good here, Sarge. Let us know what you hear."

Zep makes his way through Mesilla and arrives at Governor Baylor's headquarters as several officers enter the building. Zep walks over to a sergeant standing beside the porch.

"Howdy, Martin. How's things in Third Squad?"

"'bout the same as with yours, Zep."

"Looks like a bunch of officers with lots of chicken guts gold braid on their cuffs gathering here."

"Yep. Heared that General Sibley is on his way."

"Say, this the same Sibley as was in the Utah War against them Mormons?" asks Zep.

"Yep. Same feller. Now he's heading this way with the better parts of the Second, Fourth, Fifth, and Seventh Texas Mounted Rifle and field artillery regiments. Got several companies of Confederate Arizona volunteers along for the party as well."

"Ain't no wonder old Baylor is shining things up a mite for the General," says Zep.

"Wonder where our Arizona Rangers is goin' to fit in," asks Martin.

"They've had us trying to keep a lid on the Apaches since the blue bellies left in '61. This territory's been left wide open to Mangas Coloradas and Cochise to raid at will, left dozens dead, and spreadin' terror and fear."

"I suspect we'll go right on fightin' Apaches. Nobody knows how to do it better than us."

"I suspect you're right, Martin. Thanks for letting me know what's happenin.'"

Zep turns away from the headquarters and walks slowly down main-street to Second Squad's area.

Maybe Allie's right. This really isn't my fight. I was dealing with Apaches before, and I will be dealing with them after this affair is over, thinks Zep.

"Listen up. Here's the orders." Zep reads an official document to his Second Squad. "General Sibley's assigned Captain Sherod Hunter to lead Company A of the Arizona Rangers to Tucson. From there we're to proceed to Fort Yuma on the Colorado River and impede the progress of any Union forces from California. That's our orders, men."

"So, Captain Hunter fixin' to wander us across Arizona Territory huntin' for Yankees?" asks Corporal Jenkins.

"Yep, Corporal, that's the orders."

"Well, that means about a hundred or more of us are wandering into the heart of the Apacheria, right?"

"I always knew you were the brightest one, Corporal," says Private Seguin. The other troopers chuckle out loud.

"Shut up, Seguin. You realize we're ridin' into the hornets nest," says Jenkins.

"Alright, alright. Get your gear in order. Seguin, you and McIlhenny get the mules loaded. They're your responsibility."

"Ah, Sarge. Give us a break. Somebody else needs the mules," whines McIlhenny.

"Good, now you've got them there and back," says Zep.

The other troopers laugh out loud.

"Gear up. We move out in the morning," says Zep. He walks to his tent.

I've got to write a letter to Allie letting her know where I'm heading and when. I don't expect this to be any quick assignment, and I know that Jenkins is right. We are walkin' into the hornet's nest. Got to get there and back in one piece with all my men, if possible. Not going to be easy.

Sitting down at his tent table he pulls out his stationary box, turns up the wick on his kerosene lamp, and begins his letter.

Zep nods at the clerk standing on the porch of Governor Baylor's house as Company A of Arizona Rangers rides past in the early morning.

He's got five dollars to deliver that letter, he better do it, Zep thinks to himself. *So, what if he doesn't, what can I do about it when I'm in California?*

The rattle of loose accoutrements brings him back to reality. Gray uniformed soldiers continue to form into a line of march in front of Zep. He twists around in his saddle to look at his squad and make certain they are dressed away. Satisfied that nothing is out of order, he reviews the route in his mind.

We'll go from Mesilla to Pinos Altos, old Birchville; then to Mexican Springs; cross over the mountains through Stein's and Apache Passes; and finally make it to Tucson. Two hundred and eighty miles means plus or minus eighteen to twenty days of forced march barring any difficulties. We'll follow the old Butterfield Stage route and stop at their abandoned way stations. Damn shame the stagecoach stopped running when the war started, but we couldn't control the Indians or outlaws to keep the journey safe. Lord knows there'll be difficulties out here. I just hope not too many.

A Lieutenant sent by Captain Hunter rides up beside Zep.

"Sergeant, the Captain understands you know this area and

have done mustanging here about. He wants you to take the point. Do you understand?"

"Tell the Captain, Second Squad appreciates the assignment," says Zep.

The Lieutenant nods and spurs his horse forward.

Zep turns in his saddle.

"Second Squad's been ordered to take the point and lead the way. Move out to the front of the column. Cortez, you're our scout. Seguin, you and Jones take the lead and don't walk us into an ambush. Give McIlhenny your mule." Zep waves his arm forward and Second Squad moves out of the long winding formation of cavalry.

"At least we're out of eating dust," mutters Zep as his troopers ride to the front of the column. As he passes Captain Hunter, Zep salutes and continues at a gallop watching his men fan out in front of the gray column. Cortez, Seguin, and Jones disappear into the distance.

After putting at least a mile between his squad and the column, Zep signals his troopers to walk their mounts; it's a fair piece to Tucson.

Corporal Jenkins rides up beside Zep.

"You reckon them Apaches know we're out here, Sarge?"

"Corporal, look over your shoulder. Do you see that dust cloud? The whole world knows we're out here."

"Well, them injuns are liable to be awaitin' for us."

"You're understating the obvious, Corporal. Now, ride over to the right flank, I've got the left, and keep your eyes open."

"Yes, Sarge." Jenkins veers to the right.

Yep, Mangas and Cochise have their eyes working overtime watching us. If they hit us, it will be in little groups, hit and run. Hope they won't want to take on the entire column.

258

Guillo looks out of the barn and sees the buggy pull up to the front of the ranch house. A man steps onto the porch and knocks on the door. With a smile, Guillo watches Allie back the man up with the barrel of the Spencer as she listens to him. Lowering the rifle, she snatches an envelope from his hand. He beats a hasty retreat into the buggy and flicks the reins to trot his horse down the road. Allie looks at the paper in her hand and crumples onto the porch. Guillo sprints for the house.

"*Señora* Allie are you okay?" he asks sliding to a stop as he reaches to help her stand. She shoves the letter toward Guillo.

February 10, 1862

Dear Allie,

The Company is ordered to proceed to Ft. Yuma, Arizona Territory to intercept

Union forces possibly marching from California. Don't know how long I'll be gone. Best to figure at least four months. Let Guillo know to continue taking care of things while I'm away.

I love you.

Zepaniah

"*Ay, yi-yi. Mi compañero* is going a long way, no?"

"Too far, Guillo. I'm almost three months pregnant," says Alassandra.

Guillo leans against the porch post. A shocked look covers his face. "¡*Dios mio,*" he whispers.

The sharp report of gunfire startles Zep as he sits beside the campfire heating coffee. *That comes from the front, what has Cortez stumbled into,* he thinks staring in the direction the scout departed.

"Mount up. Seguin and Jones take the flanks. Column by two, forward," shouts Zep leaping into his saddle and motioning with his arm for the squad to follow.

Cavalry troopers dump their brewing coffee on their fires, and grab the pots as they dash for their horses. They quickly form up and follow Zep toward the sound of gunfire.

Company A's been ten days moving west in its approach to Stein's Pass.

It's the best route through the Peloncillo Mountains even if it's a potential ambush area. Zep worries his scout's stumbled into an Apache ambush. He rides weaving between scattered pines, juniper, and oak trees toward the intermittent gunfire.

Approaching the ridge of a hill, he stops, slides from his saddle, yanks his Spencer rifle from its scabbard, and on hands and knees scrambles to the ridge top. Flattening himself on the ground, Zep looks into the narrow valley below. He sees the stagecoach trail winding through the valley. Tall cliffs tower on either side. Lying in the roadway behind the still, unmoving body of his horse, he spots Cortez. The trooper exchanges gunfire with an unseen enemy hidden among the rocks on the cliff tops. Puffs of gun smoke give away their positions.

Corporal Jenkins crawls up beside Zep.

"Rest of the squad is just below the ridge, Sarge."

"Good. Hold them there. Send McIlhenny up to me."

"All right." The Corporal scoots back from the edge, turns, and scuttles down the hillside. He motions for McIlhenny to join Zep.

"Yeah, Sarge," drawls a tall, lanky soldier in a loose fitting uniform sliding up beside Zep.

"Okay, Mac, here's your chance to be a hero."

"Sarge, I didn't ever tell you I wanted to be a hero." His blue eyes stare at Zep.

"Just thought you'd jump at the chance."

"Well, you thought wrong, Sarge."

"Well, I need a volunteer and you'll do," says Zep. "I want you, Seguin, and Jones to take yourselves around behind those rocks beside the cliff top. Open fire on whoever is hiding there and let them know you mean business. Do you see how to get there?" Zep points the direction he's talking about.

"Yep. I see the way around there. How long do we have?"

"You're not there already?"

"Damn, Sarge, you do make it difficult to keep a happy disposition."

"Disposition be damned. We have to get Cortez out of there."

"Okay, okay. Wait for us to open up, then y'all can rush in and snatch old Cortez."

Zep watches him slide down the hill, gather the other two troopers, and move to the high ground. Corporal Jenkins returns to Zep's side and listens to the plan. He moves back downhill to ready the rescue of Cortez.

Waiting impatiently, Zep finally hears the Spencer rifles of the three troopers open up and signals three mounted riders into the valley to rescue the scout.

Shortly, the troopers of Second Squad stand around a rescued Cortez, now sitting on the ground back with the squad. They prepare to listen to his report as McIlhenny, Seguin, and Jones ride in to join the group. The scout jumps to his feet and attention as Zep approaches.

"Report, soldier," says Zep.

"Sarge, I was picking my way along the trail nice and quiet like, when I seen a bunch of them Apaches up along the cliff top. I believe I surprised them and sprung their trap."

"Did they all stay around shooting at you?"

"No, Sarge. Once they kilt my horse, a bunch of them shucked out of there like the party was over. Only left a handful to finish me off."

"I need numbers, soldier."

"I don't reckon that it was more than a few left to shoot at me. If I hadn't messed up their ambush, they'd of let me ride right on past, and snapped up y'all as soon as you entered the valley. Sure am glad y'all come on the run."

"Stick to the facts, soldier. How many hostiles? Give me the details."

"Well, hell, Sarge, they started shootin', I started scramblin', and perty quick my horse is down with me tryin' to see somethin' to shoot back at up amongst them rocks."

"All right, so you don't know how many hostiles. Correct?"

"Well, it was blame more than one, Sarge."

"Stick to the facts, Cortez."

"Don't know how many, Sarge."

"Okay. You flushed their ambush before it was set. Correct?"

"Yep, I plum walked into their ambush." A couple of snickers escaped from two troopers until Zep turns to glare at them.

"Glad we got here in time, Cortez. You'll ride double with Jones until the Company catches up and you can get a new mount."

"Thanks, Sarge. Sorry, I didn't see them before walking into their trap."

"Don't worry, soldier. You probably saved our hides. Corporal, form up the squad and let's get through that pass before the Indians decide to come back."

"All right, Sarge. Mount up and move out you bunch of manure spreaders," shouts Corporal Jenkins.

Zep pulls a stationary pouch from his saddlebags and scribbles a quick note.

"Seguin," he shouts as the troopers start to move forward. The soldier dashes over stopping his horse beside Zep's. "Take this note back to the column and then get back here. Don't dawdle, mosey around, mooch anything, or stop at the sutler's."

"*Bueno, el Sargento.*" Seguin's ebony eyes twinkle as he grins a toothy smile from under his full mustache, yanks his mount around, and spurs into a gallop back down the trail.

Close call today, got to be sharper, will be more traps as we go. Nobody hurt, that's good, thinks Zep as he rocks with the swaying of his horse. *We all heard that in September, 300 warriors led by Mangas Coloradas and Cochise hit the town of Pinos Altos. It was hand-to-hand combat between miners and warriors. Hadn't been for someone using that old cannon from in front of Roy Bean's store filled with rusty nails and buckshot, there might not be any Pinos Altos left. I imagine they could put a goodly number of warriors in these hills any old time they want to. Yep, it's liable to get a lot worse before Tucson.*

COMPANY A
available at your book retailer.
Enjoy the journey.
William A. Burgdorf
www.waburgdorf.com

William Burgdorf leverages a lifetime of experiences into his stories accumulated from being born along the mighty Ohio River in southern Indiana, raised in the wide, wild desert vistas of Arizona, having lived in lake-strewn Michigan, as well as the hills and hollows of Tennessee, and now in his piney woods home in East Texas. His love of, and a double major in, history along with his successful career as an adult educator prepared him to become a masterful storyteller of historical fiction. His careful attention to exacting details, colorful and memorable characters, descriptive locales, and articulate dialogue weave together stories that engage and enthrall.

"My goal is to provide a story that captures your imagination and is remembered. At the end of the day, I desire to be regarded as a good 'storyteller.'

Website: www.waburgdorf.com
Facebook: www.facebook.com/william.burgdorf

BOOKS BY WILLIAM BURGDORF

The Bierman Saga

The New Mexican
Company A

www.ingramcontent.com/pod-product-compliance
Lightning Source LLC
Chambersburg PA
CBHW071851220626
47052CB00002B/75